familiar strangers

callum noad

Second edition, published September 2017.

ISBN: 9781522013624

To all the people who are told you can't do something, you can, and you will.

CHAPTER ONE

Annabel Bancroft was the epitome of professional success. She lived the perceived 'American Dream' five thousand miles from any stars or stripes in a detached Georgian house, a brisk 15-minute walk, or the more common, five-minute bus ride from the centre of Bath. Although considered a city, Bath is as far from an urban metropolis as one could imagine. Well-minded architects cramped in stuffy London offices couldn't dream of creating Bath with all its subtle obnoxiousness. Oxymoronic concrete flats flew up replacing historical old timers as designers competed against each other to see who could design the most hideous of all the structures. It was in these flats, some 48 years previous, that a young Annabel Bancroft walked her first steps, kissed her besotted boyfriend and transitioned through every style imaginable. For almost half a century Bath proved itself as a capable home for Annabel and her friends and then, family. She met Mark, a bumbling tradesman whose intelligence didn't warrant him such a beautiful arm-wrapping in a dimly lit pub over a pint of Gem and a slightly stale packet of pork scratchings. Armed with three years of knowledge after recently graduating from

Cardiff University with a business degree in hand, Annabel had far greater conversation than the man whose only claim to success was fixing the Mayor's toilet when on work experience at Wessex Water. As the empty pint glasses began to fill the wobbling table propped between their knees, Mark began to make a move. His shameful attempt at seduction had the tables to the left and right both cringing between gulps of warm beer. Looking back, Annabel often wondered what it was about Mark, that made her give herself up so easily. It certainly wasn't his dart player physique that the torn and apparently cheap t-shirt did little to hide. Mark couldn't believe his luck as the taxi pulled up to his home in Southdown, that he still shared with his parents, with a busty brunette on his arm. Before the key had been turned in the lock, Mark had his grubby hands down his guest's underwear. The sex was good according to Mark's premature finish and average at best if you asked Annabel. Numbers were swapped, pleasantries exchanged and as Mark headed back up to bed, Annabel started to fret over the meetings she had planned for the upcoming week. Such was the contrast in their day-to-day lives, it was understandable that neither had any intention of calling the number freshly inked on their own scraps of paper. That was until, of course, that Annabel stopped buying tampons and started hiding TrueSure pregnancy tests in her basket behind the Sainsbury's meal deal she purchased every day on her lunch break. Each test, each brand delivered the same conclusion. Tick, cross, each style was different. The outcome was the same, Annabel was pregnant.

Neither party had any time to develop feelings for the other before they were forced together by the impending arrival of a human-shaped mistake and a set of overbearing Catholic parents that graded every step of their child's life. Nine months since the damp and disappointing one-night stand they shared, five since that answer machine message and just three since *that* wedding day, Savannah Bancroft-Staggs was born. For the first few months of their daughter's life, the first-time parents fussed over every breath, cry and shit but as time passed her mother's significantly higher paid job meant Mark became a full time parent. With Annabel back mixing with the movers and shakers of European finance, Mark lost all sense of masculinity as he hid amongst yummy mummies at the school gates. Although Mark ignored the opinion of his wife that he was essentially a babysitter with a penis, he came to enjoy his life with all that a top-of-the-range TV equipped with Sky Sports offered him.

For Savannah, however, life as a teenager was becoming increasingly difficult. Half of her surname was well known around Bath - teachers often remarked that 'Everyone knows a Staggs' - whereas the other half was a name more at home within the corridors of a private school rather than the comprehensive on the hill she attended through her dad's insistence. As time passed, placid minds became inquisitive. A builder Dad and banker Mum set Savannah up for a lifetime of playground interrogations with such favourites as 'Where's your mum?' and 'Is your dad gay?' Both Mark and Annabel could answer the latter with confidence and not because their sex life was anything special. Or perhaps even anything. The couple's obligatory anniversary sex had been the only saving grace in their tepid marriage, but like everything in their relationship, it eventually fizzled out. Admitting to stop making an effort was perhaps the only thing both could agree on. Mark wasn't held in the highest regard by his wife's family after years of unemployment, sofa testing and cheating allegations. Mark saw less and less of his wife after she accepted the position in Germany working as a banking consultant.

Initially, it was agreed that Annabel would fly back every Friday night so the weekends could be spent as a family away from the many stresses that working in finance brought. However, the Friday night trips to Bristol Airport arrivals gate grew rarer by the week and soon became a treat rather than a formality. Mark and Annabel soon grew out of love, some 14 years after many would have guessed, and as such he moved to find an answer to his phallic needs. It is often said that men think with their dicks and in this case, that analogy certainly rung true. Twice, many three times a week, Mark sought the services of a mobile hairdresser for reasons far more adult than a short-back-and-sides. These daytime escapades gave Mark an edge of excitement that had gone missing, adrenaline pumped through his veins every time he waited for the doorbell to ring. Savannah was the only ounce of worry on his mind as he knew, hoped and often joked that his wife would probably go shopping for a German *würst* or two on the continent. After a highly surreal mix-up with phone numbers, of which Hollywood would be proud, Mark messaged his wife, asking her to come round much earlier as Savannah was now due back from school sooner than was first expected. It was only when his wife replied to *that* message that he realised his mistake.

Charming Mark. I'm sure she's a delightful young woman if she wants to 'cum' round the house of a man who can't spell. Or perhaps that was a hideously crude joke. I'll ring you later. x

Mark re-read the message more times than he would care to admit. He quickly realised that her closing kiss was more likely down to habit rather than love. For a man who had just texted his wife with instructions intended for his mistress, he felt like he had got off easy. This was all but confirmed when Annabel rang him late that evening. After plenty of half-hearted grovelling, they both surprisingly concluded that it was important to be united in front of their hormonal teenage daughter. Annabel would continue to work abroad and visit when she could, and Mark would continue to babysit. It was telling of their relationship that a conversation concerning their futures was made on the phone rather than face to face. Normality was the real winner. If there were a prize for burying the hatchet, Mark and Annabel would win by some distance. Soon after Mark had recounted the events to his mates at *The Locksbrook Inn* over a pint or two, the news spread, even as far as his in-laws who unsurprisingly turned up unexpectedly on a Sunday morning "to check on their granddaughter." Jane and Tony Bancroft were not-so-secretly disappointed about their privately educated daughter marrying a labourer. Any opportunity for a scalding comment was acted on by Jane while Tony spoke only in sophisticated discourse to ensure Mark felt out of place. Ever since that fraught, insufferable prostration of a morning, Mark had never been able to tolerate her parents for much longer than a morning. With their daughter away working, the meetings thankfully dwindled. Yet, it was these continental forays that made money for the company and her family. Money that fed, clothed and overindulged Mark. Money that many argued didn't belong in the pocket of a man fucking another woman. Money that kept lips sealed and the truth, secret. But soon after Mark found out that having wealth wasn't the protector of all evil. Three weeks after Savannah's fourteenth birthday, on a routine doctors appointment, Mark's world shattered. He was diagnosed with terminal cancer of the brain. With just weeks to live, he made memories that he hoped would last a lifetime. After an action-packed day at Thorpe

Park, Savannah kissed her dad on the forehead and wished him goodnight. He never woke from that sleep. The weeks that followed his funeral were tough. Her mother couldn't take time off from work and as such, was seeing less and less of her grieving daughter. Savannah moved in with her paternal aunt, Jules Staggs which let life gradually resume to normality. The teen found that it was much easier to pretend life was well than to confront the issues disrupting it. For the moment, it worked for the family.

CHAPTER TWO

For the vast majority of her 17-year existence, the sound of displacing driveway stones dragged Savannah inquisitively from the pillow-heavy queen-size she lived on, to her bedroom window overlooking the road clogged with traffic. Sunday was no day for the postman to be struggling through his brimming postbag nor for Agnes from next door to sniff out the slightest smell of 'community-orientated' gossip. Today was a rest day, a family day, the weekend, days in which her ever-decreasing family would try and pretend to like each other. An effort made not for themselves but for the neighbours either side of the paper thin walls. As Savannah heard an overly familiar three knocks at the door, she slid the laptop off her thighs, leaving behind a burning sensation that every teenager has grown to tolerate and peered out of the window. What greeted her was a sight she had become accustomed to, but the sudden realisation that her mother was dead was an entirely new feeling altogether. After turning off the 'racquet' that pumped from her speakers, she pulled open the door and slumped on the stairs out of view of the front door.

"Mrs Staggs, I...."

The policeman cleared his throat and tried again. No amount of training could prepare you for these moments.

"Madam. I have some news surrounding the disappearance of your sister-in-law."

Savannah heard nothing more for the next 10 seconds or so, a pause that nearly pulled her into view.

"Can I come in Mrs Staggs?" said the policeman, finally filling the silence.

"Jules, please. Of course, yeah course please, this way," replied Jules. As the conversation moved into the kitchen, Savannah suddenly felt alone. Growing up without a constant mother figure in her life meant that she fought most of her teenage dramas alone. Boys, bitches, even her first period were dealt with a stiff upper lip and the help of Google but knowing that her mum was available if it all went wrong. Tears began to form under her tired eyes, and soon her sobbing was heard by the kitchen party. Jules appeared first hugging a roll of kitchen paper, followed closely behind by a visibly shaken policeman. Something about his manner upset Savannah even further, and her blubbering turned into hysterics. Jules felt no need to relay the information to her niece as she could tell she knew that her mother, best friend and confidante was dead. That small glimmer of hope that her mum was still alive after just 48 hours of disappearance, that small glimmer of hope that kept Savannah sane and functioning in the darkest of times, that small glimmer of hope that many told her to forget about was, just like her mother, gone and never coming back.

The days that followed meant that Savannah was introduced to dozens of relatives she had never met and some she had never even heard of. Black ensemble after black ensemble trounced over the threshold with flowers, cards and pity in hand. As the doorbell rang for the umpteenth time, Jules leapt to open the door.

"Jackie, I wasn't expecting to see you? Tell me you didn't drive all this way?" said Jules.

Jackie, perhaps dumbfounded by Jules' apparent ageing, politely smiled. Jules paused before opening her mouth.

"You did? You shouldn't have. No really. Not necessary. But yeah it is good to see you."

"Oh Julia darling, I couldn't stay at home and not help you out. I just wish it was under better circumstances per se. How's my little darling god-daughter?"

"Not so little anymore, she's in the kitchen. Come through."

Jackie followed Jules through the swarms of relatives nodding at each as she walked past before reaching the safe haven of the kitchen.

"Savannah, oh my darling, come give your Auntie Jackie a big hug."

You didn't have to be a mind reader or trained psychologist to understand what Savannah thought of a hug with a woman who she had met twice, once for her 8th birthday and once at her first holy communion the year later. Jackie read the scowl and decided to comfort her goddaughter orally.

"I'm so sorry, my sympathies darling."

Savannah smiled back at her 'auntie' while dismissing her condolences. Savannah couldn't comprehend feeling sorry for herself if anything she felt sorry for the kettle and the doorbell who had never had a busier day.

"Let me make you a cup of tea Jules, my love" mumbled Jackie as she tried to make herself look busy.

"Than-"

The doorbell interrupted Jules' pleasantries.

"Savannah, will you get that for me?"

"Jules, come on," pleaded the teenager.

For all of Jackie's annoyances, the kitchen was a haven away from the gossiping tongues and wandering eyes of the living room, full to the brim with extended family. Savannah dreaded walking through the living room to her front door. Family support was overrated.

"Savannah."

Jules' tone made Jackie laugh and then sigh to herself as she filled the kettle, an odd thing to do given she has no kids or close family to reminisce over.

Keeping her head down, Savannah made her way through the room as the cackles of laughter and chatter were hushed into subdued whispers more suited for this sort of occasion. Taking a moment to compose her before opening the door and welcoming more strangers into their family home, Savannah glanced into the hallway mirror and noticed she looked older, aged perhaps by the months of crying into her pillow. After scraping her hair back off her forehead, she practised a smile, easier said than done, and opened the door.

"Hello, my sweetheart. Don't you look the spitting image of your mother."

Savannah didn't recognise the man nor the accent. He towered over her wearing clothes that resembled one of the Hairy Bikers. If this were a game show, she would have guessed 'Eastern European' and 'worked with your dad'. The man was holding an oven dish covered over with tin foil. It smelt like a stew. He extended his arm.

"My manners. I am Daniel."

Savannah said nothing.

"I have gotten you some food, my mother's recipe for a stroganoff."

She was right. Daniel's English wasn't.

"Thanks…I thought people only brought food to dead people's homes in the movies. I'll give it to my aunt. She'll probably eat it."

"Ah okay. Maybe I watch too many American movies. May I come in?" asked the man.

"Um yeah, course. Do you want me to get my aunt?"

"No. No, bother. Please, I will find her later."

He spoke in a way that amused Savannah, gifting her with the lightest moment of comic relief. He followed her hesitantly through the room of people, pausing every few yards to peer at the family photos resting on cabinets and hanging on the walls. Savannah left him and retreated to the kitchen.

"Who was it dear?" asked Jackie, as if she knew any of the people that could turn up on the doorstep.

"Just some man. Foreign, worked with Dad probably. Where has Jules gone?"

"Oh, she's just gone to the shops to get some more tea bags. We've run out! She's put me in charge of you, but you are a big girl, aren't you! Don't need a babysitter!"

Savannah wasn't sure if Jackie was asking her or telling her but either way, she wasn't best pleased being left alone in a house full of familiar strangers or being called a big girl by a woman who has never even sent a birthday card to her 'dearest god-daughter.'

"Auntie Jackie," Savannah thought playing the family card was a good way to get her attention, "what do you exactly do?"

"Oh well, you know, this and that", replied Jackie as she took it upon herself to wash the sides.

Savannah wasn't naive and knew that meant unemployed. Unemployment leads to boredom and spontaneous cross-country visits. Throughout her life, Savannah had only heard Jackie's name mentioned a handful of times and even then it was usually followed by either the words 'drunk' or 'alone'. Her relation to the woman standing in her kitchen was weak enough that birthday money wasn't expected but calling her Auntie was considered perfectly fine. She dressed well. A pleated trouser suit with leather brogues was her outfit of choice, well suited for the time and place. Savannah expected this ensemble had been worn more than her gym gear or cocktail dress. Not because she was fat or even ugly, but because Jackie, who had now moved onto emptying the dishwasher, was hanging over the sides and weathered in the face, like an out-of-date muffin. Jackie held herself in high regard, perhaps too high for an unemployed alcoholic who thrived on other people's misfortune. The fact that the grieving, now motherless teenager felt sorry for her showed how pitiful her life had become. The silence that was filling the room became too uncomfortable for Jackie to remain quiet.

"We were ever so close, your mum and I. Known her now for what, going on 45 years."

She thought that was funny.

"We were such good friends. And then there was your dad. Oh, and weren't they suited for each other. Like two peas in a pod."

No matter how hard she tried, Jackie's Somerset twang still crept through, especially when patronising younger people.

"We had lots of fun. Me and your mum!"

Savannah wasn't sure why she had to remind the room whom she was talking about.

"I sat next to her on the school bus. Back row. How we laughed!"

While Savannah knew for certain that her mum didn't share the same sentiments, she let Jackie have her moment. Not many people would drive 200 miles to stand in a kitchen recounting stories of a dead woman to her grieving 17-year-old daughter.

"That reminds me of Mr Dorsett. He was our teacher, gorgeous he was. Your mum had a right crush on him, and we think he did on her too—"

"That's enough!"

Savannah had snapped, and Jackie had quite rightly shut up.

"My mum hasn't been dead five minutes, and you are standing here pretending that you were her best friend? I've met you twice, you don't know my family and you don't know me."

"Susannah I'm so sorry."

"Savannah! My name is Savannah. Just get out. Get back in your shitty little car and find another family to prey on."

"I didn't mean to—"

"Didn't mean to what? Make me upset? Well, you have so why don't we give you a big round of applause."

"I don't think that's necessa—"

Sarcasm apparently didn't cross over the generational gap.

"What do you want? A certificate? — 'Dead Woman's Best Friend Award, for claiming to be friends with a dead person to bag free cups of tea and custard fucking creams,' — how's that?"

"We were sisters—"

"Were. Were sisters, through blood only. There's your answer. You're a has-been."

Neither Savannah nor Jackie knew where this anger was coming from, but the latter put it down to grief.

"Your mother and I were terrific friends until she got that job abroad. She came back a different person."

Savannah couldn't quite believe that Jackie was slandering her dead mother.

"Are you serious? Are you actually serious?"

"If you let me finish my fucking sentences then I'll bloody well tell you."

"Tell me what? My mum ditched you?"

"Just me let speak you stupid little bitch."

Jackie herself couldn't quite believe that she has lost it in front of a teenager nor could Jules, who now stood at the door with a multipack of tea bags after his dash to shop. She cleared her throat.

"I think it's time you leave."

"Darling, I'm so sorry, I didn't me-"

"Get out."

Jackie's skin flushed a similar shade of red to her knocked off Louis Vuitton bag that she clutched to as she made her way through the living room. Jackie was prepared for tutting as she made her way to the door yet the room stayed silent, perhaps out of shock that a grown woman had just traded insults with the daughter of their now dead friend, relative or business partner.

With the door closing behind her, Jackie twisted the key into her ageing Morris Minor and slid into the seat. Heat radiated from every surface of the car which made her flush an even deeper shade of red than the one caused by her earlier embarrassment. Just as the car clunked into action and the gear stick shifted to reverse, the front door was yanked open by a red-faced, steaming Jules but before she had time to use every expletive under the sun, Jackie pushed her foot down hard on the accelerator. In one continuous motion, the car reversed, swung round and pushed forward, a move even professional rally drivers would be impressed by. As Jackie shifted through the gears, she did as every good driver should, and checked her mirrors, where she saw Jules' middle-aged figure gradually diminish in size. It had taken just 5 minutes of driving time before the phone inside her bag on the passenger's seat started to vibrate and hum a melodic tune. With one hand on the wheel, Jackie reached into her bag, grabbed the buzzing phone and swiped to accept the call.

"Distractions are your forte it seems," said the softly spoken man on the other end of the phone.

"Experience darling. I've worked with enough teenagers to know exactly how to cause a scene. Did you get what you were after?"

Jackie turned on speaker mode and rested the phone in the palm of her hand.

"Yes, I will transfer what we agreed to your account within 48 hours. Do stay with touch Miss Jackie."

With her finger now resting just above the end call button, Jackie moaned ever so slightly.

"I'm not one to keep away."

Bleep. Bleep. Bleep.

With that, just 17 seconds of conversation, Jackie set the phone down and turned up the radio in an attempt to block out her guilty conscious, at least for the 200 mile trip back to her lonely life for one.

CHAPTER THREE

News travelled fast in small cities and Bath was no exception. Within minutes of the news breaking on all of the local, and even some national news websites, Savannah's phone buzzed repeatedly. Never had she been so popular. Facebook notified her that thirteen people had posted on her wall in just three minutes while two people had gifted her in *8 Ball Pool.* Whether the latter was a notion of sympathy, Savannah was unsure. The messages continued to pour in as the hours ticked by; mostly from people she had never met yet who still felt the need to show closeness to the daughter of a news headline. Savannah could understand the media value placed on her head. A British woman found hanging in a European warehouse, orphaning her only daughter, was the sort of story news desks around the country thrived on. Still, the fact her mother's death was now common knowledge filled Savannah with great unease. It was far too soon to answer the multitude of questions whizzing around inside Savannah's head yet, the police insisted on sending a family liaison officer to speak with her. PC Kelly Nichols made herself at home, helping herself to a glass of weak squash within minutes of trouncing her muddy converses over the recently-vacuumed hallway carpet. The police officer matched her shoes with a pair of acid washed denim jeans and a GAP emblazoned sweat-shirt. As she sat, the teen looked her over.

"Is it mufti day?"

PC Nichols was taken aback by Savannah's dry wit and raised an eyebrow that she hoped would silence the teenager. While inexperienced as a liaison officer, PC Nichols had seen near everything, from kidnappings to domestic abuse, in her 18-year police career. Her hairstyle, synonymous within the force, light brown dyed pixie cut, had been one of the few constants in her adult life. Men had come and gone, giving her nothing other than disappointment and the need to buy another box of tissues. Setback after setback, both professional and personal, caused, the then DI Nichols to seek another type of career. Following months of tedious training, she became the newly created Family Liaison Officer at Avon and Somerset Constabulary. Just two weeks into her new job, PC Nichols found herself in the living room of the Bancroft family home with an unnerving sense of anxiousness keeping her quiet. *Be confident, be calm and be collected.* Her training was about to culminate in a conversation where neither participant wanted to be there. Savannah spoke first.

"Sorry. I guess they don't want you to wear the scary uniform. It might remind me that both my mum and dad are dead."

"Isn't that why I'm here? We don't expect you to face all of this on your own" asked the police officer.

"I've got my aunt?"

"Don't you think your Aunt would like some help too?"

"Ask her. Do I look that old?"

"Savannah, it's entirely reasonable to feel this way. This is—"

"Oh yeah because your mum going missing happens to everyone doesn't it."

"—normal behaviour, being sarcastic and putting up front. You're a sassy little thing aren't you?"

Savannah let a smile escape from within as the police officer carried on.

"It's important to open up and let people help you. Most of your friends and family won't have the foggiest idea what to say, how to help, the least you can do is let them in. Think of me as a bridge, a bridge between you and my bosses. You can ask me anything."

With Savannah staring at the floor, chewing her jumper, PC Nichols didn't wait for acknowledgement.

"How does that sound?"

"Sounds like a load of shit. I don't even know how my mum died. Where was she? When did she die? Was anybody with her? Did anyone help her or hear the last breath? Can you answer that?"

Savannah wasn't finished.

"Hm? No. Until you can tell me that, I have no interest in speaking to you. Take your squash and fuck off back to GAP."

PC Nichols could feel tears begin to form under her sleepy eyes but faced with the embarrassment of crying at her first job, the officer sniffed herself back to focus. Sliding the folder off of the table, she stood and headed towards the door. Savannah didn't think the police woman would actually leave but taking into account recent events, she had come to expect people in her life walking out on her. PC Nichols swung round on the spot and locked her eyes on the teenager hunched over in the settee.

"Look, Savannah, I'm new to this—"

"It's okay, just—"

The officer proper open the folder in her arms.

"Your mother was found on the ground floor of AgriLab, an agricultural warehouse in the countryside 8 miles outside of Riga, the capital city of Latvia. She was found by the local police force at eighteen thirty-five Latvian time on Wednesday. No other bodies or signs of violence were found at the scene."

Savannah sat up, open-mouthed, while the police officer read from the slim folder.

"Her body was taken to the local coroner's officer, which in this case was at the Pauls Stradins Clinical University Hospital in Riga, where a full medical examination will be carried out in due course, but currently police are fairly conclusive that her death wasn't suspicious."

"What does that mean? How did she die? You haven't told me-"

Savannah's speaking pace quickened with her heart rate.

"Ligature asphyxiation."

Savannah waited for the police officer to translate.

"She hung herself."

Neither Savannah nor the trained police officer spoke for the next few minutes, the silence in the room only interrupted by the noise of friction made as PC Nichols rubbed Savannah's arm through her jumper.

"My mum killed herself?"

"That's what all the signs lead to I'm—"

"My mum killed herself."

"We obviously don't know why she decided to end her own life and while it's difficult to comprehend, especially given the location of the passing, the local police force are confident in their findings and won't be opening an investigation. It's very unlikely that we'll learn any more details about what has happened."

Savannah, in a state of obvious shock, could only repeat herself.

"My mum killed herself? My mum?"

She was struggling to accept the police's conclusion. Information had been scarce in few days following her mother's disappearance with both Savannah and her aunty assuming that Annabel had missed her flight home, lost her phone or fell ill. Neither had ever entertained the thought that she was dead let alone hanging from the steelwork of a Latvian warehouse.

"Does my aunty know?"

"Your guardian was notified this morning when she visited the station to collect your mum's possessions."

"Possessions? What did she have?"

PC Nichols, licked her finger and flicked back through the folder before sub-quoting the list printed on the first page.

"One iPhone, smashed screen, a black satchel, which contained a laptop, an empty folio folder, a lip balm, purse and passport, the clothes

24

she was wearing plus her jewellery; a silver necklace, two rings and a wristwatch."

Savannah couldn't help imagining her mum hanging by a rope nor could she get the woman opposite her to stop staring. She spoke quickly.

"I think you need to ring them."

PC Nichols wasn't sure who Savannah wanted her to ring, responding only with a look of uncertainty.

"Latvia. The police. The people that found her. My mum wouldn't have killed herself; she hasn't got the guts."

"Savannah, I've worked a lot of suicides as a copper, and I can say truthfully—"

Savannah interjected abruptly.

"Something's not right."

"that people who decide to end their lives aren't always the ones who seem like-"

"She wouldn't have left me."

"You have to understand that people-"

"Is it my fault?"

"Savannah, please, you must not think that way. It's dangerous to try and second-guess your mum's way of thinking."

"I know she didn't kill herself. You need to tell them to open an investigation."

PC Nichols decided to smile and say nothing more. Sometimes the police officer wondered if people ever needed to know how their loved ones died. It seemed an odd way to remember someone. In this case, the last image of Savannah's loved one, before they flew away to wherever one believed was to be cold, limp and hung from a rope. For adults, this news was near impossible to comprehend but telling teenagers, still children at heart, that their mother had died is dangerous, unhealthy and life-defining. Savannah, sat opposite the police officer, feeling surrounded by an air of vulnerability let tears run down her cheeks. Savannah knew that no matter how many times she cried herself into near dehydration, the pain she felt inside would never subside.

"How long did it take?"

It took a moment for PC Nichols to catch her drift.

"That's hard to say. Usually it only takes a few seconds to lose consciousness. It's likely your mother passed away within 5 minutes."

"Did it hurt?"

The officer found lying natural.

"Not for very long."

"Have you ever lost somebody?"

PC Nichols fired back.

"Define somebody."

"A leaning post. Someone you can fall back on no matter how many times you let them down."

PC Nichols exhaled a short laugh.

"You don't find too many people like that. Life has a funny way of tricking us. When you need someone the most they aren't there. You fall much further when you think there is someone waiting to catch you. We trust the wrong people and push away those wanting to help."

"And how do you know who is who?"

"That's the problem Savannah. You don't."

How to speak in philosophical analogies wasn't a module on the police liaison training course and while the police officer felt Savannah was anything but 'textbook,' she was disappointed at herself for straying from the regulations. PC Nichols often thought that the black trousers and startlingly neon jacket, and later pleated trouser suits that made up her police uniform for well over a decade, felt like a cage around her. Rules and regulations stamped into authority by the top brass grappling for a power prevented police officers from effectively doing their jobs. Less responsibility yet more danger fell at the steel toe capped feet of the everyday copper and with it, a smaller wage packet to take home. After a misguided move upstairs to the CID, a well-preserved part of the 1970s, complete with casual sexism and misogynistic 'banter', Kelly Nichols deiced to part with prefix and attempted to rediscover the love she once had for her job. An application for the mounted division was rejected, but after a frank and painfully honest conversation with her seniors, Nichols applied for the role of liaison officer. With bills mounting daily, the decision to drop down a pay grade didn't make economic sense. PC Nichols hoped that the fulfilment of job would be worth more than the latest television or smartphone. Retirement was a long way off yet PC Nichols knew now that this would be her last job in the force. The prospect of searching for another job was daunting and as such PC Nichols was determined to make this role a success. Understanding, and crucially, helping people was much harder than the training course had made out and rather annoyingly didn't help PC Nichols move the conversation forward. She stumbled for a different conversation topic.

"Your Aunt told me that you're having the funeral on Monday?"

"Yeah. Monday. 1pm."

"Are you going to say anything? Some people like to read a poem, or even recount some of their favourite mem-"

"No."

"No?"

Savannah looked up at PC Nichols to emphasise her point.

"No."

"If you are sure then I guess that is perfectly fine. Have you discussed that with your aunt?"

"Look, I'm not going to stand up at the front of a bloody church full of people I don't even know and tell them all about the time my mum set off the smoke alarm baking cookies. Or the time she taught me how to ride my bike. Oh, and all the times she picked me up from school getting me a bag of sweets on the way home—"

"Some—"

"—because that would be a lie. None of those things ever happened. I didn't have a normal childhood. I grew up with a dad who would have preferred a son and a mum who preferred her job. Then he died and—"

"Savannah I think it's im—"

"I love my mum, trust me, I really do."

Just when PC Nichols thought she had calmed the teenager, tears began to trickle down her cheeks.

"But...I can't pretend we were close. She taught me the basics, the bare minimum. We didn't have girls night where we would paint each other's nails and watch *Mean Girls*. We weren't like that."

Savannah paused, her eyes glossed over as her tear ducts worked overtime.

28

"I can't even remember the last time I saw her alive."

PC Nichols placed her hand on Savannah's shoulder and shushed over through the half-words exhaled between the heavy panting.

Such resilience in the face of death wasn't uncommon, yet the almost instantaneous transition from sarcastic stubbornness to the inconsolable wreck that now faced her drew PC Nichols to just one conclusion. Broken. Vulnerable. However she termed it, PC Nichols knew Savannah was becoming irrational.

"Savannah my love, can you excuse me for just a moment?"

Savannah sniffed the tears and snot, back inside, and nodded.

The sun had come out from behind the clouds yet the wind passing through the cul-de-sac made PC Nichols wish she was wearing a coat. As she pulled her police-issued phone out of her tight jean pocket she caught the eye of a peering neighbour who politely smiled and then turned back to his gossiping wife. Holding down the centre key automatically rang the station control centre, and after a few dials, she was speaking to a familiar voice.

"Hi, Liz. Can I get you to clear my diary for Monday afternoon?"

"I can try Kelly love but I can't guarantee it'll be authorised."

"It's the Bancroft girl's mum's funeral. I need it off."

"Monday you said?"

"Please."

"I'll speak to David. Do you need to be there?"

"Liz, she's hanging on like a thread. Press is going to be there, and the last thing I need is this girl having a breakdown to see it plastered all across Mail fucking Online."

"I'll speak to David."

As the line went dead, the sun hid behind the clouds and PC Nichols felt colder than ever before.

CHAPTER FOUR

Savannah had been stood staring at the inside of wardrobe for long enough that all of her clothes had merged into one. Nothing seemed acceptable for a jolly let alone a funeral. Her collection of clothes had been hastily assembled, much like the flat-pack wardrobe that hid them away from sight. Catalogue orders were the saving grace for her aunt in charge of the shopping but they did little to enhance a teenager's style. Savannah pulled out her work trousers; black, too long and shapeless, before cutting the firm's logo out of the stitching above the front pocket. Work, if a part time job in a card shop counted as such, was a concept Savannah had all but forgotten over the last few weeks. That was until this morning when she woke to a voicemail from her manager informing Savannah that she had been sacked and should visit the store

store to collect her P45. The nationwide chain that had paid Savannah moderately since she was sixteen, was currently in the news. Administration beckoned and after the untimely phone call, Savannah wished that her snooty former manager would lose her job. The mundanity of retail, especially in a shop that sold cards and wrapping paper, numbed Savannah and made her wonder how any of her former colleagues found enjoyment and satisfaction on a daily basis. She couldn't help but feel that perhaps if she worked in *Topshop,* she might have an outfit to wear today rather than an excessive amount of discounted Yankee Candles fumigating every corner of the house. A school shirt, white but blemished with easily-hidden grass stains, and a shaped black blazer were pulled out to complete the 'look'. Before Savannah had the chance to get changed, she heard a knock on the door.

"It's Jules, Sav."

Savannah expected her to barge in like every other time.

"Can I come in?" she asked.

"Yeah."

Teenagers are often resourceful and efficient with words rather than blunt and rude. Jules had been Savannah's auntie for 17 years but her mum for little over a week.

"Are you not ready? Sav, come on, we have to leave in a while."

Savannah had not just lost her mother in the last week but apparently half of her name as well.

"I was just about to shower."

Jules would usually raise her voice but in these circumstances, she kept her words calm.

"You were about to shower nearly 2 hours ago. What have you been doing all this time?"

Savannah smirked while reaching across to grab the scraps of paper on her bed. Jules scoffed at the sight.

"Homework? I don't think any of your teachers are expecting you to be keeping up to date with school work."

As Jules moved in closer to place a sympathetic hand on Savannah's shoulder, she noticed the words 'Mum' written across the top of the paper.

"Oh Sav."

This time the nickname felt right.

"Shall we put that with the flowers?"

"No, I want to read it.."

Jules handed it back to her niece seemingly in confusion.

"Out loud. I want to read it today."

"Really? Your Mum would love that, sweetie."

The letter was spread over two pages of double sided note paper and was littered with scribbled out words and drawn through lines.

Perfection is hard to reach when rushing an obituary on the morning of a funeral. Savannah's decision to speak at the funeral was sudden and wholly self-unexpected. A sleepless night tossing and turning under the hot, suffocating sheets led to a five a.m wake up call and hours of early morning wall-watching. For those early hours, all was quiet barring the gentle whizz from her overheating computer. A small gap between the plastic window frame and her external bedroom wall pulled a cold draft into the room, that people of faith would probably claim to be a visitor. Savannah was brought up as a Catholic although her decision to write a eulogy rather than rely on poems or prayers pointed towards an agnostic, though if honest, atheist belief. Savannah found recalling memories harder than she had expected. Family days out were few and far between and as such the teen didn't have too much to write about. While her grandparents encouraged it, neither of her parents were devoutly religious and it was often joked that Savannah was only baptised to earn a place at St Peter's Primary, a school known for producing well-rounded kids. Those jokes would not be repeated today, especially when in the company of Father Derek, the local priest who had so hesitantly allowed the funeral to take place in his church given the bated press who would inevitably be waiting outside. Father Derek Morgan was a familiar face to Savannah from his time spent teaching at her school. While she wasn't sure if he even knew her name, Savannah was certain he'd be proud of the early morning reflection that gone into her scribbled down eulogy. Her mind felt clearer and she had much more room to think.

"I don't know if it's any good. I did it this morning."

Jules laughed without smiling.

"I couldn't sleep either. Get dressed, I'll put the kettle on."

Jules pulled the door closed and looked at herself in the landing mirror. She looked crisp in her freshly dry-cleaned suit yet others would think different. Once in the kitchen, she listened for Savannah's footsteps coming down the stairs. Jules worried for her niece. With the kettle almost at a boil, Savannah came into the room, looked up at her aunt and smiled through the anxiousness. For a split second, Savannah's grace and natural beauty reminded Jules of the woman they were about to bury. She had been flirting with the idea of grief since the policeman

34

broke the news and wasn't sure what to feel. Jules had lost her sister-in-law, the mother of the child now in her care, and somebody who her brother had spent most of his life. Yet somehow, the fact Mark had so infamously cheated meant mourning for Annabel riddled Jules with guilt. With now just a few minutes to spare until the funeral procession would arrive, Jules abandoned the offer of a cup of tea and stood at the window looking out onto the driveway and the small stretch of road outside their home. The rain clouds overhead moved together to form a grey blanket over the immediate surroundings, stifling all underneath. Minutes waiting soon turned to seconds and not before long, but not a minute early or late, the small procession of 3 cars pulled into the cul-de-sac. Leading the motorcade, a hearse drew their attention. Jules looked at her niece and could see the fear and trepidation in her glossy eyes no matter how hard Savannah tried to conceal her feelings.

"Shall we do this, Sav?" asked Jules, not knowing if either could. Despite burying her dad, the image of a coffin in the back of a hearse didn't get any easier. She knew well that the realisation you are near crying is almost worse than the act itself, meaning as the tears began to fall, Savannah felt comfortable in her grief. She wrapped her arms around her auntie, feeling her cosy warmth and ever so soft shake.

"Let's go."

As all responsible adults do, Jules led the way, pushing open the door and heading towards the vehicles. A man stood before them in a pin-striped black suit with a top hat on his head and a cane in his hand. Savannah suspected that he was younger than his face told her, his waxy skin aged by daily experience of death.

"Good Afternoon, Ladies," came the cockney-voice.

He motioned at Savannah with a tilt of his hat.

"Madam. My sincere condolences for your loss from all of us at Les Crawford Funeral Directors."

Both Jules and her niece were motionless yet now on first name basis.

"Please, this way."

Les motioned for both Jules and Savannah to step into the car directly behind the hearse carrying the coffin and what appeared to be an entry to the Chelsea Flower Show. The word 'Mum,' spelt out in white chrysanthemums, tied together with a pink ribbon trim, leant across the width of the hearse window. Other, lesser wreaths were spread across the coffin, ranging from the most elegant of red rose hearts to the simplest of daisy bunches. Savannah knew, from Mothers Days a plenty, that flowers were costly and wondered if any of the window decorations were worth it. After crouching into the back of the car, Savannah's nose filled with the unmistakable smell of window cleaner, and not the pine tree air freshener that hung from the mirror in the front cab. Until a complicated reversing manoeuvre that involved all 3 vehicles and a tight turning cycle forced her view, Savannah hadn't noticed that her mum's parents were in the car behind. Jane, seeing her granddaughter staring, waved from behind a handkerchief while husband, Grandad Tony kept his eyes on the road and away from the hearse in front. Les, for whatever reason, decided to walk the first 100 metres, before removing his hat and sliding into the front seat of the vehicle. The journey from their house to St Peter's Church was usually only 5 minutes yet today, it was much quicker with the majority of motorists giving way to the funeral procession. After a sharp left turn, the cars and hearse pulled up outside the church's steep steps and the clicks and flashes of intruding cameras began. St Peter's Church was near 200 years old, and its age was beginning to tell. Steeples towered above the adjacent housing estates and the lush lands of greenery broken up only by the occasional tombstone. Once out of the car, Savannah waited for her gran's cold, familiar hand and slowly climbed the steps to the church door. The grand wooden doors were open enough to allow sunlight to bathe Father Derek, stood just inside the doorway with golden light across his face. Ill health had cast doubt on whether he was still a capable priest for the local parish yet one could not falter his enthusiasm and determination to the cause. His back arched over, and his head drooped lower than it should. Savannah had know seen the colour of his hair changed over the years, from a light hazel to the snowy blonde we see now, yet his toothy smile never wavered. As they greeted each other, the priest, dipping his finger in the font of holy water, offered a blessing to the teenager. Out of respect for both the priest and her grandmother, and encouraged by old habit, Savannah instinctively obliged.

The familiarity of the church and in particular, its beautiful interior, complete with authentic frescos, gave a warmth to the expanse that would not exist otherwise. Memories of baptisms, communions and school masses filled the room from its modest width to impressive height. Savannah spotted a few familiar faces as she walked to her front row seats, including old teachers, school friends and PC Nichols, the liaison officer from the police, all of which chose to keep their heads down as she walked past. As they waited for the funeral start, it became apparent that wooden pews weren't made for the comfort. Reaching into her pocket, Savannah pulled out the scraps of paper, unfurled them each individually and practised her lines. Father Derek paced up the aisle before he slowed to speak to Savannah and Jules. "We are about to start. I'll let you know when it is time for you to come on up."

Without waiting for a response, Father Derek walked the gentle incline to the microphone, tapped it twice to check it's functionality then spoke.

"Please stand."

The pews were packed full of regular churchgoers and those who had come specially to pay their respects. Barring the elder people, each member of the congregation rose to their feet as the coffin was carried up the aisle. Savannah, stuck behind the several tall men, couldn't beyond the first few rows, even after turning. Halfway down the aisle, Savannah watched as her grandad came into view. Leading a group of six men, each looked sombre as they rested her mum's coffin on their shoulders. The organ, so secretive it was hidden out of sight, pumped out a melodic hum that Savannah couldn't place even though it sounded so familiar. After setting down the coffin on a stand at the front, Tony joined his wife and granddaughter while Jules left Savannah to join her family on the other side of the aisle. Successions of 'Amens' and hymns followed before Father Derek beckoned Savannah to the podium.

"And now, I'd like to invite.."

He glanced down at his page.

"young Savannah to the stage to share some memories of her mother, who we sadly lay to rest today."

Savannah stood before he was finished and moved up to the podium, the scraps of paper wetting in her clammy hands. As she cleared her throat, Savannah spread the speech out on the podium. Looking out at the crowd, she decided against any set up and went straight in.

"Mum. We weren't that close. You know that. I know that. But you had part of me. I'm not sure when or how you took it, but part of me, part of my heart lived inside of you. I'll miss you, and I'll miss that until we meet again. I wasn't sure what I wanted to write to you, I don't know if you can even hear me. I didn't want to embarrass myself in front of all of these strangers."

Savannah looked up to see outbreaks of nervous giggling ripple across the room, each person hoping they weren't one of the aforementioned strangers.

"But then I thought, fuck it."

Jules should have been horrified that her niece had sworn in a place of worship yet even she found herself snuffling laughter under the scornful eye of the priest standing directly ahead.

"Work was perhaps your one true love in life, Sorry Dad.."

Pausing, she pointed to the ceiling.

"..and you strived to be a success. My mum, a female, was one of the most influential people in finance and for that, I was always immensely proud. Sure, she didn't teach me how to ride a bike or to braid my hair into cute plaits. We never baked a cake together or watched girlie films while painting our nails. We never spoke about school or friends or boys. But she taught me something else. Something far greater. She taught me that you can succeed. You can achieve whatever you set your mind to. She often said that everything seems impossible until it's done."

Savannah cleared her throat once more.

"I'm a disappointed with myself. Disappointed that is has taken until this to see everything she did for me. She wasn't around to tell me to stop skiving from school or to make me work harder in maths. But her achievements and morals live with me. I'd like everyone to remember my mum as the force for good she was. Not the person who let go of all she had but couldn't see. I yearn every minute, not for my mum, but for answers. And I know I will find them. Whether that takes a day or a thousand, I won't stop looking. Then, and only then can my mum, my inspiration, my friend rest in peace."

CHAPTER FIVE

Most of the twenty-four pound, sixty pence weekly wage that found its way into Savannah young savers account was wasted on public transport to and from work. While it was only a twenty minute round trip, Savannah shelled out £4.80 for a bus fare as unlike most of her friends; she didn't look young enough for a child ticket. Savannah was often caught in limbo, and her age was no different.

It was early morning, and the summer sun that become uncharacteristically consistent this June had not yet risen high enough to heat the bus shelter that nestled itself between the lines of hedges at the junction end of Old Kings Road. A narrow plastic bench, a usual godsend for legs too tired to stand, was part of the reason Savannah often found herself turning up late to work. With no electronic board announcing the next bus, and a timetable so outdated it was wholly incorrect, keeping her eyes on the street corner was her only way to spot the speeding bus, a feat made impossible while sat. Today, however with no time pressures and waiting managers, the teenager slumped over the bench and checked the news on her phone. It had been little over a week since her mother's funeral. The media hype had settled down, and her family faded back into national obscurity. Her old manager had phoned back, presumingly after stumbling across the employee that she had sacked grieving her dead mum in the paper, apologised and offered her old job back. Savannah knew full well that she didn't want nor need the job and politely declined before making plans to collect her last wage slip and holiday pay. The road, which usually fizzed with traffic, was still and Savannah was able to hear pedestrians before she could see them. An elderly lady, wrapped in a headscarf and unnecessary amount of layers for the forecast, approached the bus stop with her shopping trolley reluctantly pulling behind her. Savannah looked up to recognise Mrs Braithwaite, the now-retired owner of the corner shop that regularly swapped her pocket money in exchange for pick 'n' mix, coming ever closer.

"Ah aren't you an angel," said Mrs Braithwaite as Savannah stood up and freed her seat.

"No problem."

Savannah hoped that her face wouldn't be known as the dead woman's daughter as it was common knowledge that old ladies love nothing more than to gossip at a bus stop.

"Off to town then my love?"

Mrs Braithwaite's west-country accent was homely and maternal and far stronger than Savannah's slight twang.

"Yeah, just for a bit" came the blunt reply. She was in no mood to talk.

"I've just got to pick up some pieces. It's my Ian's little one's birthday on the weekend. I've got to stop off at the post office first then I'm going to pop into that new bakery down the bottom of town and get one of those caterpillar cakes. Aren't they cute, my love?"

Savannah had no energy to continue and decided to ignore the obvious ploy for conversation and just smile. Peering at the teenager's face, she continued.

"Got a list the length of my arm. You off to the pictures?"

Savannah despised the use of that phrase as everyone in their right mind, old or young, knew it was called the cinema and had been for several decades.

"No, I've got to pick up my P45 from work" replied Savannah, doing her best to indulge teenage stereotypes.

"P45!" screeched Mrs Braithwaite in a pitch only dogs could register.

"3 weeks holiday pay though. I'm not that hard done by."

"Oh, my love, that ain't bad at all. They must be bonkers to get rid of a lovely looking girl like you though."

Savannah was sure that looks didn't come into the decision but appreciated the sentiment regardless.

"I missed too much work. An absent worker isn't a good worker apparently."

Mrs Braithwaite stopped Savannah in her tracks.

"Sweetheart. I thought I recognised you. Now, look, you've got to tell me how your mum ended all the way out there."

43

"If I knew that then I wouldn't—"

Savannah stopped herself as the bus pulled around the corner then stuck her arm into the road to hail it down.

Hydraulics pulled the bus to a stop and as the electronic doors collapsed inwards, a wave of musky air was pushed into the waiting passengers' faces. Mrs Braithwaite hobbled aboard the bus and flashed her over 65 pass at the driver's glazed over eyes.

"Return to town, please."

Savannah yearned for the day she could buy a single.

"£4.80 love."

Savannah tossed the change into the tray before tearing the ticket from the machine. The bus was packed, and as neither pregnant nor old, she was forced to stand, squeezed between the bodies of two Japanese tourists. The journey to town was short, if not interrupted by multiple stops and awkward attempts at leaving the bus through the crowd. Tall townhouses-cum-office space either side of the park whizzed past before a series of tight turns brought the bus station into sight. Bath bus station could only be described as a giant tin of beans unless of course, you were the architect, in which case the building is a carefully designed mesh of steel and glass. As Savannah stepped off the bus eyes lingered longer than they should have. The concourse, unusually busy for mid-morning, echoed whispering voices from wall-to-wall. Glass lining the back wall caught the rising sun, splintering light and heat into the already stuffy ticket hall. National headlines didn't often involve Bath, and the city was certainly making the most of it. Savannah ignored the hushed silence and kept her head down until she reached the relative safety of outside paved forecourt. Celebrate!, 'the UK's number one

44

card retailer,' was housed opposite the bus station, nestled in an alcove of the new shopping development. While only a few years old, the outdoor mall had the look of something much older. All new buildings in Bath were subject to rigorous planning regulations, one of which was to use limestone to fit in with the surrounding structure steeped in history. Multi-million developments were no exception and as such, pale brickwork splattered with pigeon shit juxtaposed against the brightly coloured shop facades. Savannah stood toe-tapping at the zebra crossing, waiting patiently to be beeped across the road to the modest cheque. As the lights flashed red, traffic on either side of the path grounded to a halt and the more confident of crossers sped ahead of the crowds. The beeps began, and soon Savannah was approaching her former place of work.

Celebrate!'s logo, a birthday cake with candles spelling out the brand name, stood proudly over the half-hearted window displays. A red carpet extended out onto the street, an attempt to mimic special occasions and make the customer feel welcome. Savannah had no doubt that it was the brainchild of some big boss who had most likely never been forced to vacuum it every Saturday morning wearing a polyester t-shirt and internally recycled fleece. Staff left quicker than new ones could be found and trained which often meant queues to pay stretched the length of the store. Today was no exception. Red banners with 'SALE - ALL STOCK MUST GO' hung from the ceiling while below, similar stickers adorned the general bric-a-brac on shelves and in the brimming baskets. The one sole cashier, a spotty face teenager that Savannah had never seen before, looked daunted at the mounting queues of quickly angering customers. She sidestepped the queue and lent into the side of the till bank.

"Alright mate, can you get the manager out for me?" asked Savannah.

"I'm sorry—"

His voice cracked under the pressure of this unexpected request.

"—you have to queue up to be seen."

Savannah could hear the queue tutting even over the in-store radio that pumped out the same pop songs on a loop through the speakers.

"I used to work here, mate. Just get Dawn yeah?"

The lad gulped, nodded then pressed the bell beneath the desk.

Intimidation was another string to add to Savannah's ever growing bow.

Four happy and two not-so-happy customers were served before Dawn Bracknell, 'Celebrate! Regional Manager of the Year 2007,' paced out of the back door. Managers weren't subjected to the fleece, t-shirt combination that the regular employees were. A black skirt and striped shirt the only visible benefit of several months of online training courses. Dawn looked good for her middle-age. Her fiery red hair brushed immaculately into a fringe that was neither in nor out of fashion, framed her pale face. The striped shirt, complete with name badge pinned above the top pocket as per company guidelines, hugged her slight frame. Dawn's face dropped as she saw her former employee.

"Savannah. How are you?" asked Dawn, clutching a clipboard that was never too far from her side.

"I've been better. Just trying to keep life as normal as possible."

Savannah got the impression that she wasn't listening.

"No. Good," came the reply.

Savannah looked around the store to avoid the eye contact.

46

"Yeah, great. It's busy in here."

"It is. We need you back. Can you start in 10?"

Savannah laughed a little too hard.

"I think I'll just take my money if that's okay."

"Is money all you teenagers think about?"

Dawn was laughing as she handed over an envelope but Savannah knew she was being serious.

"Life doesn't pay for itself, Dawn."

"And shops don't run themselves, so I best be off."

"Thanks, Dawn."

"Take care Savannah. Keep in touch."

Dawn patted her former employee on the back and sped off to make herself look busy leaving Savannah to take the red carpet into the street.　　　　A hazy, amber glow lit the tall Georgian townhouses that formed around the moderate sized, well-maintained park. Rows of branded deck chairs filled the gaps between giant outdoor connect-four frames collapsed on their sides, and picnic mats held down by hampers of potato salad and pompous pop drinks. Cutting through the park was the quickest way to *Gailey's* at the top of town and as such Savannah found herself zig-zagging through gaggles of families enjoying the sun. Picnicking in the park was something that her family had never done and now, never would. Taking a right at the park gates brought Savannah into sight of the high street and in particular, *Gailey's*. The last week of the summer holidays wasn't complete without a visit to *Gailey's* to stock up on stationery, notebooks and a new pencil case. 'Back to School' window displays showed a diverse bunch of kids in pristine uniforms clutching books in a way that would most likely encourage classroom torment if their school was a real one. Savannah headed inside, remembering fondly those tense visits in which her Dad insisted on a black pencil case when the rest of her class had pink ones with lights and whistles.

"Hello."

Savannah looked up to see a beaming, larger woman wearing a heavily stained blue top with 'Happy to Help" stretched, almost illegibly, across the chest. With air conditioning at an almost arctic level, Savannah had no clue why this woman was sweating so excessively.

"Yeah. Hi. Maps?"

"Maps." said the employee before repeating it four times over as she thought about it.

"Yeah like a travel guide."

"Oh travel guides, 2nd floor next to the cafe on the left."

"Okay, thanks."

"Would you like me to show you where they are?"

Savannah declined, partly because the woman needed a rest and partly because she didn't want the unpleasant smell to follow her upstairs.

"No..it's okay thanks."

"That's fine by me. Now is there anything else I can help you with?"

Savannah knew her script; she was forced to use it at Celebrate! too.

"No. It's just the maps I'm after."

"Well, then you have a good day!"

Savannah could still hear the ringing of the woman's voice in her ears as she stepped off the escalator onto the second floor. *Gailey's* 'Travel' section was conveniently located right ahead of Savannah and not to the left of the cafe as her new friend had suggested. With the selection on offer, Savannah was glad she wasn't planning on visiting outer Mongolia of any of Africa otherwise she would be leaving empty handed. A quick scan of the shelf revealed only one suitable product, and upon realising this, Savannah plucked the book from the pile and headed downstairs to pay. The queue was much shorter than the one in Celebrate! and it wasn't before long that she found herself standing in front of the same sweaty employee from earlier.

"Oh fancy seeing you here!" she chuckled to herself.

Savannah didn't respond to the joke.

"Did you find everything you were looking for?" she chirped as she took the book and searched for the barcode.

"Clearly."

"Oo. 'The Very Best of France and Germany.' You off on your holibobs?"

"Yeah, something like that."

Describing Savannah's trip as a holiday couldn't be further from the truth.

"Do you have a GaileySaver card?"

"No."

"Will you be paying with American Express or cheque today?"

"No."

"Will you be paying with Visa or MasterCard?"

"No."

"How will you be paying today?"

"Do you accept chocolate coins?"

"I…I..don't—"

The woman looked around for a manager.

"No? I'll have to use cash then—"

Savannah enjoyed being on the other side of this intensely irritating interaction.

"—how much is it?"

Savannah glanced up at the screen, counted the cash from her purse to her hand and then dropped each coin into the waiting hand of the cashier.

"Would you like a receipt?"

She couldn't help herself.

"Oh fuck off you sweaty bitch."

Savannah felt exhilarated. She'd lost count of the number of times she'd been sworn at by customers, and while she felt bad, this time felt like revenge. Savannah envisaged a quick getaway from the store and didn't factor in waiting at the door to have her bag checked by the jobsworth security guard. Savannah could feel the sweaty bitch's eyes burning into her neck and daren't look back at the pain she had inevitably caused. Outside the store, the sun was at its highest point. Three balding men, all homeless and selling similar magazines, sat cross-legged beside a public toilet block, burning in the summer heat. Housed in a faux brick building, the toilets were electronic and required 30p to use, an attempt to stop people much like those sat outside, from using them. Savannah had needed the toilet since she stepped off the bus yet 30p seemed expensive just for a wee. As she walked down the main street, Savannah saw much of the same. Bath was full of coffee shops, ranging from the bog-standard chain cafe to the pompous monkey-picked coffee houses, and it wasn't much of a walk before she found Dixon's, a well-known chain. As the automatic doors slid open, Savannah could feel the ice-cold air conditioning on her skin. It felt pleasant in the summer heat. Boards behind the bar advertised limited edition frappe flavours at not so limited edition prices. These summer themed offerings, photographed in a highly unrealistic way, were pictured alongside Savannah's favourite treat, a Caramel Mocha. While the £3.99 for whatever size Piccolo was, slightly tempted the now bursting teenager, the toilet's seemed a better option. After squeezing through tables and pushchairs, she found herself facing an alphanumeric lock on the bathroom and a laminated sheet of paper reading 'For Customer Use Only.'

"Oh for fuck's sake," muttered Savannah under her breath, cautious of the children nearby.

Rather ambitiously she tried spelling the name of the store and turning the handle, yet the door stood resolutely shut.

"You need to buy something to use those toilets," shouted the patronising 'barista' behind the bar prompting everyone in the coffee shop turn and stare.

That 30p seemed cheap now. With no option other than to buy a drink, Savannah gave in, ordered a caramel mocha frappe, paid via her contactless card and waited for her drink to be blended. Savannah was the only person stood at the bar yet the barista still felt the need to shout 'Caramel Mocha' at the top of his lungs once he had finished drizzling her cup of flavoured ice with sauce.

"Thanks. What's—"

"Toilet code is Dixons followed by the number 1."

"£3.99 for a piss."

"No limits."

Savannah, disgusted by the barista's crudeness, yanked her frappe from the tabletop and walked over to type in the code she was so close to guessing.

With hands washed and the toilet now flushed, Savannah opened the door and left it resting on the latch to purposely piss off the pedantic man now blurred by steaming milk. Dixon's was busy enough that all of the tables were taken yet quiet enough that there were still dozens of chairs free. She moved close to the table of the only-regular looking guy in the cafe. He was wearing a long black coat over a smart jacket and seemed too engrossed in the spreadsheets on his computer to care about a neighbour. Upon seeing Savannah attempt to sit down, he ripped a headphone out of his ear and looked up.

"Can I sit here?"

Without saying a word, he smiled, moved his bag to his side and pulled the chair out.

"Thanks."

Savannah felt awkward sitting next to him typing away while she sat there and slurped her drink staring into the distance. With little to entertain her and an uninspiring view of the high street looking back at her, she reached into her bag and grabbed her newly purchased travel book. Pictures of the Eiffel Tower, a nameless vineyard and the Berlin Wall adorned the very colourful front cover of 'The Very Best of France and Germany.' Turning the page revealed the contents on the right-hand side and a plastic pouch containing a road map on the left side. The map would have extended to the size of the entire table, and as Mr Laptop Man was covering most of it, Savannah was only able to see the roads of Northern France and on the reverse Eastern Germany. Flicking through the book's colour coded sections was easy enough, and it didn't take much skimming before she found the Germany section. Alphabet order, deemed the most logical ordering of cities found Savannah stopping her page flicking just after Berlin.

"Cologne (Köln in German) is a modern, vibrant city steeped in history that is lit up in colour every springtime when Carnival comes to town. The skyline is dominated by the Cathedral, a reflection of the city's past, yet modern structures, many home to leading industries, cement the city as a hub for European business. World class sport, art and culture make Cologne a must see destination on your travels."

What the book failed to mention was that Cologne was the home-away-from-home for Savannah's now dead mum for much of her adult life. It was home to the colleagues who knew her and the 40-story SchulzVossen building where they all worked together. Cologne was where she would find the answers to her many questions. Her mum had been dead for over a month now, and not one question she had raised had been answered by the police or her support worker. Her mum was a banker who lived in a cul-de-sac and worked in a 'modern, vibrant city' in Germany. Nothing she had been told made any sense. Savannah woke up each morning with the same question, 'Why was my mum in Latvia?' Frustration soon grew into anger. With nobody willing to help her, Savannah was faced with only one option; to travel to Cologne. Naivety was something she hadn't yet accounted for. Google told her that a plane ticket was too expensive yet from Dover, tickets on a ferry to France and train from Paris then Cologne, were financially achievable. Well-researched, her journey was meticulously planned. Her measured anger soon dissipated into anguish — should she tell Jules? Her plan was foolproof. With answers, came closure and Savannah could live her life. With the money from Celebrate! heading into her account, Savannah wanted to grab Mr Laptop Man's computer and book her journey then and there. She was confident. Savannah asked herself each night 'What could go wrong?' and each time she could think of no obstacles. As she ignored the plan's absurdity and refused to acknowledge her ever-changing moods, the man opposite removed a headphone and looked up from his screen.

"Excuse me, what was the toilet code?"

She responded with a smile.

"I left it open on the latch."

Laughing as he stood, he went to speak.

"Do you mind watching my laptop for a moment?"

Recognising her opportunity, Savannah nodded and waited for the toilet door to lock. As it did, she span the laptop to face her and typed quickly.

CHAPTER SIX

"Whereabouts am I dropping you?" huffed Jules as she struggled to fire
up the engine of the ageing Renault Clio.

"Just by the main building, with all the restaurants and shops in."

As Jules nodded and on the third attempt, the key turned all the way, and
the engine kicked into action. Lights on the dashboard lit up, and the
small screen to the left of the steering wheel displayed the Renault logo
before switching to the navigation screen. She started flicking through
the various presets stopping at the motorway section.

"Leigh Delamere motorway services?"

Savannah nodded as Jules press the start route option in the corner of the
screen.

"13 miles! This is going to cost me a fortune in petrol, Sav."

Savannah grabbed the aux cable from the glove compartment and jammed the ends in Jules' phone and the plug on the car radio. The need for conversation was smaller when the Specials were rocking out over the speakers. Savannah didn't have the effort to argue over music, and as the Specials were the soundtrack to her Aunt's life, she played nice. After just six songs into their greatest hits, Jules exited the motorway and followed the signs towards the services. As she swung around the corner, the sun hid behind the tall trees and allowed Jules to see her niece's blank face in the reflection of the windscreen.

"You look like you are going to be sick Sav."

Savannah could see the reflection too and knew she looked ghostly.

'Nerves I guess."

"Are you really that nervous love? What happened to my gutsy niece? What have you done with her?" laughed Jules taking one hand from the wheel to shake life into Savannah and very nearly verging off into the opposite lane.

"I'll be fine."

Pulling into a disabled bay in front of the main building, Jules yanked hard on the handbrake.

"Is here okay love?

"Yeah, thanks for bringing me."

"Not a problem, my love. Now, you said Laura's mum is picking you up from here later? Do I need to ring Karen to check?"

"No, she knows where she is picking me up from." lied Savannah.

"Alright. Well, good luck! And have a lovely time later on."

Unclipping her seatbelt, Savannah reached over the middle of the car and gave her aunt a kiss on the cheek.

"Thanks. Love you Jules."

Savannah's tone was sentimental but her aunt didn't pick up on it.

"Love you too Sav."

Savannah grabbed her bulging back pack from under the feet, opened the door onto the pavement and jumped out of the car.

"Remember to tell them about your experience at Celebrate!, that's what they are looking for."

Savannah smiled, shut the door and headed inside the building with her heavy bag on her back and a head full of lies. She turned around to take one last look at her aunt, but through the crowd of people and frosted automatic doors, she could see only the back of the Clio spluttering away. She was alone, albeit not far away from home but she was alone nonetheless. Jules had been tricked into the impression that she was driving her niece to a job interview and not to the first step of her elaborately planned trip to Germany. It was a rare weekend in which she had possession of her niece. Under the details of her will, Annabel's sister, Jackie, had legal guardianship of the orphan. Savannah, quite understandably in Jules' opinion, resisted moving. A few weekend visits, viewed as a period of transition, had Savannah fearful of a permanent move. Soon, the adaptation period would end, and the teen would be forced North. Knowing that her life was due to change beyond belief was one of the catalysts for the trip. Savannah was under no illusion that she was running away. She was fleeing her family and crossing borders to find closure. For weeks, Savannah toyed with the idea of telling Jules, but the thought of rejection and punishment exiled her into secrecy. Savannah wasn't traditionally, or even academically, clever yet she knew it would be naive and stupid to tell someone. If just one mouth blabbered, her plan would be foiled. The bag that added yet more weight to her shoulders, packed under the guise of an innocent teenager sleepover, contained everything she'd need for a quick trip to Germany. Her folded money nestled neatly in the back pocket of the bag with her passport. 3 clean t-shirts, underwear and socks padded out the bottom with travel size toiletries, nabbed from the cupboard under the bathroom sink, stacked on top of the travel guide she had picked up from town. With no real job interview to attend, Savannah needed to find a quick way of getting to Dover Ferry terminal. From there, she could board a boat to France. Most of the travel websites Savannah had stalked during her research had advised buying a ticket at the terminal instead of pre-booking online. Single passengers were taxed heavily unless they purchased tickets on the day. Her money wasn't infinite and as such she followed the internet's advice. If she wanted to escape the clutches of her family, who'd most likely notice she was gone some time the next day as she failed to return from a sleepover, Savannah needed to be on her way to France before the sun set over Dover's famous white cliffs.

Service stations were such a cross-section of society yet today, due to the international football match being played later that evening in London, the inside food court was full to the brim of balding middle-aged men whose beer bellies appeared five metres before they did. Remarkably slender framed women, proving opposites do attract, sat next to husbands, some daring to nibble away at their partner's full-English breakfasts. Most of the women didn't seem interested in the sports news cycling on the grainy television sets at each corner of the food court leading Savannah to assume that they were solely chauffeurs for the day. Gossiping groups of secondary-school aged kids filled the rest of the food court while the not-so-lucky loners of the same school, stood at the side looking in at what could have been. Regardless of social standing, each teen was wearing a light blue t-shirt with the name of their school and "Spain Sports Tour" printed on both the front and back. Each t-shirt looked different; some were rolled up, some tucked in and some even tied into a crop top, acceptable now that their visible mid-drift was far away from parental eyes. Savannah had envisaged catching a lift with the family of a vicar who, with time off from the vicarage, were on their way to Southern France for a well-deserved break yet the coach load of kids heading to Spain via Dover seemed a more realistic option. Looking around, Savannah had noticed coach after coach pulled up in the designated bay and as such, realised she'd have to stick close to the school group to know when they were leaving and crucially, by which coach.

Leaning against a faux pillar that had no structural importance, Savannah waited for her new friends in blue to make a move. Having been stood in the same spot long enough to see the story on the current refugee crisis reported six times, Savannah was growing impatient with every passing second. Her stomach growled in hunger as the smell of *fry'n'shake* burgers hitting the grill wafted around the service station. If options were aplenty, Savannah would never choose a *'fry'n'shake'* burger. Their burgers were greasy, fatty and stale much like the clientele that stood in a queue winding down the side of the food court. A brightly flashing neon sign above the counter almost enticed Savannah to quiet her rumbling stomach, but a booming voice behind her put all thoughts of food to the back of her mind.

"St Swithin's College. Time's up. We are ready to leave."

He paused as Savannah looked around to see the gossiping pupils scared into silence. The towering man booming out instructions was tall and stocky. He was athletically built yet wouldn't look comfortable on an athletics track. A beard, grown before it was fashionable, hid the bottom

59

of his face but did little to mask the remnants of his recently purchased burger. He wore a similar top to his pupils but with STAFF emblazoned across the back and in a size that no student could fill without having the school nurse on their back. As he spoke, he answered his own question. "Good. The coach leaves in four minutes."

Savannah had under five minutes to mix in with the colour-coordinated crowd. Now was her opportunity. Most of the kids jumped to their feet and began pushing each other through the small opening in the food court fencing partition. The noise was almost unbearable. Savannah felt much older than these teenagers, her days of buzzing like a swarm of bees squeezing out of a hive were long gone. Truthfully, she was much closer in age than she'd have liked to admit. The mob moved down the concourse, cutting people up as they battled to be at the front of the group and subsequently back of the bus. Savannah didn't need to keep close; the noise carried for miles. A sea of blue t-shirts swept Savannah outside and in sight of the coach and a trip to the docks. With a young face, Savannah hoped the teachers would consider her as one of their own. With no other options but to try her luck and jump aboard, Savannah joined the back of group pushing their way towards the door. As the door approached, she felt a shove on the back of her shoulder. "Hurry it along Missy."

The same man who had been shouting at his pupil's earlier now considered Savannah as one of his own.

"Sorry," said Savannah who stood upright with growing confidence.

"Sorry, what?"

"Sorry, Sir," corrected Savannah, a phrase that she had practised many times during her school life.

"Better. Now, where is your t-shirt? Did you not pick it up from Mr Humphries earlier?"

"No Sir."

"Do you expect everything to be handed to you on a plate Miss..?"

"Bancroft."

Savannah lamented herself.

Shit. He'd have a register.

He huffed his smokey lungs then motioned his head in the direction of the door. As he sighed, he longed for better days.

Savannah slipped past the teacher and tentatively stepped onto the bus. Thanks in part to her roadside grilling, she was one of the last of the students to board the bus meaning only staring faces, and not free seats, were aplenty. Moving up the bus, Savannah ignored the gawping faces and sat next to a fresh-faced boy who seemed smaller than the backpack that she was now pushing down between her legs. The interior of the coach was mainly black panelling with faux wooden planks lining the aisle right down to the driver's seat. Cool air blasted out of the vents just above the tightly pleated leather seats that were now almost all full. The heady fabrics that were such a fixture of the old coaches that Savannah caught to school every day were nowhere to be seen. This was posh and so was the company. Savannah could hear the same gossiping teenagers from inside, doing the same but this time she was the subject.

"Who even is she?" said one.

"Not a clue. Probably some whore Mr Manley is bringing along."

Savannah resisted a glare of acknowledgement as by doing so made her more liable to answer. The aforementioned Mr Manley, an apt name for a person of his size, stood at the front of the coach scanning the seats with

61

squinted eyes. In his right hand, he gripped a blue t-shirt, still packaged, while in his left hand, a microphone which was held up to his mouth.

"Miss Bancroft?"

Savannah raised her hand and smiled. Her plan was working.

"Ah, Miss Bancroft."

He dropped the microphone on the seat next to him, and side stepped up the aisle, blue t-shirt in hand. His narrowing eyes told a different story than his forced smile.

"Miss Bancroft. A noble effort."

Savannah was scared into silence. He seemed out of breath.

"Close but no cigar. After you" whispered Mr Manley as he stood back to motion Savannah out of her seat. She thought quickly.

"I don't know what you mean Sir" lied the teenager.

Mr Manley exhaled a deep smokey breath and crouched down to her level.

"You can get off quietly, or we can make a scene. One that involves the boys in blue and night in a cell. Neither of us wants that Miss Bancroft." The threat of police action was enough to make the teenager grab her bag and barge her way down the aisle. Mr Manley followed her until she was away from the coach.

"I don't have the time to ask what the hell you thought you were doing but thank your lucky stars that I'm not stood here with 2 coppers. Come to office first thing next term, and I'll speak to you then. I've rang your mum, she's on her way to pick you up. Don't talk to strangers and pay for the trip next time."

Savannah was confused, shocked and embarrassed.

"Sorry, Sir."

Savannah wasn't sure who Mr Manley thought she was but with the door closing between them the first plan, and what seemed a viable option, had failed. Savannah knew she'd be waiting a long time for a lift off her mum, nearly as long as he'd be waiting for Savannah in his office. As the coach full of waving kids headed off to sunny Spain, the realisation of what she was doing hit home. Despite feeling hard done by, Savannah knew that most people wouldn't be as kind. Maybe if Mr Manley had known the whole truth, Savannah wouldn't be shivering in the crisp morning air but on the way to a police station where a cell and bollocking from her aunt would await. Luck was on her side.

Savannah headed back inside the main building and retreated to the toilets for thinking space. After pushing open each cubicle door, Savannah found a shit-less one at the far end of the room. As the door creaked shut, she attempted to slide the lock closed, but like most public toilets it was broken, leaving Savannah propping her foot against the door to stop any uninvited incomers. The grey walls of the cubicles were covered in amateur graffiti and mobile numbers. Savannah felt grateful that she was too innocent to understand the plethora of abbreviations next to the numbers yet it didn't stop her guessing what they might mean. Using the solitude to collect her thoughts, the teenager let herself calm down before the smell of shit and piss became unbearable. Taking her foot off the door, it swung open. A line of women had been waiting for the only shit-free toilet, and as she walked past, the look of delight was evident on each and every one of their faces. After washing her hands in the scalding hot water, Savannah heaved her backpack over her shoulder and headed for the exit door.

"That was a good effort, mind. One of the best I've ever seen."

A balding man with few sprouts of hair left on either side of his face, sat in a cheap-looking leather massage chair currently on demo mode, was looking directly at Savannah. His gaze was focused but wishful.

"You talking to me?" asked Savannah ignoring Mr Manley's advice of never talking to strangers.

"Who else? Brave effort, although I knew what you were doing straight away. It made me laugh, it did."

Savannah felt uncomfortable. Strangers had been watching her. She kept her head down and paced away from him.

"Where you going love?"

Savannah ignored him.

"Alright, then pet. I was only trying to help."

Savannah considered her lack of options. Turning, she sized him up.

"Tell me how I can get to Dover then. I need to get there tonight."

"I can help you love. I'm heading down to Folkestone, but I can drop you down by the docks."

"Is it close? Folkestone?"

"Don't you worry about that."

Savannah wasn't sure if she could trust this man, but his soft Welsh accent and lack of alternatives was enough encouragement needed for Savannah to follow him outside.

"Here she is," said the Welshman as he patted the cab's front exterior. *Whittingham's of Cardiff* was stencilled above the windscreen in a sparkling silver font. The lorry was as expected. A blue front cab pulled the insulated wagon that attached behind. Savannah got a hand up into the cabin that was quite clearly his home-away-from-home. Football scarves draped the back wall with numerous other *Bluebird* memorabilia placed randomly on the dashboard. A plaited blanket stretched the length of both the driver and passenger's seat making it hard for Savannah to find her seatbelt. Folders full of paper on the seats formed a barrier between host and guest while empty fast food packaging hid in every crevice.

"Right. Dover, here we come."

"Dover." replied Savannah, confirming the destination to herself.

The engine powered on, and the lorry began to roll away.

"Oh, I'm Alain by the way."

"Savannah."

"Savannah. Lovely name."

"Thanks."

"Thank your mum and dad. You didn't choose it" chuckled Alain, his eyes focused solely on the tight turns that took them onto the motorway.

"I suppose."

"So Savannah, are you going to tell me what drove you to get in a strange man's lorry and head for Dover?"

Savannah laughed at the sureality of the situation.

"How long do we have?"

"3 hours. Long enough?"

"Just about."

CHAPTER SEVEN

Vehicles of every shape and size, and their similar passengers, shoehorned into 3 lanes of standstill traffic, looked over to their right at the
incident-free carriageway and the high-speed cars that whizzed by. An
accident ahead had stopped journeys in their visibly marked tracks
causing closeted angst and frustration to emanate outwards and towards
the crumpled Ford Focus a few hundred metres away. Savannah knew if
she were to succeed in getting across to France undeterred, she'd need to
be cruising across the English Channel before the sun set and the last
ferry eased out of Dover. The last thing she needed was for traffic to stop
her dead. Journeys were considerably, and perhaps understandably,
slower when your lift was required to pull a 16-foot long trailer full of
pet food down the M4. The need to weave through traffic, a skill many
frustrated drivers had honed over the years, was high, yet nigh-on

impossible in a lorry a quarter the size of a regulation football pitch. With traffic squeezing on at every junction, the long journey was only getting longer.

"Gridlocked. It'll be standstill now right down to Heathrow."

The driver's brow furrowed below the deep wrinkles that lined his forehead. His skin, tainted brown with experience that could never be washed away, wrapped tight around his slight frame that was a rarity amongst his colleagues. Sitting on your arse all day, albeit working, isn't recommended by most doctors, nor is the consistent diet of Steak and Kidney pies, wrappers of which littered the floor beneath Savannah's feet. His weathered hands were split, one grasped the steering wheel while the other changed gears on the elongated lever shift that asked too much of the engine. When Alain did speak, his Welsh voice lingered in the silence longer than it needed to. Every word was a few letters longer when Alain spoke them. Savannah was sick of the silence and decided to muster up some conversation.

"I bet you spend your life stuck in traffic."

"Part of the job my love. At least I'm getting paid."

Savannah kept her eyes focused on the road ahead but could feel herself feigning a smile. Alain waited for a reply but knew it wasn't coming.

"Do you work?" he asked.

"Used to. Card shop—"

"Celebrate?"

"Yep. Got fired."

"Fired?"

Alain went higher than his voice should have gone.

"Yeah pretty much."

"Not stealing from the till was it? I'm not going to have to lock away my valuable am I?"

Savannah looked to her right and caught a look of worry on the face of her driver.

"Nah. I kept missing work, so they let me go."

"Fair enough. Not everything in life comes serves on a plate ya know."

"Sorry Sir"

Alain had no choice but to laugh off the sarcastic comment.

"Feisty little one you aren't you!"

"Only when I have to be."

The conversation was moving at the same speed as the traffic surrounding the lorry. Both felt obliged to speak, for different reasons entirely, yet neither could muster up the effort to exchange falsities. Life on the road was a lonely one. Alain grew to embrace his new life in the wake of his ever-so-timely a few years previous. He had been the most average of all Joe's, semi-detached house, 3 kids, 2 weeks in Tenerife, before it all came crashing down. Alain spent most of his days, and often nights, in the confined space of a driver's cab that was well-known amongst drivers to be smaller than a prison cell on death row. Conversation didn't visit often. Home comforts were non-existent if not for the laminated photos of his children and a Cardiff City football scarf, both of which were stuck to the back wall with blu-tack. The panelling and holstering through the middle was, much like Alain, falling apart yet trying to remain functional. Aside from the minor decorations, just a sign hung on the wall thanking visitors for politely not smoking, a sign ignored if the smell was anything to go by. Curled road maps, each a different year, were stuffed in the compartment by the passenger door. Maps at more than an arms reach away from the driver showed Alain to be confident on the road. With the radio off, the only sound in the cab came from the click of the indicator as Alain moved over to the right-hand lane much to the dismay of the beeping motorists behind him. The road began to open up and not before too long did their lorry pass the mangled Focus that spread itself across 2 lanes of the motorway. Alain wasn't impressed.

"There's the bastard. Hours late just because somebody can't drive a fucking car."

Alain's choice words reminded Savannah of her dad, who would swear non-stop if Bath City lost, and lose they often did.

"Sorry love. I shouldn't swear around kids."

"I'm hardly a child."

He repeated himself with different tact.

"A teenager then. I shouldn't swear around teenagers."

Savannah held in her laugh.

"You know swear words are a lot funnier in a Welsh accent."

"You aren't the first person to tell me that, and you certainly won't be the last. Us Welsh? We fu—"

Alain caught himself.

"—bloody love a swear word."

Much like the road, Savannah reluctantly opened up.

"Were you born in Wales?"

"Cardiff. Born and bred."

"That explains the scarf."

"The mighty bluebirds. I had trials with them years ago. They liked me down there."

Savannah had heard similar tales from her Dad and decided to play along.

"Oh yeah?"

"Broke my leg in one of my first games. We didn't have shin pads back then. They stretchered me off, and that was it. I never played for them again."

"But you still watch them?"

"When I can. I don't think you can fall out of love with football no matter how many times it decides to fuck you over."

Savannah, faced with a severe lack of footballing knowledge but a desire to know more about Alain, decided to change the subject.

"How long have you been driving lorries?"

"4 years. I had started at a national firm before I got this job in Cardiff."

Savannah didn't want to pry into Alain's life too much but a career change at his age was odd. Given that there was still a lot of road between them and Dover, she provoked him.

"Only 4 years. Weird."

"Weird? What's weird about that?"

You could tell by the Welshman's pitch that he was expecting to be grilled further.

"It just is. How old are you?"

"44."

He looked much older.

"Right, so who decides to change their career at 40."

"You sound like my dear old Mum, you know that?"

Savannah wasn't really sure if he was genuinely annoyed, and with eyes locked on the road ahead, it was hard to gauge what he was thinking.

"If you really must know, my circumstances changed, and I needed a new job."

Savannah felt surprisingly comfortable around this middle-aged stranger given he had picked her up from a service station less than an hour ago.

"Oh, so you were fired."

"Nope."

Savannah thought she had him sussed.

"Not fired then—"

Air quotes appeared.

"—made redundant."

Alain smirked and glanced across at his passenger who he was beginning to regret picking up.

"Nowhere near. Are you going to carry on guessing?"

"Or you could just tell me."

"Where's the fun in that?" asked Alain, eyes still focused ahead.

"Witness protection?"

Nothing.

"Stolen identity?"

Alain was silent. Savannah was feeling playful.

"Did you go wandering in a supermarket and lose your mum?"

Still nothing. Alain, while indicating left, glanced from mirror to mirror and caught Savannah's eyes just before the far mirror.

"Why don't you explain to me why you happily jumped into a strange old man's lorry en route to Dover, and presumably Europe, when you should be playing with Barbie dolls?"

The tables had turned. Savannah's sense of comfort had been yanked from beneath her feet.

"Barbie dolls aren't really my thing anymore."

Wit had always been Savannah's first form of defence.

"You know what I mean. How old are you?"

"Old enough."

"Good answer. Do your mum and dad know you are running away?"

"I'm not running away."

Alain changed the subject.

"Do your mum and dad know you are in my van?"

"I think they know somehow."

"And they are okay with it?"

Alain was visibly shocked. He continued.

"I wish I had parents like that when I was growing up."

Savannah's face was motionless and void of any emotion.

"So do I."

With two kids back at home, Alain recognised every possible teenage emotion even in its smallest form.

"I was working away from home. I used to flog stationary for a company based in Swindon. Door-to-door business. I'd visit offices up and down the M4 trying to sell everything from paper clips to whiteboards. You name it we sold it."

Savannah looked up.

"I wasn't bad at it either. I always reached my sales targets, and I was paid quite well for what I did, bonuses too. It was beginning to become pedantic but look, I had a family to feed and a house to pay for."

With each word he spoke, Alain looked increasingly mournful as his mind recalled memories he had put to rest.

"December it was. The last day of work before Christmas break. We'd planned to take the kids to Florida Disney the next day. It was a surprise, they didn't know a thing. I wanted to surprise my wife with her Christmas present too, so I booked for us to have lunch that day, got it off work and everything. She didn't have a clue. I'd booked a nice restaurant and got some flowers on the way home from work. Boss let me have the afternoon off so I'm driving home, just about to pull in and I see my brother's car in the driveway."

Savannah could guess where this story was going.

"I thought, well fuck me he's only gone and got us a gift this year the tight bastard. I opened the door, shouted out to see where they were. Nothing. So I went upstairs, no sign of them in the kids' room. Didn't even think to look in our room."

The ending she feared was coming.

"I must have thought to get changed because I chucked my coat down on the bannister and went back down the hall to our room. You'd never guess it though — what I saw."

Savannah felt like she could but kept the state of confusion.

"My own brother and my wife. They were so fucking busy, they didn't even notice when I entered the room."

Alain left it so long that Savannah felt obliged to speak.

"I'm so s—"

"My own fucking brother."

Savannah bit her tongue. The joke was there.

"What did you do?"

"I hit the fucker. I made sure he would never forget what he did. He ripped apart my family. My wife had to pull me off him."

Alain wasn't finished.

"I had to get out of there, so I ran away. And I ran, and ran, and ran."

"Wife. You keep calling her your wife. Are you still married?"

"As far as the Queen is concerned, we are. I'd love to see her again, help her."

Alain, even after four years of reflection, still loved his cheating wife. Savannah had questions aplenty.

"Do you regret it?

"Running away?"

She nodded.

"Every day. You never realise how much you'll miss something, or someone, until they're gone."

Hearing his advice, Savannah should have been doubting not just herself but her journey. In reality, she had never felt stronger. Alain was corrupted by nostalgia, he chose to remember what he wanted and not the whole truth.

"What if she's moved on?"

"She won't have. I know her. Deborah wasn't like that."

Savannah felt like a therapist, and while she was grateful for the lift, she couldn't really be bothered to argue with a broken man.

"Maybe you should visit her. It might not work, but you should at least try."

"That's the dream. Unlikely, I know, but—"

"The most distant of daydreams are the ones we keep closest to our hearts. That's what my mum used to tell me."

"Used to?"

If this was primary school, Savannah was being handed the conversation ball.

"She's dead. My dad too."

"Oh sorry, love. I didn't mean to—"

"It's fine. You didn't kill her."

"Is that what you are running away from? Grief?"

"I'm not running away."

She was defiant in her answer not just to Alain but to herself.

Alain said nothing.

"If you were in my shoes then you'd be doing the same."

"And what shoes are they?"

Savannah didn't know the answer. For once in her life, she had nothing to say.

"I don't want to talk about it."

She could feel tears beginning to form in her eyes but keeping her eyes strained meant not crying, which next to Alain which would be mortifyingly embarrassing. Looking up from her lap, she followed Alain's lead by focusing her eyes on the road. Straight ahead, looking past the queuing cars, Savannah could see just one thing. A sign.

Dover. (J7)

Next exit.

CHAPTER EIGHT

Pulsing brake lights added additional colour to the amber haze that emanated from the summer sky as queues of car approached the ferry terminal. Smoking funnels beyond the main building put an end to the questions of *'Are we there yet?'* that had been the soundtrack to many a journey. Families that many hours ago bundled too much 'stuff' into the boots of their people carriers were frustratingly close to the start of their continental trips. Yet, even with ferries that wait for no-one before departing, traffic slowed progress to a halt. The wide lanes that led cars from the motorway funnelled into an official entrance some 100 metres ahead of Alain and Savannah meaning that soon the 16-foot long lorry that had trudged down the M4 and beyond would soon be squeezed through the gap into the security checkpoint. The journey has been long and taxing, both on Savannah and the vehicle itself. Queues of summer holiday traffic and incidents a plenty stopped the lorry from reaching the upper bounds of its speed capabilities. Inside the cab, the conversation had been equally stop-start. Through her charmless wit, Savannah had endeared herself to the driver although Alain wasn't sure his passenger felt the same. But still, without Alain and his awkward conversations about life, Savannah knew she would still be slumped outside the service station miles away, and certainly not metres away from a continental crossing. With every minute that passed, the lorry edged closer to the entrance.

"What time is your ferry?"

Savannah, with not a second of hesitation, looked down at her watch and lied through her teeth.

"7:30."

"You've got plenty of time then. Does it say where I should drop you?"

Savannah had no ticket to check.

"No, it doesn't. Anywhere is fine though. Thanks"

"I'll ask this gentleman" came the reply.

Alain, checking the interior mirrors lined his vehicle up with the lane markings and crept forward to the barrier. A stumpy man in a pleated uniform stood next to the fence, manually raising and lowering it as and when each vehicle passed his inspection. Alain cranked the handle to open the window before sticking his head out of the small gap.

"Alright, bud."

Whatever the guard was expecting, Alain's strong Cardiffian accent wasn't it.

"Haulage and Cargo, take the second left and carry on to the blue zone."

"Just a drop off mate."

"In a lorry?"

"In a lorry."

"Well it's a tight turn down to drop-off, I'm not sure—"

"Follow the signs to drop-off? Okay then mate."

Resigned to defeat and irked on by a lack of desire to argue with a Welshman when on just £7.30 an hour, the guard set down his clipboard and yanked up on the barrier.

"Cheers then mate."

Alain sped forward and headed towards to the drop off zone cutting up several smaller cars as he turned towards the bend.

"You didn't have to do that. I can get out wherever."

"I promised to take you to the ferry, and that's exactly what I'll do."

"Thank you."

With a heavy backpack to carry, Savannah wasn't going to argue with the driver. After a series of tight turns, Alain took the straight road then cautiously followed the large purple signs to the drop-off zone. The ferry terminal was wide, spanning the entire width of an almost full car park. Towards the front of the car park, nestled between the pay kiosk and terminal entrance was the marked drop-off zone, an area too small for a 16-foot long haulage lorry. With little thought, Alain pulled the vehicle to one side and parked with half of his truck hanging out of the designated spaces. Alain smiled as he lifted the handbrake.

"Voila. Your destination awaits."

"Alain, I'm not sure I'll ever be able to properly thank you."

"Ah, nonsense. No need to. I was heading down this way whatever."

"I don't have much but—"

"Right you can stop that. Get out of my cab before I make you pay."

Savannah didn't really want to pay nor spend much longer in the slightly smelly lorry so slung the heavy bag over her shoulder and opened the door. As she stepped down, he spoke through the open door.

"Oh, love?"

Savannah turned around once more.

"They ain't cheap—"

He was grasping a rolled up ten-pound note.

"—those ferries. It's gonna cost you."

As Savannah was shocked into silence, a booming voice came from her blindside.

"You can't park there mate. Not in that beast!"

Alain had an answer for anything.

"Give me 2 minutes mate. Just about to head off."

Savannah felt she had to speak.

"Alain, I really can't."

He motioned for her to take the money, but out of respect and pity, she lied yet again.

"I've got a ticket."

"If you've got a ticket, then I'm Britney Spears."

"I'll be okay. Thanks, Alain."

"Be safe, love."

"I will. I hope you find happiness."

"You too, love. Go get them."

Savannah shut the door on the driver's cab and tightened the backpack on her shoulders. With the door closed, Alain ignited the engine and found his gear.

"Savannah—"

Alain's voice could be barely heard over the engine.

"—catch!"

With smoke blurting out of the exhausts above the lorry, the ten-pound note that Alain had held in his hand flew out of the window and onto the ground. Before Savannah had time to register what had happened, the lorry had sped down the road as he headed back towards the motorway.

"You've got a good Dad in that one."

Savannah turned to see the same security guard that had just told them to move looking directly at her. He began to speak once more.

"I couldn't get a ten-pence off my dad let alone a tenner."

"He's kind. Perhaps too kind."

"Kindness kills."

"Ticket office?"

"Just inside the building. On your right, pet."

With the weight of her bag weighing heavy on her slight frame, Savannah hoped to make the journey from road to sea as quick as possible. A red-brick facade dated the building yet automatic doors leading into an open-plan glass plaza were more telling of the terminal's age. The balmy-summer air that had been stifling for hours was replaced with climate-controlled air conditioning once inside the concourse, a welcome relief on the hot summer day. People of all ages were milling inside the open-end terminal. On one end, doors led out to the ferry boarding buildings while the other took you back out to the car parks. A manned ticket booth stood lonely next to the lines of automated machines. Savannah tried her luck with the robots. Her budget, based on hours of website-trawling, allowed her enough money to purchase a one-way off-peak ticket across the English Channel. Savannah had used similar machines at train stations, but even to the novice, the interface was easily comprehensible.

Start / Démarrer.

Tickets / Billets

Day / Journèe

Savannah selected the correct date.

Time/Heure

No times found. Please try again.

Aucun horaire trouvé. Veuillez réessayer.

Savannah followed the machine's instructions and tried again.

No times found. Please try again.

Aucun horaire trouvé. Veuillez réessayer.

By the third attempt, Savannah had deduced that the machines were useless and dragged her bag over to the woman sat behind the ticket booth.

"Hi—"

"Good Evening, welcome to RLEN crossings, how can I help you?"

"—yeah hi, I just tried to buy a ticket on the machine, and it wouldn't let me get one."

"When does the RLEN crossing that you wish to travel on depart?"

Savannah wondered if this woman was a robot as well.

"Today, the next Calais ferry."

"I think we have sold-out of walk-ups for today's ferries. Let me check the system."

Savannah stared at her feet as the woman's acrylic nails tapped against the keyboard. Several minutes of typing had passed before the woman spoke again.

"Okay, so the next one I can get you on to Calais is Wednesday at 4:40pm, and that will be £67.00 or you can pay in Euros with the conversion fee—"

Savannah had stopped listening. Wednesday was 3 days away and 3 days too late. Running away was much harder with an ocean in the way.

"—but that comes with the included onboard cabin food vouchers."

"Are you sure you don't have anything left for today?"

"I'm sorry, but we are very busy this time of year. Shall I book you in for Wednesday?"

"No. No, I'll…I'll leave it."

With nowhere to go and time up against her, Savannah pulled her bag across the shiny floor to the row of benches that laid vacant in the middle of the concourse. She need time to regroup. If she weren't bound by the chains of uncertainty, Savannah would have chosen to start her journey when kids were still at school and most parents still at work. Looking around the building was a constant reminder of the life that she had never had, and now, never will. Red-faced parents, with cases in tow, sidestepped through the crowds wondering when the stress-free promise of their holiday would begin. It was a sight to behold. The lucky parents of the most rebellious of kids were forced to harness their children in an attempt to stop escape attempts and their respective, rather embarrassing tannoy announcements. Directly in front of Savannah, a crowd began to form of holidaymakers desperate to be one of the first onboard. Each and every set of eyes were trained on the departures board that hung down from the low ceiling. With the next and last ferry of the night, to leave in just 35 minutes, the plucky teen knew she was running out of options. A bell tone sounded out from speakers above the screens, only just loud enough to be heard over the excitable chattering below.

"We are now boarding RLEN crossings service 2712 to Calais."

Savannah wondered if any actual humans worked at the terminal as the robotic voice began to speak again.

"We kindly request all driving passengers on the RLEN crossings service 2712 to return to your cars via exit A. Walk-on passengers are required to board via Gate F. Thank You."

Savannah's face began to heat up. Just hours into her highly planned, utterly unrealistic journey, the lack of alternatives had stopped the teenager dead in her tracks. She knew Jules would be out looking for her within minutes of her reported disappearance. If the daring teen were to avoid a premature reunion with her locked bedroom door, then Savannah would need to be on the docked ferry that was filling with passengers by the second. Walk-on passengers were likely to have a ticket, a ticket that Savannah didn't have. It was easier to get a ride over 100 miles for nothing than it was to get onboard a boat she was all too happy to pay for. An army of uniformed middle-managers made themselves look busy by guiding the melee of travellers away from the cafes and shop and to their respective gate. Savannah felt alone, lost in the crowd. Her eyes glassed over and focused on the emptying expanse before her. Her ears involuntarily tuned to the conversations taking place beneath the signage. A family, dressed head-to-converse in hand-me-downs, blocked the way. From behind the tallest child came a head of greying hair, ushering her children to 'mind out of the way.'

"Now then, are you going to listen to me or am I going to have to chuck that bloody iPod into the sea?"

The lady's voice was northern, stern but with a gentle softness. Savannah was transfixed. Scooping all of her bags into one hand, she continued to yap.

"Who has the ticket?"

The stroppiest of her bunch piped up in a cracking but geographically similar voice.

"Dad's got it."

The briefest of reliefs took over the stress. A glance at her children, and then at her watch returned it.

"Dad's got the ticket, right. Where is your father?"

Savannah noted the lack of plurality. The kids didn't respond.

"Jack, where's your father?"

"Gone to the shitter."

"Watch your language, Jack, I won't be having any of that in a public--"

Just as Jack scowled, his father returned stopping his mum mid-sentence.

"There you are, Roy. We've got to go. You've got the ticket?"

"Yes ma'am I've got the ticket."

The dad's desperate attempts to be one of the kids had gone unnoticed by everyone but his wife.

Savannah could feel herself staring, and while she enjoyed watching the family, she knew her time as Big Brother was up. She needed to move fast now that she had a plan. The departure hall was now almost empty. A long snake of people queued patiently by Gate F. With no ticket to her name, Savannah excitedly joined the hundred or so people waiting to funnel through Gate A. Frosted automatic doors opened out into a series of queues that each culminated at a yellow line, several metres from a passport checking booth. With the ferry due to leave in the next 10 minutes, the passport checks were merely a game of spot the difference rather than a questioning that you would come to expect at the American or North Korean border. Nearing the front, Savannah slipped her backpack off her shoulders and took out her passport. It had been a challenge in itself to sneak the passport out of the locked cupboard where her aunt kept important documents, IDs and a secret stash of toffee kit-kats. A young woman wearing a burka waved Savannah forward from the yellow 'Do Not Cross' line. She took the passport from her hand and flicked to the photo page at the first attempt. Within a second, the officer had slid the passport back through the slot.

"Safe travels."

"Thanks."

Savannah pushed the passport into her tight jean pocket then followed the path past the booth to another set of doors where a man sat perched on a stool. Quickening her pace, Savannah headed towards the door and the man with more hair on his face than on the top of his head.

"Ticket please."

Savannah could smell the sea breeze from behind the doors. She was so close. It felt colder by the door. A combination of the arctic air conditioning and draft spilling in from the propped open door chilled the air. Savannah had just one chance, only one plan. She daren't think what would happen if this failed. Nobody passes through a passport check by accident. A night in the cells was surely a realistic possibility. They'd think she was a terrorist, maybe worse. The man, with eyes on his clipboard, held out one hand. He'd probably heard it all before.

Savannah opened her mouth.

"My Dad's got it."

He nodded without looking up from his lap.

"Stay together love. They aren't as friendly in France."

Ignoring the casual racism, Savannah pushed open the door and took a deep breath. Never before had she been so excited to be in a car park, to hear the songs of seagulls or to see smoke billowing from a ship's funnel just metres away.

Savannah knew her journey was far from over but that didn't stop a smile breaking out from ear to ear. Europe's continent was blocked only by a narrow stretch of water. And she had a boat for that.

CHAPTER NINE

Just as quickly as the crowd formed in the vast concreted forecourt, it dispersed leaving the teenager alone between the queuing cars, vans and buses. Getting through passport control seemed the hardest hurdle, but with queues of traffic revving their engines with holiday excitement, Savannah knew her next task would be far from easy. Standing on a roadside sticking out her thumb would have worked further afield but metres from security and police forces, Savannah ruled it out. The lanes of traffic were organised by vehicle type, heavy load lorries nearest her, people carriers and hatchbacks nearest the ferry. A quick glance at each road ruled out the majority of waiting vehicles. Savannah would find it hard to hide in a Mini. The lanes were 15, if not 20, vehicles deep and followed each other nose to tail with not much space in between. Her options were limited to one of the vans at the furthest end of the queue.

Any closer to the main building and she'd be spotted. Even the vans carried risk beyond thought. With time not on her side, Savannah headed along the pavement to the middle lanes. A group of middle-aged pot bellied men had formed along the pavement fence each lighting up their own cigarette before passing the lighter to the next. With these men, van drivers of the most accurate stereotype, pre-occupied by their own smokey haze, Savannah seized the chance. An off-white dirtied transit van was the last of its kind in the ordered lanes. Four wheels of different treads hung low below the mud-stained body and splintering roof rack. Peeling decal proclaimed the van to belong to 'Broderick and Sons' - Scotland's most reliable cross-border delivery services. Savannah wondered if they had ever transported a parcel her size. Just tall enough to see into the windows and assure herself it was empty, she timidly checked each door without success. If this was to be Savannah's one-way ticket to the continent, the back doors needed to be unlocked. Keeping her eye on the smokers by the fence, one of which she hoped was the driver, Savannah crept around the side of the van. Once in sight of the doors, she exhaled a deep breath of relief. Not only were the doors unlocked but slightly ajar. Savannah couldn't believe her luck. Without hesitating, she pulled the handle outwards with her other hand wrapped around the open door. Full of wooden planks and an old-Victorian style lamppost, the van was far from the cushy seats that would be enjoyed on the ship ahead. While spacious, the van wasn't tall enough to accommodate Savannah's average frame forcing the teenager into a crouch before she slumped to the floor. With the door slightly open, Savannah could see the smokers drop their fags as the rain started to fall down on their heads.

"This is too easy." said the teen under her breath.

Savannah eased the door shut. Savannah's confidence was growing. "Too fucking easy."

As a pair of quickening footsteps came closer, the rain intensified, pounding the top of the van.In the subdue darkness, the pounding felt ominous. She hoped for the best.

CHAPTER TEN

Enough light squeezed through abrasions in the van's bent roof that
Savannah's face felt warm even in the cold darkness around her. Her bag,
much like herself, was crammed into a gap between planks of wood and
the corrugated wall. For a summer's evening, the night felt cold. Summer
months in England were famously inconsistent and often inclement.
Once schools across the country break for a well-earned rest, it is easier
predicting lottery numbers than the weather forecast. Savannah yearned
for warmer climates and while she wasn't expecting sun, sea and sex on
her continental foray, longer evenings and sun-kissed streets wouldn't be
ignored. Still, rain hammered against the roof filling Savannah's ears
with a ringing that, along with the smell of treated wood, couldn't be
blocked out. With the rain showing no sign of letting up, Savannah slid
further into the centre avoiding the drips of water that trickled down from

the roof. No matter how many different positions were tried; cross legged, crouching, kneeling, Savannah knew that the journey would be far from comfortable. With no warning, the engine spluttered to a start, and the van began to crawl forward. Savannah hadn't heard anyone get in nor make any noise in the front cab. She wondered if the partition separating the driver and, unbeknownst to him, his cargo, was sound proof. The crawl quickened to a measured speed and soon inclined up what Savannah assumed was the boarding ramp onto the ferry. Freedom now smelt like a diesel stained ocean from the inside of a dirty transit van. As the smell subsided and the bump of the road was replaced with a gentle sway of a boat, Savannah took a deep breath and closed her eyes. Despite her meticulous planning, at no stage of her research did she envisage sitting in the back of a van trying to board a ferry. Savannah found herself laughing at the thought. With detailed information on which coach would take her to Paris and which train would take her to Germany, the journey once in France seemed comforting to the girl in the back of a van. Savannah's booking blip would soon be forgotten and the answers to the questions she'd held since her Mum passed away would be closer than ever before.

Opening her bag, Savannah counted, and recounted, the €150 in her purse. It was enough for her coach ticket, a train fare and spending money, all of which she had saved from her last wage at Celebrate!. Savannah took the money out and once sure it was all there, tucked it away beside the notes she had factored in to buy a ferry ticket - British pounds that couldn't be used where she was going. Without placing too much value on her own head, she knew that soon her Aunt would raise the alarm and people would start searching for her. Her face would be beamed around the country if the not the world as her schoolmates back

91

home battled with each other for the best 'I care about my friend' face, online status or search effort. It would piss her off immeasurably, and truthfully Savannah was quite glad she wasn't going to be there.

* * *

Having seen the latest weather forecast, Rick was pissed off that his boss had assigned him a Dover to Paris crossing knowing full well that he had three days off booked in after this job. Rain, as part of an incoming continental thunderstorm, would slow the motorway traffic gridlocking his entire journey into the French capital. For now, the ferry crossing gave Rick the opportunity to stretch his legs. The day had started early for the Scotsman, as it often did. Living in Dundee had it's benefits, yet not many did he remember as the pocket alarm beside his single bed screamed out before the sun had bothered to rise over the Scottish skies. It had been over eight hours since the van driver had kissed his mother goodbye on the porch of the suburban bungalow they had shared since his 'ma's' divorce with Rick's third step-dad. Despite being made to drive far longer than he legally should in a day, Rick's boss had booked a bed and breakfast for his employee once he had arrived in the French port. It wasn't Rick's first visit to that particular establishment and as such knew that he'd be leaving with a bad back and empty stomach. Couriering was the perfect job for Rick. A decent wage allowed him to care for his mother and live a comfortable existence with little questions asked. His work kept him away from people, people who'd question his single, lonely life. Pulling up at the port, Rick followed the monotonous boarding procedure to a tee. He was well-rehearsed in what to do, and despite a timely arrival, he found himself at the back of the queue to board the ferry. Glancing down at the dashboard, a flashing clock showed that he still had time for a fag before the ship would start to board. Grabbing the packet of cigarettes and lighter from the cup holder, Rick pushed open the door and slouched out of the van.

"Ah here he is…" came a deep Scottish voice from within a group of men perched on the railings behind his van. Driving on the same routes at similar times most days meant Rick often saw the same faces at the dock. The man took a drag of his cigarette before resuming.

"Mummy's little boy. I'm surprised she's let you out of the house after last week."

Rick continued towards the railing, flicked open his cigarette box, pulled out a fag and spoke in the group's direction.

"And rob me of seeing my favourite dodgy dealers? No chance."

Rick's smirk disappeared as he put the cigarette in his mouth and moved to light it. The group of men laughed off his remark but knew Rick's description of them was accurate. Despite not actually liking each other, all of the men in the group knew far too much about the others to ever risk getting on their bad sides.

"Rick, you lanky twat. Where you off to today?" asked a softer voice from within the smoke cloud. His attempt at name-calling not registering on the people he was trying to impress.

"Some warehouse near Paris. Another night in the van I reckon."

A short, stocky man piped up.

"You might bump into your mum down on that Moulin Rouge."

Rick, increasing his grip on the lighter, refused to acknowledge the comment. His aggressor continued.

"She still doing all that? Fucking those junkies for a tenner and a Capri-sun?"

Rick couldn't hold it in.

"Fuck off Sparky. Ain't you got any Syrians that need smuggling?"

"You better watch your mouth Ricky-boy…"

Sparky leapt from his perched position on the railings although he wasn't much taller now stood. His head and body appeared to be one; his neck was nonexistent, replaced instead by a series of chins, the result of years of Rustlers microwaveable burger consumption. His face, devoid of any distinguishing features, raged into an almost purple shade.

"…I think you're forgetting who you are talking to. One little phone call and you'll be locked up like the rest of those freaks."

Rick drew a long inhale of vaporised tar, spat his half-burnt cigarette on the floor and crushed it dry with a stamp of his mud-specked boot. Sparky spoke up once again.

"Safe trip then, Rick. All the best to your ma."

With his eyes firmly on the floor, he turned his back on the insult and paced back to his van, stopping only to notice the closed door. Sodden clouds stretched out over the queues of cars and into the disappearing horizon in a shade of grey that endangered Rick's days off.

"Oh, what a beautiful day."

* * *

Savannah felt the van stop, and an aggressive yank of the handbrake before the door slammed shut with a force that reverberated through the bodywork she was slumped against. Inside of the van, the air had become suffocatingly stuffy despite the ever-cooling summer night. A sheet of corrugated iron cooled her back while the amber glow that partially lit the back of the van escaped through one hole on the side of the van. Just the smell of wood remained; the planks themselves slipping into the darkness. As she stretched her legs out straight, Savannah listened as the chattering voices outside the van were silenced by the sound of an impending announcement.

"Tranquil-plus passengers are invited to check in to their cabins using Elevator B2. All other passengers are asked to take any other passenger elevators to the comfort of the main deck where hot coffee and tea will be served. Thank you for choosing RLEN Crossings. To see the world, comfortably."

The comfort of the main deck was appealing to the teenager squeezed up against planks of wood in the darkness of a stranger's van. If she could make it out of the van and into an elevator undetected, Savannah would have a far easier voyage across the English channel. She knew that now was as good a time as any to get out and disappear into the crowd of passengers on the upper decks. The noise outside the van had subsided, the chatter that had stopped her leaving thus far moved elsewhere. Kicking the wood out of the way, Savannah pulled herself across the floor of the van to the back doors. Her face, scrunched in a gurn of resolve, pressed up against the metal door, she listened for anything that would stop her leaving the van. Blocking out her heavy breathing, only the gentle sloshing of the waves revealed itself to her keen ear. Her teeth, chattering with nerves, bit down on her roughened lips. Savannah, buoyed by unfounded courage, slowly wrapped her fingers around the handle and pulled it towards her. As the handle clicked, the left-hand door begrudgingly opened, pushing a wave of sharp, salty sea air into the van. With one hand on the door, Savannah pushed the door open further, her eyes frantically scanning the surroundings. Looking ahead, she saw nothing but open water. The back of the boat was open, the last glimpse of England disappearing into the mist. Now fully open, Savannah dropped her legs over the side of the van, reached behind to grab her bag and inhaled a deep breath of sea air.

***

Rick enjoyed the serenity of the ocean. He liked the smell of the sea and the gentle spray that splashed across his face as he stood gazing out into the watery nothingness. For all that he enjoyed the ocean, he equally hated summertime ferry crossings. Holiday happiness in the form of squealing children and fake parenting filled his ear drums and caused a frustration like none other. He had never been away on holiday. Until he got this job as a courier, he had never been out of his town let alone the country. For a grown man, the vastness of the world scared him. His insularity was a comfort, an immunity that inadvertently put him at risk in the wider world. Rick was a danger not just to himself but to those around him. The holiday happiness was silenced.

"Tranquil-plus passengers are invited to check in to their cabins using Elevator B2. All other passengers are asked to take any other passenger elevators to the comfort of the main deck where hot coffee and tea will be served. Thank you for choosing RLEN Crossings. To see the world…"

Rick had heard this announcement more times than he could remember and could mimic the voice, complete with a patronising tone, almost perfectly.

"..comfortably."

He had made the expensive mistake of buying the watered down coffee from the upper deck before and as such wasn't in any mood to join the holidaymakers upstairs The deck was empty if not for rows of cars and vans that positioned themselves between the yellow lines painted on the floor to varying degrees of success. It was a cold night, and with the wind funnelling through the back of the ship, Rick, in just a t-shirt and shorts, turned to head back to the warmth of his van.

"What the fuck."

His brain didn't want to believe his eyes. Rick's mind was running through every possibility, his breathing quickening with every step. He dropped to a crouch, cowering at the side of his van. Keeping his eyes on the door, he watched as it slowly crept open. Rick waited with bated breath, his palms sweaty in both anger and trepidation. As the door edged open further, the hanging ceiling lamps lit the van's special cargo. Rick's heart rate picked up again, not out of fear, but excitement.

"A girl. A sweet little girl."

***

After time submerged in the darkness, Savannah welcomed the brightness even if her squinting eyes did not. Gradually, the surroundings revealed themselves in all their industrial glory. Looking to her left, Savannah saw empty vehicles, the ocean rolling back and forth and the promised lifts. To her right, she saw him. Her eyes did not linger on his sweating face for longer than a second before his size-six boot flew into the side of her head. Blood, not wanting to be part of what was coming next, escaped from her nose. Savannah was stunned, her eyes squinting once more. Stumbling to her feet, he advanced. His teeth gritted, his fists clenched. She ran. Her feet had moved barely a step before his clammy hand grasped onto her wrist. He yanked back and pull her into reach. Her screams were muffled by a hand across her mouth. He didn't relent. In one movement, he span her back around to face him before pulling her closer. She stared into his beady eyes, her fear only evident through the cold sweat trickling down her now, quivering back. With every resistance and hint of a fight, his grip tightened. His arm twisted hers

97

Rick had stood guarding the back of his van since he slammed the door shut some hour before. Few workers came by, and those that did knew not to question such a familiar face. With one hand leant up against the van's chipped bodywork and another holding up his now belt-less trousers, the unexpected ringing of his phone needed more thought than expected. His leaning hand, now redundant, reached into his back pocket and lifted the phone to his ear.

"Boss."

"Rick, you bastard, I've had Suva Sounds on the phone all bloody day. They are saying that you've damaged most of their stock. Are they trying to bullshit me or have you fucked up again?"

Rick knew what was coming.

"Boss...I.."

"Oh for fuck's sake. I can't trust you with bloody anything. Not for all the tea in China."

"I'm sorry..I didn't think.."

"Yeah, that's the bleeding problem with you, Rick. You don't bloody think. Next time you're in the depot, we'll have to have a chat."

Before Rick had a chance to reply, a foghorn blasted through the deck.

"Look, boss..I've got to go. I'm about to get off the ferry."

"Well, go carefully. I can't afford to have all this stock to replace."

Rick went to speak, but his boss had already hung up the phone. Rick welcomed the sound of the foghorn on every crossing, not just in the middle of an awkward phone call. Alongside the flashing red lights on the side of the deck, the sound indicated that the ferry was close to docking and that all passengers should return to the cars. Within minutes of the horn, the floor filled with hundreds of people all with little idea as to where they had parked their cars. Rick stayed at the back of his van, watching the vehicles in front fill with excitable children and their tiring parents. He blamed his parents for a lot in life, much in the same way that they blamed him. His parents were both in happy relationships until the drunken night that led to his existence and with a baby hard to hide, both marriages fell apart. Rick's dad, not wanting to be tied down to a one-night stand ran away leaving a poor and bitter single mum. Seeing all of these happy families reminded Rick of what he had ruined not just for his mum, but for himself.

"Excuse me, Sir. I kindly ask you to return to your vehicle to prepare for disembarkment."

Rick, startled by the employee's tap on the shoulder, maundered back to his van without saying a word. By the time Rick had reached across for his seatbelt, the cars at the front of his queue had already started crawling forward. Moving off, the steady flow of the traffic led Rick meandering down ramps, his view dazzled by flickering brake lights against the darkening French night. Signs to the motorway and then onto Paris pointed ahead though Rick found himself indicating into the road on his right-hand side. He was aware that he had to deliver his special cargo before he could follow the rest of the traffic onto the motorway. Unlit, Rick slowed into the corners of the mud road, his eyes scanning the surroundings like a hawk with prey. The sides of the road dropped away, banking down a hill into an overgrown meadow wasting away below. Glancing in his mirrors, Rick pushed down on the brake and stopped his van within a metre of the road edge. Swinging open the door, he lit a cigarette between his lips, the minty smoke sobering his thoughts. Looking down the steep, grassy verge, he wondered where this ruthless side of his personality had come from. Sensing regret setting in, Rick spat his cigarette onto the floor and pummelled it into the earth with his now blood-speckled boot. He paced around to the back of the van and adopted a new psyche. As the door opened, he saw her lying unconscious in the same place he had finished with her. Her jeans still pulled down to her ankles. Grabbing her feet, Rick pulled the girl towards him and leant her torso against the side of the van. His hands, shaking and cold, yanked her jeans back onto her slight hips. Unhooking the belt, the girl's limp and lifeless arms fell down in unison. Attempting to stand her up, he heaved. His bony arms wouldn't allow it. After pausing to muster the strength required, Rick managed to drag her body out of the van and onto the sodden floor. Her face, muddied by the dirt, frozen still, void of innocence. He crouched, pulled up his hanging trousers and used both hands to push her body to the edge of the hill. Standing tall, he placed his boot on the back of the girl's spine. Almost instinctively, his boot ploughed into her side before the insipid body started tumbled down the hill. As he watched his 5-minute tryst roll away from him, a smile crept across Rick's face.

"Right then. Back to work."

After 2 spluttering ignition attempts, his van kicked into action leaving Rick free to set his sat-nav for Paris. With that, he pressed the gas pedal to the floor and accelerated into the night.

CHAPTER ELEVEN

Savannah's weary eyes crept open, just in time to see her clothes, money and rapist speed off into the distance. Her eyes could only follow the van so far before the rapist took a turn onto the main road and out of sight. Mud stained on the side of her face irritated her skin. The pain in Savannah's head was like nothing she had felt before. Throb after throb of discomfort cluttered her mind, and Savannah felt as if she could think of nothing more. Her head felt heavy. Lifting it from the ground was hard and only worried the teenager more. With the rest of her body now in sight, she looked down at her bruised and battered legs, littered with cuts and splinters. Her clothes were ripped and dirtied. She pushed herself up and sat looking out at her extended legs. Her jeans were unbuckled. She couldn't help but remember. She wanted to forget.

Savannah used her body weight to push herself up onto her feet. Despite standing, her throbbing head showed no signs of relenting. Her legs felt lethargic and useless as she sized up the hill leading back onto the road. With the night ever darkening, Savannah wanted to reach the main road before the sun had set beyond the luscious velvet lined hills on the horizon. Both her feet and hands were muddied enough that the soft ground didn't faze the teenager. Using her fingers like claws, Savannah crawled her way up the hill, stopping only to catch her breath and wipe her hands and shoes on the drier, longer parts of grass. Reaching the top, she paused and looked down at the markings her body invariably made as it tumbled down the hill she had just agonised up. Her mind refused to answer the questions itself was conjuring up. With nowhere else to turn, she followed the path to what she hoped would be the main road. Savannah couldn't think clearly. Feeling herself, she tentatively patted her legs for bruises. As she reached her jean pockets, she sighed in relief. Her decision to tuck the passport into her jeans rather than inside of her backpack was most fortunate. The sun had started to set yet still hints of amber escaped into the night sky. Soon enough, her nose filled with the smell of petrol and the sounds of the main road came into the distance. Savannah, again alone with her thoughts, started to blame herself.

"Why am I so stupid?"

Not that they could hear her whispering, she stopped speaking as a car whizzed by at a speed easily above the speed limit.

"I'm the perfect victim. Of course he's going to.."

She paused, but this time the road was clear.

"..rape me. How am I supposed to go to the police and explain the story without letting them know I smuggled myself into Europe."

The seriousness of the situation suddenly daunted on her. Her steps were slow and measured. She didn't know where she was going or if she wanted to go there. The main road, illuminated by towering street lights spaced metres apart, continued on for as far as her narrowing eyes could see. Her legs ached, but her feet refused to stop moving. Dented metallic signs, that glistened under the streetlights, pointed straight towards the motorway and left for Calais as the road split up ahead. Savannah was standing at not just a metaphorical crossroads, but a real one too. Her journey from here on in would be much harder than she could ever have planned.

What on earth am I going to do? How much longer can I walk until my legs just stop working? I'll just find somewhere to sleep and decide what to do tomorrow. I could get on a ferry back, I'd be back before Jules even realises I'm gone. She'll have no clue where I've even been. But then I'll be sent up north. Like a piece of cargo delivered to that nutcase. Chill, Sav. This is fine. I'll walk to the nearest town and find somewhere to sleep. Nobody is going to turn down a girl on her own. Okay. Just a little bit further.

With her mind working overload, she decided to take the road on the left. It wasn't as well-lit as the main road yet still enough light spilt onto the concrete that Savannah could walk with no fear in her steps. Brushing the drying mud from her face and clothes as she walked into sight of the town, Savannah looked far better than she felt. Her legs, still bruised and cut, ached as she rounded the corner into the crux of the town centre. Splinters of moonlight specked the uneven tarmac that formed the boulevard. The buildings, which at first glance seemed to belong to a higher class than the night's inhabitants roaming the street below, leant inwardly as if their sole aim was to meet in the middle of the road.

Paying closer attention, Savannah noticed that these buildings, once considered the envy of their time, were losing the battle between character and age. Their decaying, chipped facades allowed the world to gaze in at their timber skeletons. The residents, like their homes, had seen better days. The streetlights picked up again, illuminating the road down to a Church that straddled both lanes. Without the lights, her search for a place to rest would have been infinitely harder. Instead, the signs of B&Bs and hotels glistened under the faux light. The closest to Savannah towered over the rest. A large, dated building stood squeezed between what Savannah deduced as a butchers, from the hanging pig's heads in the window, and a pharmacy, with a solid green cross flashing intermittently. The door to the building was ajar, left unlatched as if to welcome in anyone despite the sign on the door marking no vacancies. Savannah squeezed in behind the door and crept past the row of slanted pictures that hung on the hallway wall. Floorboards beneath her feet creaked with each step. Old-style gas lamps, fitted with electric bulbs, flickered irregularly, casting light onto the cobwebs that hung from the rotting timber beams above. The hallway turned a corner, expanding into a room full of beige, floral-upholstered sofas, each sunken at different depths of decay. Mustard coloured-curtains covered the three rectangular windows shutting out any view of the outside. In the corner of the room, a desk, with a large, open note book sat on top, blocked another doorway. A bell, polished, unlike the rest of the room, was glued to the desk's corner. Savannah moved to the desk, stopping only to look at the laminated room rates displayed on the wall. She had nothing. Every single hard-earned cent had be left in the back of his van. Savannah didn't count on her rapist returning to drop it off. Hoping to look younger than she was, Savannah brushed her gritty hair behind her ears. It didn't take long after she had pressed the bell for an elderly lady to appear behind the desk. Her leathered face, wrinkled and cracking, lacked any emotion or indication. Savannah broke the short silence.

"Bonjour."

Her French was limited and didn't extend to much else.

"I have travelled a long way and I don't have any mo—"

"Non."

The lady scoffed at Savannah's suggestion. Her brow furrowed in disgust before she repeated herself.

"Non. Non. Non"

Savannah, not surprised by her answer, smiled and thanked her.

"Merci Madame."

Undeterred by Savannah's will to leave, the French landlady carried on to speak however now spoke firmly in heavily accented English.

"You aren't welcome here. Your kind. The campsite is not far. Go there."

"My kind?"

"Travellers."

Savannah was used to racism. Growing up with a black dad and a white mum meant that she was often subjected to playground name calling. She recognised it more when she was at work. She'd be ignored and overlooked even when her white colleagues were much busier. Resigned to defeat, Savannah left the building through the same creaking corridor as she had entered although now made as much noise as she could on the creaking floorboards and by slamming the door behind her. It was a Saturday night, and the streets were still busy. Crowds, spilling out of the bars and bistros, gathered on the street, most with a cigarette in their mouths. Unfamiliar chatter filled the air, the foreign language spoken far too quickly and incoherently for Savannah's GCSE level French to process. Crazed eyes followed the teenager as she quickened her pace to the brightly lit hotel on the other side of the road. Despite the heavy crowds, no cars were to be seen and she crossed easily. *Hotel d'espoir* with its black tinted windows and a grand oak door stood proudly amongst the older buildings. Three illuminated stars hung precariously above the door, all tilting in slightly different directions. Savannah, as she went to pull on the oversized door knocker, noticed a buzzer fixed on the left side. Buzz. Savannah could hear the ringing behind the door. She waited for an uncomfortable amount of time before tentatively pressing the button once more. On the second occasion, the ringing was met by hurried French expletives and hastened footsteps.

"Ok..Ok..Ok." came the muffled voice from inside.

As the door eased open, Savannah stared intently as a stretched, skinny man looked in disdain at the sight in front of him. Losing every shred of professionalism, the man started belly-sniggering.

"No."

Savannah squeezed her words in between the man's laughter.

"Bonjour. I am looking for a room."

"No."

Still, he laughed and still, she tried.

"Just for tonight. Chambre?"

"You think I will let you come here?"

Savannah wasn't sure if his decision was a contentious one.

"Please."

"It's bad enough having you in the campsite. Let alone in our town."

Savannah latched onto his idea. She'd never been camping before but by now, it was her only realistic option.

"Campsite. Please, where is it?"

"Follow the road over the river. Go past the university and head back to the sea."

Savannah repeated it back to him but couldn't finish her sentence before the door had slammed shut in her face.

***

The loud cackles of French nightlife had been hushed as Savannah's weary legs paced out of the town centre. Her mind, fully focused on reaching the campsite, internally repeated the directions given to her some time before. She had passed the university on her left, a grand building guarded by a high bush perimeter. Flags, spaced out along the hedgerow, could all but twitch in the calm night. Thick concrete dropped down to the road where cars and lorries hurtled past at breakneck speed, slowing just enough to straight line the wide roundabout, spoking out into various, ambiguous directions. Savannah was alone on the pavement, and despite the hooting of several horns as men in machines whizzed past, she felt no fear. If anything, Savannah felt excitement, a gentle swirling of adventure in her stomach. She was approaching the roundabout that looked distant 5 minutes before. Her nose again filled with the smell of sea air. Without much thought involved, Savannah followed the road as it wrapped around the roundabout. As the road curved, the streetlights grew ever distant. Waterlogged gravel replaced the pavement on the side of the now quietening road. Fencing, previously so ordered and tight on the main road, looked broken and unkempt as it snaked into the distance. Gravel become grass as Savannah's shoes squelched in the sodden sward. Avoiding the mud, she cut across the road, stopping only to look both ways. Her eyes strained in the darkness yet even in the pitch black, Savannah could make out a few people dotted

on her side of the road. Their loud voices, foreign to France, carried in the silence. Feeling their gaze, she walked by quickly hoping to avoid becoming a part of their confrontation. Hand written signs, attached with zip ties to the fence, pointed out the campsite. A sense of relief overpowered everything else Savannah was feeling. Her legs, boosted by the possibility of rest, felt energised once more. She continued on, noticing a large group of people stood by a wide opening in the fence. Again, she walked on quickly, though this time the conversation stopped as she passed. Feeling unnerved, Savannah scanned around for anything helpful. A sign for the campsite, identical to the one 100 metres back, rested against the fence though this version was pointing in the reverse direction. It had clicked in her mind even before Savannah had fully registered the sign. The vast opening behind her, surrounded by the group of people, was the entrance to the camp. Encouraged by an unfound determination, Savannah wasted no time in changing direction. Wanting nothing but rest, she felt ready for anything. The conversation didn't stop as the resolute teenager headed for the blocked entrance. Savannah hadn't heard the language before yet the group had a similar skin tone to hers. Savannah relied on her French once again.
"Excuse moi."
Without a glance, a man in the centre of the group stepped back, freeing a pathway to the entrance gate. Surprised yet stoic, Savannah went to walk through. Her journey, just two steps old, was stopped as a swinging arm blocked the path. Looking up at the arm's owner, Savannah swallowed her breath. He spoke.
"Be careful."
With that, the arm came down, and the path was free once more. Brushing off the remark, Savannah crossed over the entrance way and

took tentative steps past a large tarpaulin marquee. Walking into the camp, the light from the roadside slipped away. She could see nothing significant but a small fire burning on the floor several hundred yards away. With the night now full of chill, Savannah headed for the warmth the glow would bring. As she walked, dust beneath her feet kicked up with every step. Voices, the same kind as those outside chose not to reveal their sources in the darkness. With the fire nearing, the amber flare washed its surroundings with light. Around the fire laid mats, each ripped and torn slightly. Nearest the fire, the mats were covered by bodies scrunched into a tight crescent moon shape. Savannah, laden with exhaustion and obvious pain, looked around for an empty space. Finding one, she rounded the fire and crept between the people to her vacant mat. Feeling the heat from the fire as it spat warmth towards her, Savannah slumped down onto the floor and stretched her tired, cut legs. The voices, so alien to her, softened as her eyes began to close.

CHAPTER TWELVE

Adnan was walking almost as fast as his heart was beating. His stinging eyes, raw from the sudden awakening, were sobered by the fresh, coastal breeze. As the space in front of him opened up, Adnan's walk quickened to a run. He dodged past tents, jumped over pegs and ducked under washing lines, all the while ignoring his body's plea to stop and catch his breath. His feet slipped as he raced down the slope causing a spraying of dust to cover an unfortunately placed tent. Adnan could see the commotion ahead, slowing himself as he weaved through bewildered onlookers. He pushed through the growing crowd, shooing them away from the spectacle that slept before them. He had come straight from his home after being shaken awake. He had dreamt of this moment many times. Peering over the crowd, he could see her. Her face was blackened with ash, her legs cut and bruised. She was naked if not for her underwear. He called out.

"Adhhiba!" *Go.*

"Adnan. Hal min almmkn dhlk?" *Adnan. Could it be?*

The crowd turned, allowing Adnan to come in closer. He crouched down next to her body, brushing the clumps of dust and mud from her hair. The crowd waited, some more patient than others.

"Adnan? 'ahdhuh hi?" *Adnan. Is it?*

Adnan could feel the stares. The people closest to him waited for an answer. He stroked her hair, waiting for the word to come to his mouth.

"No."

Disappointment-induced dispersion left Adnan and his friend alone with the sleeping girl. Both men looked unsure as to what to do, their eyes locked on the problem in front of them. Adnan's friend broke the silence.

"She is foreign, no?"

"Of course. We must dress her, treat her as if she is our own."

Adnan took the girl's hand and sat her up. The action alone was enough to wake Savannah. Her eyes, squinting at the morning sunlight, crept open to see the two men standing over here. Adnan, wanting to calm the girl, spoke with a softer voice than usual.

"Hello. You speak English?"

Savannah looked first at the man talking and then at his friend. Despite understanding what he had asked, just moments after waking up, she had not the words nor will to reply. Her hand, black after itching her ashen face, pushed away from the man's grasp. Adnan watched as the girl registered her nakedness, recoiled in fear and scrambled to her feet. She cried out for help.

"Get away from me. Please. Somebody help me, get away from me."

Adnan, who had half expected such a reaction, was visibly shocked by her aggressive paranoia. He spoke softly as he pleaded with the girl.

"We are not going to hurt you. We want to help you."

Savannah had been here before. It was all too real. The masses of people around, most still crouched inside their tents, refused to acknowledge her screams.

"Somebody? Anybody? I need help."

Adnan's friend spoke up.

"We will help you. We will clothe you, send you on your way."

Savannah had no reason to believe these men. She went to bed fully clothed and woke up all but naked. Savannah wasn't sure who to trust.

"Who are you? Tell me now, or I will ring the police."

Savannah had no phone nor did she have any clue where she was. She wasn't sure if the men had believed her bluff.

"We will help you. I can't explain here. There are too many gossiping tongues. Come with me, and I will explain."

Savannah remained coy. Her hopes of reaching Germany depended on getting out of Calais. She was sure she could go it alone. Adnan refused to give in.

"If you don't want help then at least help me."

Savannah listened on.

"Let me be a Father again."

She turned her back on the pair and looked out at her surroundings. Green topped tents, mostly makeshift using pieces of industrial fabric, covered the dusty field for as far as Savannah could see. Rubbish seeping out of plastic bags and refuse sacks littered the narrow walkways between each tent. Lines of washing hung low between the poles. Clothes muddied by the ground soaked in large tubs of brown water.

Corrugated iron structures, so few that each could be considered a landmark, lingered just above the multitudes of tents. A concrete wall, tagged with colourful graffiti, bordered the left side of the campsite. Topless kids chased each other between the tents, oblivious to the dangers around them. A film crew, all dressed in black cargo trousers and branded fleece, tiptoed around the camp and its inhabitants. Their lenses, now focused on the children playing, started to record. Turning back, Savannah faced the two men yet again.

"Is this the.." she mumbled.

Adnan cleared his throat.

"The Jungle."

Savannah didn't move.

"It is. Don't worry. We will look after you."

Savannah walked towards the men. Her exposed body felt cold while the sun hid behind the long grey clouds.

"Come. My place is not far."

Savannah followed the men through the camp and past hundreds of pairs of wandering eyes. Her outfit, or more lack of, didn't raise as many eyebrows as Savannah was expecting. It seemed that clothes weren't a necessity to the people living in the camp. Adnan led Savannah to the perimeter of the campsite where eight tents faced inward looking at a dusty circular patch. She could see several faces inside each of the tents but most were hiding behind the solid tarpaulin sheets. Adnan smiled and called for his children to come out of the tents. One by one they introduced themselves to Savannah, each in their own unique way. The last to do so, and by far the smallest, ducked out of the way of a high-five and blew a raspberry in Savannah's face. She couldn't help but smile. Adnan was not impressed.

"Loic…"

WIth a face so stern, just Loic's name was enough to force the boy into an apology.

"I'm sorry about him. He's always been cheeky."

"It's okay. My cousin is like that."

"Your name?"

"Savannah."

"Ah, a beautiful name. I have a rule here. I ask no questions of nobody unless they want to talk."

Savannah's silence showed she preferred the first option.

"You must be cold."

"Quite. I had clothes."

"Ah Miss Savannah, in the Jungle, sleeping where you did, clothes aren't likely to survive the night. You are lucky you did."

"I guess."

"You guess what?"

"Never mind."

Savannah hesitated before she asked a lot of Adnan.

"I'm trying to get to Paris. Can you get me there?"

"Paris. The city of love. Not many people here are looking to goto Paris. We must get you something smart to wear."

Savannah was grateful but confused by his over-generosity.

"Anything will do."

"For Paris? You talk nonsense."

"Why are you helping me?" asked Savannah.

Adnan crouched beside a tent and started searching through a black bag of pre-packaged clothes.

"Because you need help."

"But why me? Why did you hold me as I woke up?"

"You were not who I thought you were."

"Who did you think I was?"

"That is a question for another time."

"You said something about wanting to be a father again? You have kids here. Are you not a father to them?"

He sighed.

"My daughter."

Adnan stopped rummaging through the bag and looked Savannah square in the eyes.

"We travelled from Syria. I was a teacher, at a good school. I earned a lot of money for my profession. But those in power didn't want people like me in their country. We weren't welcome. My family had to leave. We tried for a better life, and this is where we ended up."

He hadn't yet stopped for breath.

"It was our second night here. My daughter was walking around the camp. To make friends. I told her to be back before dusk."

Now he stopped. His eyes left Savannah's.

"She never came home."

"I'm so sorr—"

"I have never given up hope. I never will. You can understand that when I hear a dark skinned girl is sleeping alone naked by the entrance gate, I think not of you."

Savannah completed the sum in her head.

"You thought I could be your daughter."

"Correct. But, I still help you. You might not be my daughter, but you are somebody's."

Reaching into the bag once more, Adnan grabbed two plastic packets and chucked them outside of the tent. Inside the packets were a pair of pleated grey trousers and a short-sleeved white blouse. After zipping up the bag, Adnan ripped open the packaging and held each piece of clothing against Savannah.

"A perfect fit."

"I really can't take it. People here need it."

"Your compassion is kind Miss, but nobody has a use for this type of clothing in the jungle. It is not for us."

Savannah, caught between a real need for clothes and unease at taking them, sighed as she was handed the shirt. The shirt was starched, pressed and clean. She slipped the shirt onto her shoulders and fumbled with the buttons. While Savannah stepped into the trousers, Adnan reached into a separate bag, taking out a pair of black, pre-laced plimsolls. For a place that was running low on clothes, the outfit matched rather well. The shoes were a tight fit, but the options were limited, and Savannah felt relieved that she was in clothes once again. Adnan had moved back inside to his tent where he was handed a small red book from a young boy. He ruffled the delivery boy's hair and sent him on his way.

"Name. Savannah Bancroft Staggs."

Savannah hadn't registered what he was saying. Adnan, with a crooked smile on his face, looked up at his guest before continuing.

"Date of birth. 10th January."

Savannah stopped him in his tracks.

"What are you doing? How do you know who I am?"

Adnan did nothing but laugh in an overtly obnoxious way.

"Miss Savannah. When you come into the Jungle with a passport."

Adnan raised his voice higher than usual.

"A British passport! You do not expect to see it again. The Good God Allah is looking down on you. You have been blessed."

Savannah, raped and abused hours before, did not feel blessed. Her tone was authoritative. She wasn't to be messed with.

"Give me that."

"A girl from Britain in the Jungle, looking to travel to Paris. I taught English for many years, read many books, but it is your story that intrigues me the most."

"This book isn't for reading."

"Savannah, I have helped you. I must ask these questions to see if I could help you mo—"

Adnan's sentence was suddenly interrupted by the arrival of three, tall policemen. The leader of the trio walked with vigour. His two subordinates followed behind, their faces red with heat. It was becoming a hot day, and the uniforms they wore weren't designed for that. A monobrow, visible underneath the lead policeman's cap, furrowed as he surveyed the area. His boot-covered feet shuffled into a stance that exerted power. The others followed suit.

"Madame. Les journalistes ne sont pas autorisés ici. Vous devez revenir à la zone désignée."

Savannah's basic French skills weren't advanced enough to make sense of his commands. He repeated himself though this time he spoke in a firmer tone.

"Madame. Les journalistes ne sont pas autorisés ici. Vous devez revenir à la zone désignée."

Journalistes. Savannah was sure of what she had heard. She was grateful. Not only did the French word sound similar to the English but the policeman had addressed her as a journalist. Unlike most others, he didn't think she was a refugee.

"Allez!"

The policeman powered forward and motioned for Savannah to follow him. Looking to her side, she could see Adnan. He looked downbeat. As the officers swept her forward, she caught Adnan's eye and mouthed 'Thank You.' He had, perhaps unwillingly, helped Savannah more than either of them could ever have imagined. Adnan smiled falsely as he watched Savannah disappear into the distance flanked by three of her very own bodyguards.

As they weaved through the tents, the most senior policeman turned to Savannah and started speaking in French. Her reaction caused him to stop, then speak again in almost perfect-English.

"You don't speak French?"

"Non."

Savannah, attempting to be funny, had confused the matters worse.

"So you are English?"

"Yes."

Savannah remembered she was a journalist.

"My office is in London."

"You know to remain close. How did you find yourself in that part of camp?"

"I was doing a story. That man was telling me about his daughter."

"You mustn't believe all their tales. Every man in this camp has a story."

"Stories worth telling."

"For you, maybe. But we are bored of it. Nobody cares for these immigrants."

Knowing an actual journalist wouldn't confront an officer of law, however bigoted he may be, and wanting to remain on the policeman's good side, Savannah felt powerless to argue.

"Maybe."

"We must walk quicker. A bus leaves shortly."

This was the first she had heard of a bus, and while she wasn't sure where it was heading, she was happy that there was a way out of the jungle. Her passport had made her a prime target.

Savannah rounded the corner and recognised the entrance gate from the night previous. The gang of threatening men that had blocked the entrance last night had been replaced by a small group of journalists, each dressed smartly in similar clothes to Savannah. Most had messenger bags hanging across their bodies which Savannah assumed carried laptops and other props she didn't have. The group smiled as Savannah approached. She had never met any of these people before yet felt naturally comfortable around them. Savannah's charade was a fortunate one. For the first time since she had left home, she felt at ease. Before a chance to stand out amongst a group of French speakers presented itself, a pristinely white Volvo minibus pulled up alongside the entrance gate. The driver, a short, stumpy man jumped out and ripped a ham and cheese baguette from the packet. The door electronically slid open allowing the 8 or so journalists, and one faux, to bundle into the van. As she sat down, a petite lady with bleached blonde hair tied in a pony tail, motioned to Savannah's blouse while mumbling in French. Reaching behind her back, Savannah felt the tags of her shirt still attached. With her face embarrassingly rosy, she ripped the label from the blouse and thanked the lady in French.

"Ah..Merci."

Brushing the crumbs from his stretched top, the driver pulled himself back into the minibus and reeved the engine. A young journalist, with sweat patches staining his light blue shirt, reached across to the door and pulled it shut. Savannah's window seat afforded her a view of the Jungle as the van crept forward. From the van's heightened view, she could see the fire where she slept last night. Now, she was in a van with a group of people who thought she was a journalist. The noise of children playing was still audible as the van indicated to turn left at the roundabout. Savannah, who had started to recall her own family memories, caught the reflection of herself in the window. She wasn't the person that had left home so confident she'd find the answers she was looking for. It had been just two days, yet Savannah had already been raped, abused and ransacked. She had lost all of her money and clothes and necessities. It wasn't long before she again wondered if it was worth the stress. Even with luck on her side, the trip had become so much harder than she envisaged. Savannah had found someone to take her to Dover and someone to dress her. She knew that at some point, her luck would run out. How much longer would she be able to pretend that the rape didn't exist, to pretend she wasn't a victim of her own inquisition. For now, Savannah found it easy to put it to the back of her mind. She hoped that once the reality eventually set in, she'd be home with the answers she wanted, and the family that she already missed For now, she was in a van with a group of people who thought she was a journalist hoping that it would take her home. She thought it unlikely. As the driver interrupted the peace, she knew for certain.

"Mesdames et Messieurs. Prochain arrêt, Paris."

CHAPTER THIRTEEN

Luscious green valleys rolled into the horizon beneath the snaking road that had taken them from Calais. Spurts of yellowing shrubbery splintered the grazing meadows. The sun, at its highest point in the clear sky, warmed the glass windows to a temperature too hot to touch. On board, Savannah leant in with every corner and turn as the minibus zipped by on the empty roads. Fields packed with crops in regimented lines framed the van as the road straightened out. It was nearing midday yet the streets were quiet. Every so often the van would speed up, overtake a tractor then slow back to cruising speed. Besides themselves, traffic on the road, much like the conversation, was few and far between. Savannah sat in silence, her mind wandering in and

out of focus. Field after field grew visually tiresome after being treated to so many. She had not said a word since thanking the petite blonde to her right for pointing out the labels still in her blouse. The conversation behind grew louder with every mile. Savannah couldn't understand a word of it yet that didn't stop their yapping from being an irritant. Since becoming a journalist, albeit a fake one, Savannah felt a need to be more adult. Dressed smartly she could easily pass for someone much older, someone who wouldn't sulk in the corner of a bus. In a move that would have pleased her socially-confident Dad, Savannah turned and tried to catch the eye of the blonde journalist. She was enthralled in her conversation and showed no signs of wavering. Not wanting to be rude, Savannah waited patiently. She watched as the lady pulled her hair from out of a pony tail, letting it drape down her shoulders. Her outfit was a finer version of Savannah's. The blouse a carbon copy, although her trousers were fitted and accessorised with a designer belt. By her side, a branded clipboard nestled on top of a brimming shoulder bag. As the road turned from smooth concrete to rough gravel, the blonde journalist turned back around, her eyes meeting Savannah as she did so.
"Hello."
The journalist wasn't expecting the conversation. She had already turned to face the opposite the window by the time Savannah had finished speaking. Turning back towards her, the real journalist flashed a smile.
"Hello."
Savannah had planned the next question.
"Who do you work for?"
"Liberté. And you? I haven't seen your face around here before."

To Savannah's surprise, the blonde's English was almost as good as her French.

"A small company. We are relatively new."

Savannah didn't sound convincing, yet the journalist seemed to buy it.

"Ah, okay. Where are you from?"

"Our office is in London."

"What takes you to Paris?"

"I'm finishing a story."

Savannah wasn't lying.

"Where did you train?"

She wasn't trying to be nosy, yet Savannah regretted catching her eye.

"I came out of school and joined the local paper. Been climbing ever since."

"I'm Emilie by the way."

"Savannah."

Emilie extended her dainty arm for Savannah to shake.

"How long until we arrive?"

"Oh, not long now. Soon you'll be able to see the city."

Savannah smiled yet said nothing allowing Emilie to fill the silence with more small-talk.

"Where are you staying in Paris?"

"I'm hoping I'll only be there for a few hours. I have to be in Germany."

"Germany? You are well travelled."

Emilie giggled before speaking again.

"It must be an interesting story."

Her tone was inquisitive, yet Savannah was in no mood to share the details.

"Hopefully it will be."

Slightly taken aback by Savannah's reluctance to share, Emilie wished Savannah luck and turned back to the French chattering behind her. With the journey nearing its end, Savannah thought as to her plan once she was safely in Paris. She had made notes on her journey, but like her money and clothes, they were inside the bag that was being looked after by her rapist. From the drop off point, Savannah would have to make her way Gare Du Nord train station. She had remembered that detail from her planning. With no money to hand, she faced an all too familiar problem. Her frustration forced her to think aloud in gritted whispers.

"How can I get on the train if I don't have any bloody money. What the hell am I going to do?"

She knew she was close. It was a simple journey from Paris to Cologne, one that if afforded, would bring her within touching distance of the answers she so desperately needed. Looking down the middle of the van, Savannah could see through the windscreen and out to the road ahead. The traffic was plentiful yet not enough to slow their progress. As the van climbed over the crest of a asphalted hill, the city of Paris revealed it's distant splendour. Jagged industrial buildings punctuated the immediate skyline while glimpses of the ornate city appeared between. Despite the traffic, the road widened allowing much faster vehicles to fly past on either side of the van. With every mile, the city skyline came closer. Through the suburbs, high rise structures, homes for those who had moved to Paris with dreams much grander than their current reality, blocked the view momentarily. As they emerged from beneath the buildings, the obscured sun flashed through the van littering heat as it went. Ahead, the Eiffel Tower stood obnoxiously, looking down on the rest. Even in the baking sun, the buildings emanated greyness; spots of colour as rare as a cloud in the sky. Undisplaceable dome-roofed churches, some with towers sprouting from their sides, gave competition to the rigidly rectangular Notre Dame cathedral. Smoke billowed from ceramic chimneys camouflaged between tiled roofs. As the van journeyed into the beating heart of the city, the hustle and bustle of Parisian life could be heard outside. Beeping horns, cat calls and street-side cafe chatter complimented each other as they hung in the polluted air. From the seats behind, Savannah could hear bags zipping and papers shuffling as the real journalists readied themselves. With little to pack away, Savannah gazed out of the window as the van pulled over on the opposite side of the road. Before her stood a modestly sized building, wide in length not tall in height. The building was at least three stories high, though even that looked small when compared to the monstrous structures out in the suburbs. Romanesque columns held up the front of the neat building. Despite its age, the stonework was clean. Faux balconies and gated windows, not uncommon in their kind, added to its flamboyancy. Well-kept trees, still infant in age, and a flaccid French flag added colour to an otherwise beige exterior. A plaque, a few polishes shy of golden, proclaimed the building as belonging to *Liberté Media*. As the van stopped and the door slid open, Emilie, followed by her French colleagues, bundled out of the van. Using the large glass windows as a mirror, they tidied their outfits By the time Savannah had thanked the driver and stepped onto the pavement only Emilie had not headed into the building.

"It was nice to meet you, Savannah."

"And you."

"I wish you luck with your story. See you around."

Savannah, growing more confident by the hour, smiled back.

"Auvoir Emilie. Merci"

Savannah watched as the journalist headed through the columns and into the building via the revolving doors. While it was true that Savannah was alone once more, for the first time since leaving home, she walked with conviction in her stride. Following the flow of people on the pavement led Savannah to an intersection for both pedestrians and traffic. Gard Du Nord, sign posted on thick white arrows, was to the left. Despite the hot summer's afternoon, her path was shaded, her walk cool. Savannah, in her smart outfit, felt mature beyond her years marching through Parisian side-streets. Approaching a busy road, Savannah spotted another sign post, pointing off in a different direction. As she crossed Rue la Fayette, Savannah gazed both up and down the long street. In both waus, Parisians and tourists alike gathered outside cafes and bars, enjoying the aestival afternoons. Unlike England, where the pub gardens would be full of unscrupulous practices, those sat enjoying their drinks were polite and quieter. Savannah enjoying seeing people so smiley. Either weather or drink-induced, she wasn't sure but it was clear that their joy was infectious. Continuing on, Savannah found more cafe's and bars before arriving at a pretty square, the greenery caged in by an ostentatious fence. Large, solacing oak trees allowed for picnics in the shadowy coolness below. For those relaxing, hamper open, champagne bottle popped, life seemed simple. Savannah watched as a young couple opened their second bottle of champagne, each sip likely costing more than Savannah's train ticket. Still, she walked on to the station with hope far greater than it should have been. Passing a church on her left, Savannah noticed a building, *'Hotel Celia - Gard Du Nord'* on the opposite side of the road. The name was a giveaway, she knew she close. As she approached the edge of a busy intersection, she could numerous signs for the station pointing towards a small, cobbled street. After waiting for a lull in the traffic, Savannah joined the tide of other pedestrians looking to cross the road. From the other side, she could see directly down the short, cobbled street. Gard Du Nord train station was imposingly grand. It was difficult for Savannah to comprehend its size until she had walked further down the road where the cobbles opened up into a courtyard. Taxis waited patiently outside the station, ready and waiting for the next influx of passengers. A sculpture, unnecessary and odd was dwarfed by the large rounded windows that split the building into thirds. A young man, sat cross-legged on a piece of cardboard, begged for money as people darted past. Savannah watched as hurried tourists lost their minds rushing into the station. Savannah's mind, however, was focused.

CHAPTER FOURTEEN

Inside, the air was hot and sticky. The smell of sweat and body odour lingered in the air far longer than was pleasurable. Painted metal beams arched over the limitless expanse creating a roof that reached high above the floor. A brick wall, furthest from the empty middle ground Savannah found herself in, held both an arrivals and departures board. Walking over, Savannah noticed the ticket barriers blocking the platforms and a well-lit ticket booth flanked by empty queue ropes. Gazing up at the flickering screens, Savannah spotted her target train.

"Essen. 19:35. Via Brussels, Liege and Cologne. Perfect."

Savannah squeezed between a tour group and headed towards the ticket booth. As she joined the back of the three person queue, Savannah caught her own reflection in the glass panelled facade. She liked what she saw. Amongst the hoards of tourists in the station, and particularly the 2 sunburnt Brits in front of her, Savannah felt superior. She didn't have the look of an orphan who had run away from home, smuggled herself across the channel and woke up in a refugee camp. Approaching the counter, Savannah felt good.

"Hi."

Savannah had assumed that the stumpy lady, hoisted up on her office chair behind the glass, spoke English. Chopped brown hair came to her shoulder while her striped uniform barely wrapped around her figure. Her badge, polished silver, named the ticket agent Bernadette.

"Bonjour."

"How much is a ticket to Cologne?"

Bernadette did not seem pleased as she squinted at her computer screen.

"On which service?"

"Umm. The seven-thirty."

"You mean the nineteen-thirty-five service?"

"Oui."

Savannah was trying to be polite, yet her use of French was rude enough for Bernadette to look up from the screen.

"Sorry."

"One-way or return?"

"One-way."

Bernadette stopped and looked up at Savannah again.

"A one-way ticket is forty-five euros…"

Bernadette carried on speaking yet Savannah had stopped registering what she was saying. Her mind was racing. She knew she had no chance of finding that money. Bernadette was waiting.

"Madame?"

Savannah let her mind wander.

"Madame. There is a queue."

"Sorry. I was thinking. Are there any cheaper trains to Cologne? Less money."

"I will look."

Bernadette, using just one finger, typed into her computer. With each search, she would sigh and start typing again. She shook her head while speaking.

"All one-way tickets to Cologne are forty-five euros."

Savannah, in a moment of desperation, had an idea. Bernadette was growing impatient.

"Which shall I book?"

Savannah needed time.

"I will be back. Later on."

Bernadette smiled out of courtesy before sliding a folded timetable through the gap in the counter.

"Merci."

Savannah grabbed the pamphlet, slid it into her pocket and avoided eye contact with the now substantially larger queue behind her. Her idea was novel yet not entirely unfounded. Savannah trudged out of the station unusually buoyant for somebody who had just been priced out of something so vital. The sun had mellowed and the afternoon was now much cooler. Savannah's inspiration had left, and for that reason she was glad. She slumped down against the wall, lying her legs out straight. Making a cup with her hands, Savannah tried desperately to catch anybody's attention.

***

Despite knowing exactly how much she had, Savannah decided to count it anyway.

"one…two…three…four….fifty..two..two…four euros, 54 cents."

With no watch, Savannah wasn't sure how long she had been slouched against the wall, but guessing by the light, she had been there for at least 3 hours. Her time had been wasted. She was over forty euros off being able to buy a ticket and with night approaching, she wanted to be out of sight. Her outfit hadn't helped. She didn't look like a beggar and people weren't treating her like one. Other than the two policemen on their rounds, Savannah had attracted little attention. She'd been asked to move on yet with little English, the policemen weren't all that effective. As the night grew darker, Savannah began to play closer attention to the people circling the courtyard. On a bench metres away, a black lady sat watching Savannah intently. She'd leave and then return to the same seat, still with eyes on the teenager. If he were male, Savannah would have scurried away yet this woman intrigued her. Still, she looked. Savannah stared back so attentively that two 50 cent pieces had fallen into her lap without much of a realisation. As she totalled her money, the lady advanced. Coming closer,Savannah could see her in more detail. Her skin was much darker than the teen's, her hair much longer. The dark-skinned lady wore an outfit that wouldn't have passed her Aunt's pre-party check. A denim skirt came high above the knee while her string vest did little to hide her pushed-up boobs. She was caked in makeup. Savannah watched as she came far too close to be talking to anyone but her.

"Vous ne gagnerez pas d'argent de cette façon."

Again, Savannah cursed her unpractical french skills. Her empty-faced stare answered for her.

"English?"

Savannah nodded.

"I said...you won't make any money that way."

"Tell that to my five euros."

"Five euros?"

She laughed as she dropped down to Savannah's level.

"French people. They don't like charity. If you want something in this world, then you must get up and go get it."

"You were watching me. Why?"

"I was like you once."

"Oh."

"An English girl begging outside Gare Du Nord in Paris? We all have our stories."

Savannah stopped herself from speaking.

"I'm Angelique."

Staring into her lap, Savannah stayed silent.

"You don't have to talk to me, but you mustn't stay here. The night is falling, and the police don't look favourably on beggars. Especially not foreign ones."

Savannah snapped back.

"And how would you know?"

"Walk with me, and I will tell you."

With her begging efforts proving far from fruitful and a night on Parisian streets a genuine possibility, Savannah was warming to the idea of having a friend.

"Walk to where? I need to get a train."

"It isn't far."

Angelique couldn't resist bantering with her.

"And besides, with five euros, you aren't getting any time soon."

Savannah knew she was right. Following Angelique, she stood to her feet. After sliding the little money she had into her pocket, she brushed her blouse that had been dirtied by the ground. Instead of walking back down the cobbled street, the pair stayed left and came to a much larger road. From their position, the road looked endless. Savannah, recognising the help she was being given, made a conscious effort to be polite.

"Are you French?"

"Yes. I was born just outside the city. In the suburbs."

"I think I drove past them on the way here."

"Not much to see, going back now it is a piece of shit. But that was my childhood, and I thought it was the best."

"Did you go to school?"

Angelique couldn't help but laugh out loud.

"Of course I went to school. We were poor, but we weren't that poor."

"Your English is good. My French isn't nearly as good."

Angelique looked at Savannah, her mouth slightly ajar.

"You can speak French?"

"A little bit. I did it at school for a few years."

"Go on."

Now, Savannah was embarrassed.

"What shall I say?"

"Anything."

Racking her brain, Savannah settled on the one line that came up on every French exam.

"Bonjour. Je m'appelle Savannah. J'habite à Bath en Angleterre."

Both girls burst out laughing as they waited for the traffic lights to turn the same colour as the Brit's face.

"Savannah. Like in Africa."

"Oui."

"It's nice to meet you Savannah."

"And you."

Like those she saw earlier in the day, the street was also lined with cafes and bars that spilt over onto the pavement. Smells, too exotic to pinpoint, reminded an already hungry Savannah that she was starving. As they approached another crossroad, Angelique pointed out a small park nestled in between 2 lanes of speeding traffic.

"It is this way."

The park was small but perfectly formed. Grass covered all but the gravel entrance while three benches under a shading tree provided relief from the setting sun. Angelique motioned towards the bench nearest them.

"Let's sit."

"Do you come here often?" Savannah asked.

"From time to time. When I need to collect my thoughts. It's quiet."

"Do you have a job?"

"A job of sorts. I make money for myself."

"Are you a drug dealer?"

Angelique, stern faced, replied sharply.

"No."

"Oh, okay. Sorry."

"What do you do?"

"I was about to go to university. I had a job in a card shop."

Angelique queried her use of the past tense.

"Was?"

"Yeah. Was. Don't suppose I'll go now."

"Why not? Dare to dream."

"Things happen, plans change."

"Can I ask?"

Savannah came back quick.

"Ask what?"

"What happened? What changed?"

Savannah laughed on a short, outward breath.

"How much time do we have?"

"I'm not going anywhere."

"I'm not sure. I don't even know you."

Angelique rubbed her hand on Savannah's back.

"It's okay. I understand."

Silence came over the bench as neither girl knew what to say next. Cars of all sorts and sizes accelerated past the park yet the sounds of the stuttering engines were numbed by the park's tranquility. Both girls watched as two young lads sat down on the bench furthest from them. Their conversation was jovial, their spirits were high. Angelique, clearly uncomfortable by the silence, broke it.

"My parents were murdered when I was 14."

Savannah, in shock, turned to look at Angelique, but her eyes were focused on the floor.

"We lived in a high rise building. My dad, he was the leader of the residents association, everybody liked him. My mum would bake. She'd bring her cakes and bread to the meetings. They were famous."

She stopped to clear her throat. Her voice was cracking.

"One day, there was an argument. Somebody moved into the building that shouldn't have. My dad got them evicted. It was what everybody wanted yet only he said anything. They left, and we didn't hear anything from them for some months."

"You don't have to tell me any—"

"Then, the night before my school's awards presentations, they came back. He came to our house, broke the door and let himself in. My parents slept in the first bedroom. He opened their door, walked in and.." Angelique mimicked a gun firing with her fingers.

"Bang. Bang. I heard the gunshots. I hid under my bed."

Savannah could see tears beginning to form under her eyes.

"If I had gone, if I had been quicker then maybe they'd still be here."

"You can't blame yourself."

"I waited then ran to them. I took the phone, I screamed for help. Nobody came until the ambulance arrived. By then, it was too late. I held my mum's hand as she left me. My dad was already gone."

"I'm so sorry, Angelique."

"I have no family here. My parents had moved from Ghana before I was born. I went to live in an orphanage, but nobody, not one person, liked me there. I was the only black girl. You'd think they'd welcome the outcasts. At 18, they pushed me out. I didn't have a job, any money, no friends. What was I to do? I came here."

"To this park?"

"To the streets. I worked. I worked hard, and I started making money. I didn't want to work, but I had little else to do. Nobody employs a homeless, black girl."

"But your English is so good.."

"Everyone speaks English here. It is only your country that doesn't speak another language."

"But now..are you okay?"

"Now? I live in a flat. One bed, only little light. But it is all I can afford."

"And do you have a job?"

"A job of sorts."

"On the streets?"

"Oui."

"You've done so well."

"It doesn't seem that way."

Savannah, after hearing such a tale, felt obliged to share her own.

"My dad died 3 years ago."

It was Angelique's turn to look at Savannah.

"Cancer. They caught it late, and he only had weeks to live. We tried to make the most of it but…"

Savannah felt tears coming.

"but..it's hard to act as if everything is normal you know? We all knew it would happen, it was just when. Every night I went to sleep I feared it would happen as I slept. He died 3 weeks after his diagnosis. That day, I never wanted it to end. That was the last day on Earth with my Dad. I couldn't cope. My mum, she worked abroad in the week, so I lived with my Auntie. For months all I could think was of all the things we'd never be able to do. He'd never walk me down the aisle. He wouldn't scare off my first boyfriend. He wouldn't ever be able to kiss me goodnight again. I haven't felt the same since."

"I get that. He had died, but I felt like I was the one who paid the price."

"Exactly."

Savannah stopped herself as she built up the courage to continue.

"Life was normal again for a while."

Angelique watched as Savannah wiped a tear from her eye.

"Then my Mum went missing."

"Missing?"

"She worked in Germany. Ever since my dad died, she would come home on the weekends. One day, she didn't. We tried calling but she didn't pick up the phone. Again, we called. Still nothing. We stopped trying her and phoned the police instead. They marked her as missing and contacted the German police to coordinate a search. They tracked her card being used in Latvia. After that, nothing."

"Latvia?"

"Yeah. A few weeks later, they found her. She was hanging in a factory near the capital. Police ruled it a suicide."

"Suicide? Why would she kill herself if she knew you'd be alone?"

Angelique had shocked herself with the unfiltered remark.

"I'm sorry. I shouldn't have said that."

Savannah wasn't angry. She was glad someone else saw it the same way.

"No, it's fine. She wouldn't have. I just know she wouldn't kill herself."

"So what happened?"

"I struggled."

"But you are here?"

"We weren't particularly close, my mum and I. I couldn't move on with so many questions still buzzing in my head. I just want to know more about her. I want to know what she did after work for fun, who her friends were. I want to see where she lived, where she worked. I want someone else to believe that she didn't kill herself."

"So you are going to Germany."

"Yep."

"Yet you are in Paris. "

Savannah half-lied.

"I planned this. It was the easiest way."

Angelique tried to lift the conversation, laughing through her words.

"Did you plan to beg outside of the train station?"

Savannah hadn't finished her story.

"I didn't plan on getting raped."

Angelique's hand grabbed Savannah's instantaneously. She could only manage one word.

"No?"

Savannah, snuffling through the tears, managed more.

"I got to Dover. I had the money for a ferry ticket. I had it all written down. Which ferry to get, which train, which bus. It was planned and researched. My last wage from my old job was to pay for it. But I couldn't buy a ticket for the ferry. They wouldn't let me. I needed to get across the Channel. I had to."

Angelique's grip on Savannah's hand tightened.

"It was too easy. I walked through and got in a van. They weren't looking, and I only needed to be inside until we boarded the ferry. I could get off and walk out. I'd be back on track."

"What happened?"

"I made it on board. The deck cleared, I tried to leave."

"Please, Savannah. You don't have to go on."

Ignoring both Angelique and her emotions, Savannah carried on. Her eyes were glazed over.

"I opened the door, and he hit me. His boot. I was knocked back into the van. He tied my arms together, pulled my clothes off. My first time. I felt nothing. I cried. He finished. I stopped. I said nothing when I could have

140

said anything. He dumped me on the side of a road in Calais. Everything I had was still in his van. I lost my money, my clothes, my phone. Everything."

Angelique tried to be positive.

"Yet you made it here!"

"I made it here by refusing to acknowledge I was raped. Every ounce of pain from those 10 minutes I've stored in the back of my mind. I don't know how to confront it, so I don't."

"Telling me was far braver than you think."

"Brave? I let it happen."

"Nothing you could have done would have stopped him. You mustn't let yourself think like that."

She sniffled her tears.

"So, yeah, my plan was ruined slightly."

As the pair let the tranquillity of the park take hold, the symmetrical lampposts that bordered the open space simultaneously lit up. With the sun fixed on setting, the sky turned dark. Angelique, realising the time, let go of Savannah's hand.

"Savannah. I'm sorry, but I have to go."

"Go where?"

"I have to work."

"Oh."

Angelique felt guilty leaving this girl alone, especially given how honest she had just been.

"Come with me. You'll have to wait, but then I can help you."

With the only other option being to return to her begging spot outside the station, Savannah agreed to follow Angelique.

"Are you a Christian, Savannah?"

"I'm not sure I am. I was brought up Catholic."

"Well, you will know that God always has a plan for people.I believe that He has made our paths cross tonight. We can help each other."

Savannah appreciated the comforting thought.

"I hope so. I really hope so."

CHAPTER FIFTEEN

As the pair left the fenced-in greenery, both girls were unsure what to say. Entering the park, Savannah felt slightly nervous around an older girl who had been watching her intently. Leaving, however, Savannah felt like she had gained a sister. Telling her story had lifted the burden from her aching shoulders. She felt freer, and she was sure that Angelique did too. Savannah was comfortable by Angelique's side, even if she didn't know where she was going. Between two buildings, a partially lit stone staircase climbed out of sight. It had been a dry day, yet the stone steps felt greasy. Side by side, the girls clambered up the empty stairs. Reaching the top, Savannah noticed how quiet the streets felt. It was a pedestrianised space, yet the hustle and bustle she had come to expect was missing. Cafe's and bars stood empty. Their tables, tightly packed together on slanted courtyards, waited for customers. *Cafe Tabac* rounded the corner of the street and a side alley they were heading for. Two boomerang-shaped signs, lined with red fluorescent strips, protruded from the building proclaiming tobacco for sale. Stop warning posts, leaning out of the concrete, acted as guardians of the mopeds chained together. Angelique taking Savannah's hand led her to the entrance of the curved alleyway. Unkempt plants and unpicked weeds adorned flower boxes affixed to the buildings that leant into the alley. Three refuse bins, presumably from *Cafe Tabac* next door, had attracted a swarm of flies intent on sampling the cafe's rotten delicacies. Savannah had wanted to stay nearest the well-lit, road end of the alley yet Angelique pulled her out of sight.

"You must stay here. If you walk into the street, you will be at risk of danger."

"Danger?"

"Yes. They aren't the sorts of people you want to be mixing with."

"Promise me you will come back."

"With all my heart.'

Angelique's phone started ringing, an electronic chiming that must have grown irritating over time.

"Oui. Je serai bientôt là"

The conversation was brief but was enough for Angelique to now appear rushed.

"I'll be back soon."

Angelique disappeared out of sight as she headed back to the main road. All was still.

With nothing to do but wait, Savannah walked further down the alley. Her inquisition took hold as she peered into windows and open doorways. It didn't take her long before she had reached as far as she could walk. A fence, consisting of several broken planks of wood, blocked her path. Pressing her ear to the fence, Savannah could hear the vibrations of trains on tracks, thundering through the city. Turning back, the teenager avoided the garbage bags that had been torn apart by hungry birds. Taking a piece of cardboard from an open bin, Savannah ripped it lengthways and placed it on the sullied ground. After a while on the floor, her bum was numbing. She had much preferred the park bench and started to wonder why Angelique hadn't made her wait there. From what Savannah had seen of Paris, she liked the city. It was pleasant, mostly clean and the buildings captured a sense of what life would have been like when they were built. She could see herself here. Chatting in the bars, enjoying a bottle of wine with her professional, hard working friends. She hadn't been dealt the greatest hand in life, but Savannah was determined to make it a winning one. Time ticked on, and still, Angelique had not returned. The night was now at it's darkest tone. Sounds, rowdy and masculine, had started to heighten from the out-of-sight street. For a girl alone at night, the noise was proving to be quite the intimidation. Her desire to get to Germany was forcing Savannah to question her new found friend. She wondered what was a reasonable time to wait before other options should be considered. Still, Savannah wanted to trust her friend. Feeling a drop of rain on her shoulder, Savannah gazed up at the sky. Grey clouds had lightened the darkness yet the rain looked imminent. She trudged back to the bin and grabbed another piece of cardboard to rest upon her head. Before she had a chance to make her makeshift shelter, the heavens opened, and thick droplets of rain fell from the sky. Her piece of cardboard was completely aqueous within minutes. With her hands over head, she ran to the bin and fetched more pieces. Turning, she almost slipped on the wet, slippy surface. Walking back to her spot, she spotted a lamp-cast shadow against the wall. The silhouette, human-shaped, spread along the wall nearest the road. Savannah instinctively slowed her steps. Moving slowly, Savannah watched as the shadow drew closer. Rounding the slight corner, she kept close to the wall. Out of the corner of her eye, the teen became distracted by a flicker of movement. Something was most definitely there. Her heart was beating fast. It was too broad to be Angelique returning. Fenced in by a dead-end, Savannah had no choice but to advance and hope it was nothing. Creeping forward, he spotted her before she did him. Savannah froze still. She feared the worst. He came round, his right leg trailing behind his left. He shouted out.

"Combien?"

Savannah knew the translation not what he meant by it. Defenceless, she watched as he came closer.

"Belle femme. Combien pour une nuit?"

He held out euros, folded between his knuckles. He waving it at Savannah as if for her to take it. He didn't stop moving nor talking.

"Sexy lady."

At that moment, and only then, did Savannah learn something about Angelique that she, rather naively, hadn't picked up on. She was a prostitute. And the man standing in front of her, advancing with every second, thought she was too. Savannah, seeing the money, walked towards the limping man. She was close enough to smell the alcohol on his breath.

"Bonjour Madame."

Savannah, staring into his eyes, was disgusted with what she saw.

Feeling no fear, she let him speak.

"Kissy kissy," he whispered as he mimed kisses with his lips.

"Never."

Savannah pushed him to the floor and sprinted towards Cafe Tabac. Looking back, the man was climbing to his feet and coming towards her once more. She contemplated both directions before running down the more crowded of the two boulevards. Pushing past people and squeezing through tight gaps annoyed the other pedestrians but Savannah wanted to be as far away as possible. Her legs felt like jelly. She was running on very little energy and wasn't sure how much longer she could keep up the speed. With every metre ran, she wondered if it was far enough. As her legs tired and she considered stopping, a hand reached out of the crowd, halting the teen. Screaming, Savannah tried to shake off the hand's tight grip.

"Savannah. Stop."

The voice was familiar.

"It's me. Savannah!"

Angelique pulled Savannah into a hug.

"Where are you going? Why are you running?"

Savannah looked at the prostitute.

"You didn't tell me that was what you did. You're a hooker?"

"A hooker with more money than you."

"Dirty money. I was in that alleyway, and you knew all too well that they would think I was there to have sex with them."

Angelique showed no signs of remorse.

"You seemed encouraged. I thought you needed money."

"From shagging a retard?"

Angelique's words were hastened.

"Savannah. I didn't mean to—"

"Looks like we aren't that similar after all."

"Please..let's not do this here. Come with me."

Savannah was shouting.

"With you? With you? I don't want to be a prostitute thanks."

"Come to my flat. We can eat and you can shower."

"Is it a flat? Or a brothel?"

Angelique looked despondent as she spoke to Savannah's back.

"You are being unfair."

Savannah, on self-reflection, was being far more pompous than she had the right to be. It suited her narrative to be this way but with little else in the way of options, she quickly recalculated her approach.

"How far is your flat?"

Angelique smiled.

"Not far."

***

Angelique's flat was unassuming in that it was accessed through the back door of a twenty-four-hour convenience store. She knew the staff well. They all greeted her by name as she cut through the store and into the back area. A metal door latched with a padlock, had the hallmarks of a prison cell, not a home. Angelique took a small key from her bra and opened the padlock. Creaking open, the door revealed a steep set of stairs sans handrail. Angelique motioned for her guest to head up first. Savannah pulled herself to the top where a room immediately opened up. The carpet was rough but clean. A beige chair, complete with solitary cushion resting upon the thick armrests, squeezed into an alcove. The space for a fireplace had been boarded in and replaced with a small chest of drawers. It fitted well. An ad hoc kitchenette was bundled together in the furthest corner of the small flat. To the left of the oven, a stripped bed nestled neatly next to a thin, MDF wardrobe. Beside the storage, an open doorway separated the main space from a modest bathroom. Until now, there was no need for a door. Angelique's flat was small but compact. It had everything she needed. Angelique stood hovering in the middle of the carpet, looking to Savannah for approval.

"So? What do you think?"

"Yeah. It's nice."

"It's not the Ritz, but it works you know?"

"Yeah. I like it."

Savannah wasn't entirely convinced by the decor.

"You must be exhausted. Have you showered since..?"

Angelique wasn't sure how to say it. Savannah interjected.

"Since I was raped? You can say it."

"Yeah. Since then."

"No."

"There are towels in the bathroom."

Given how rude she had been outside, Savannah didn't deserve this level of hospitality.

"Thank you."

Once out of sight, Savannah stripped her gifted clothes and folded them neatly before setting them on the closed toilet seat. She twisted the tough tap, unleashing a powerful jet of hot water from the shower head. Savannah had been craving cleanliness since she arrived in Calais. Stepping in, she was not disappointed. Dropping her arms, she let the boiling water wash over her skin and through her hair. Looking down, Savannah watched the water turn brown as the last remnants of mud washed away. Her legs, bruised and beaten, were a reminder of everything she wanted to forget. Conscious that Angelique wouldn't have unlimited hot water, Savannah shut off the shower. Instantly cold, she wrapped her body in the thin towel found under the sink. A pair of pyjamas had been left by the door in the time Savannah had been showering.

"Are these for me?" she called out.

"I'm not going to let you sleep in that blouse and those hideous trousers."

Angelique's kindness knew no bounds even if it didn't know sizes. Her pyjamas dwarfed Savannah. Angelique was much taller, and the matching pink top and bottoms reflected that.

Savannah came through the door, laughing to herself. It didn't take long for Angelique to join in.

"It's a bit big."

"Am I really that much taller?"

"I guess so."

With the shower now free, Angelique stripped down and turned on the water. Savannah sat cross-legged on the bed wondering how she came

150

to this point in her life. At school, her teachers would often ask what she was planning on doing after she had finished her A-Levels. Not once did she consider running away from home as an option. Angelique was quick. She had slipped into her own pair of pyjamas and, like Savannah kept her hair in a towel. Angelique joined Savannah in sitting on the bed.

"Did it feel good?"

"The shower? More than you can imagine."

"I'm glad. It's not the best, I'm sorry."

"It worked well."

Savannah paused and considered what she was about to say.

"Why do you do it?"

Angelique played dumb.

"Do what?"

"Work the streets."

"We spoke about this earlier...it's hard to get a job."

"When you were homeless, I understand. But now? You could apply anywhere. You speak better English than most people I know. You could work at a hotel. As a tour guide. Anything"

Angelique smiled through the compliment.

"You want the truth?"

"Only that."

"I can make more money working for 2 hours each night than I could if I worked all week."

Savannah felt let down.

"Money. That's the reason?"

"You can't live without it."

"But what sort of life are you living? A life where any man with sixty euros can fuck you."

Despite the tirade, Angelique appreciated the honesty.

"I know."

Savannah sprung up from the bed and dropped her towel into the bathroom. Angelique, removing her towel hat, tied her hair into a scruffy ponytail.

"You must be exhausted."

Savannah nodded.

"Top and tails?"

"You say my English is good, but I don't know what that means."

"Like this."

Savannah grabbed a pillow and rested her head at the bottom of the bed.

"Goodnight."

Angelique, giggling at Savannah's curled toes very close to her head, shut her eyes.

"Goodnight Savannah. Bienvenue a Paris."

***

Spreading her legs, Savannah welcomed the space after a night cramped against the wall. Her numb arm pushed her body up from the bed. Angelique, in the small flat, couldn't be seen. Savannah croaked.

"Angelique? Did you sleep well?"

Silence greeted Savannah. She tried again.

"Angelique?"

Swinging her feet around, Savannah lifted herself from the bed. With no sign of her host in the main room, she peered into the bathroom.

152

Angelique wasn't there. Moving back to the bed, Savannah noticed a piece of paper, folded on the kitchen worktop. Opening the paper, a fifty euro note fell onto the floor. Savannah wondered if she was still dreaming. The writing was messy and smudged. She read aloud.

"Savannah, Au Revoirs are much harder than Bonjours. I was happy to have met you. Bonne Chance in Germany. This should get you there. When you find what you need, check on me. Qui vivra verra. Angelique. x"

Only once she had seen it written down did Savannah notice the first five letters of her new friend's name.

Angel.

CHAPTER SIXTEEN

Taking the train timetable from her pocket, Savannah skimmed through the times. Although notably unreliable, Angelique's oven clock, flashed *10:34*. Picking up a pen from the worktop, she circled 11:55 in the grid of departure times. If Savannah managed to make that train, she'd arrive in Cologne just after three o'clock, well before her mum's workplace would shut for the day. Without wanting to waste any time, Savannah scribbled a note on the reverse side of the paper, folded it in half and dropped it on the kitchen surface. By the time she had arrived at the bottom of the steep stairs, the shop was brimming with customers. Despite her slender figure, she found it hard to squeeze through the shoppers. Pushing open the chiming door was a welcome relief as the tepid Parisian morning hit Savannah's clean skin. There was an evident chill to the air. The rising sun hadn't been given a chance to warm the morning but was evidently trying. Following the noise of a crowd out of the side streets, Savannah found herself lost. She couldn't remember the route she had walked with Angelique and with no phone to map the route, Savannah risked missing her train. Her stomach that had been growling in hunger since she woke up, called out for food. Wandering aimlessly up the boulevard was proving useful. Crescent Moon Bakery occupied a tall, slim building between a bank and bistro. A red and white striped awning hung over the bricked facade. Peering into the windows, Savannah's stomach rejoiced. Inside, the bakery was a hive of activity. Workers buzzed around carrying trays of dough up and down a small flight of stairs. Sweet smells filled her nose, reminding Savannah of her aunt's home baking. Aunt Jules would often bake chocolate-chip cookies ready for when Savannah came home from school. Jackie did nothing of the sorts. Entering the queue, the abundance of goods forced Savannah into a difficult decision. She was next and still hadn't decided. It was a nice problem to have.

"Bonjour."

The cashier was short and not too dissimilar in age to the customer across the counter. Her fair hair was tied in a bun, hidden under a hygienic net. She smiled as Savannah deliberated.

"Pain au chocolat. Two. Please"

Her begging efforts hadn't been useless after all. It was all in change yet the cashier didn't seem to mind as Savannah passed it over.

"Merci."

Gripping the full bag of pastries tightly, Savannah waited until outside in the warming sunshine before tucking into her freshly-baked breakfast.

She had been craving not just food but something sweet for days. Savouring every bite of the flaky, buttery goodness, she cared not about the crumbs falling down her top. As she walked, Savannah enjoyed the heat on her face. Her hunger-induced stomach growls had now been replaced by nervous tinges. Her journey was almost complete. Looking ahead, the signs that had guided Savannah to the station first time around had picked up again. Following the directions to the right took the teen onto a familiar path. She recognised the route from her time with Angelique. Walking much quicker than she had done then, Savannah weaved in and out of the much slower crowd. Every so often, she would reach into her pocket and check the money was still there. It was just fifty euros but to Savannah it felt like gold. Not before long, she had arrived at the road leading to the station. Lorries, delivering fresh produce to the dozens of cafe's and bars that lined the street, covered the prettily patterned cobbles. Savannah walked taller than she did so yesterday. Birds, nesting in the spaced out trees, sang their morning songs as the sun dripped over the white-stoned buildings. The day was perfect. As she crossed the courtyard, Savannah looked across at a man begging in her spot. He looked tired. Savannah didn't think twice. Heading over, she collected the change from her back pocket.

"Hi. Are you hungry?"

He didn't speak English, but his eyes spoke of desire.

"Have this."

Passing the man the bagged croissant, she dropped the few remaining coins into his metal cup.

"It's not much, but I hope it helps."

Savannah grinned to herself as she pushed through the large station doors. It felt good to be nice. A large, digital clock fixed to an information post told the time as half-past eleven. Savannah had time to catch her targeted train. Savannah, seeing the ticket booth queue growing by the second, hurried over to the far side of the station. Joining the line, Savannah looked through to the window. Bernadette, presumably starting her shift, collapsed into her familiar chair. With no desperate teenagers in front, the queue moved fast, and soon it was Savannah's turn.

Bernadette, eyes fixed on her screen, called out.

"Prochain!"

Savannah came forward, taking the fresh orange note from out of her pocket. Bernadette's eyes rolled over as she spoke.

"Are you going to buy a ticket today?"

"11:55. Cologne."

Bernadette shuffled her glasses to the end of her nose and glanced at the clock.

"You are cutting it close."

Savannah slid the fifty euro note through the gap in the glass. She listened as the ticket, in its three parts, flew through the printer. Bernadette filed the cash into the tray before passing the excess money, five euros, and tickets through the gap in the glass. She looked up at Savannah, sarcastically smiled then spoke every syllable.

"Platform 6A. Please have your passport or identification card ready for inspection. Bon Voyage."

Passport. Savannah had heard correctly. She hadn't even considered her passport would be checked. Her excitement turned to fear as she considered whether her auntie would report her missing. If she had then a simple passport search would halt Savannah's journey at the final hurdle. Savannah grabbed the tickets and span away from the ticket booth. Following the signs, she reached Platform 6A ten minutes before the train was scheduled to leave. Looking lost, a uniformed guard, directed Savannah into an airport-style security control. She walked through. With no bags, the process was quick. Past the scanners, a security officer, trapped in a tinted glass box, asked Savannah for her passport. There was no way out now. Sliding the passport into his hairy hand, she held her breath. He swiped the passport into his computer and stared at the screen. Holding the passport to the light, he scrutinised the details carefully.

"Travelling alone?"

"Yes."

"What is the purpose of your visit?"

"I'm visiting a friend."

Using both hands, the officer shut the passport and pushed it back through the gap in his box. She was free. An electronic gate opened, inviting Savannah onto the platform. Her seat on the pointed-nose scarlet-coloured train was in the furthest carriage from the gate. The platform was longer than she had expected. Climbing on board, an inspector checked her ticket and pointed out her seat. Her seat was garishly coloured, a shade of pink that looked radioactive even in the dimly lit carriage. Savannah, occupying the seat closest to the window, hoped not a soul would come and sit next to her. On board, her carriage was quiet barring the obnoxiously loud conversation between a businessman and his phone a few rows behind. To her left, a table seated a trio of smartly-dressed men all crowding around a small laptop screen. Their presence, so close by, made Savannah feel at ease. A woman, dressed in a baby blue maxi dress, listened to her music while staring out of the dirtied windows. Back home when travelling to her aunt's up north, Savannah would often do the same and block out everything around her. An announcement crackled through the speaker above

Savannah's head. The train was due to leave. As the clock inside the station turned to midday, the latecomers jumped on, and the train rolled out of the station slightly behind schedule. From her seat, she watched as the high-speed train hurtled past Paris' most famous landmarks. Soon, the city turned to countryside, and the only sites of note were small barns and silos. Of the four stops before Cologne, Savannah had heard only of Brussels. It looked frantic as they arrived. The businessmen in her carriage had been replaced by even more, similarly suited people. An hour or so after Brussels, the train came into Liege. Savannah marvelled at the modern station. Beams of crystal white concrete curved over the tracks and high into the sky. From by the black, yellow and red tricolour flag hanging from the ceiling, Savannah deduced that the train was still in Belgium. Setting off once more, Savannah tinged with excitement. Their next stop, Aachen, was not far. Savannah could see little of the city when approaching yet the signs inside the station were all in German. She was close. By now, she was one of four people left inside the carriage. They remained in silence as the train powered through the German countryside and past towns not significant enough to stop at. She had been listening carefully to each announcement but only now did the mumbling voice tell her what she wanted to hear.

"Damen und Herren. Die nächste Station ist Köln. Bitte stellen Sie sicher, dass Sie alle Ihre persönlichen Sachen haben."

He repeated it in French before the English translation.

"Ladies and Gentlemen. The next stop is Cologne. Please ensure you have all your per—"

Leaping to her feet, she waited by the door for the train to slow to a stop. Through the small window in the door, Savannah looked out as the countryside became the city. Brick walls, ruined by graffiti, separated the track from unkept homes behind. An observation tower loomed large in the distance. Hearing the brakes screeching, Savannah watched as the train slowed into the grand station. The roof arched over the wide platforms, a glass wall enclosing the space. Groups of people, spread across the platform, waited for the doors to open. They did so, automatically, once the train had stopped allowing Savannah to step down onto the marble floor. Following the signs for the exit, the teen emerged into a large courtyard where a city map was pushed into her hand by a brightly-clothed helper. Hundreds of people milled around the steps to a scaffold-covered, red-netted church. Around the courtyard, the architecture was confused. Heavily-concreted blocks stood side by side with glass cubes and mixes of the two. It felt dated. Spotting a bench, she sat and unravelled the pocket map. On one side, the attractions and highlights of the city were listed alongside grid references and colourful images, the other was a map bordered by discounts to restaurants and museums. Savannah ran her finger down the alphabetised list, stopping at the 'S' section.

Schaafenstraße — D6

Schlidergasse — F3

SchulzVossen — G5

G5. Flipping the map, she pinpointed G5. Her path was straight once out of the square. Savannah, seeing the way out of the crowd, headed for it. Walking past a restaurant, she wondered if her mum had ever eaten there. Savannah had heard so much about this city. She had always planned on visiting yet until now had never found the time. For years, even when her dad was alive, she had dreamt of surprising her mum with a visit. This time, she had no one to surprise. Out of the square, Savannah followed the road past a McDonalds that had been shoehorned into a traditional,

German building. She continued following the road until she found what she been desperately seeking, across from her on the other side of the street. She wasn't expecting a building of that size. In her mind, the office was to be a small concrete block lacking windows and good enough air conditioning. In reality, it was monumentally different. She gazed up at the glass-wrapped, rounded skyscraper. King-sized letters, spelling out the building's tenants SchulzVossen, sat precariously above the top floor. Glistening tinted windows covered each of the building's many floors. At ground level, the building widened into a perspex plaza that opened neatly into a gentrified piazza. Dodging the spouting water fountains, Savannah's felt closer to her mum than she ever had been. She could imagine her mum, sat where she was, enjoying the German sunshine; sharing lunch with a co-worker. Reaching the foot of the tower, large glass panes, too impractical to be called doors, swung forward and backwards as people slid in between. Her whole journey had been building to this doorway. A doorway that she would soon discover, would change her life forever.

CHAPTER SEVENTEEN

Briefcase-carrying power people welcomed the air conditioning as they stepped inside the SchulzVossen lobby, away from the summer heat. Swept inside, Savannah found herself gaping in awe at the futuristically styled reception area coloured universally white. Marbled, cream quartz spanned the entire length and height of the back wall. A desk, elaborately shaped as if defying gravity, housed a small number of computers, phones and accompanying users. Strips of lights, excessively bright, lined the high ceiling held up by off-white, stone columns. Past the desk, a sculpture of a naked woman with fire for hair, stood tall if not out the way. Through a high opening in the wall, rushed workers waited for one of six lifts. Other than the leathered sofa's nearest the entrance, the lobby was cold and clinical. Savannah, after travelling through countries to be here, did not feel welcome. As people pushed past her, she wondered if she'd be recognised. Her mum's office would surely be adorned with pictures of her childhood. It was only a matter of time. Approaching the desk, Savannah waited for the receptionist to finish his phone conversation. In her now dirtying blouse and trousers, she didn't stand out of the professional crowd. As the man put the phone down, he looked up and smiled with an expression that told Savannah he hated his job. Despite having had plenty of time to think, the well-travelled teen wasn't sure what to say.

"Hallo."

"Hi. I've got a question."

His voice matched his flamboyant, peroxided hairstyle.

"Please."

"My mum used to work here. And I was wondering if I could maybe meet her some of her colleagues—"

He stopped Savannah as the phone rang once more.

"One moment, please."

Savannah stood against the desk, waiting for the gentleman to finish, what seemed to her, a personal call. He ended the call with a mwah.

"Sorry. Please go on."

"I have some questions. For her friends. If I could meet them.."

"Miss. We don't disclose information like that."

"She's dead. My mum."

He didn't know what to say.

"I just wanted to see somebody. I want to know what she's like."

"Miss. I am sorry, I cannot help you."

Savannah was riled.

"I've travelled from England to be here, from bloody England and now you are telling me you can't help me?"

His face quivered as he repeated himself.

"Miss. I cannot help you. I'm sorry."

"Can't help me? Or won't help me?"

"Miss. I have other people waiting. I'm sorry."

Savannah could sense that his apology was not a genuine one. Succumbing to yet another setback, she walked away from the desk, sighing heavily as she collapsed onto the hard, leather sofas. With nothing else to do, she enjoyed the air conditioning and the sight of too many people squeezing into one life. As she froze in stare, a figure moved to stand directly in front of Savannah, blocking the view with her stodgy frame.

"Downstairs. Records Administrator. He'll be able to tell you who your mum worked with."

Savannah looked up. A lady stood close to her, facing the other way. She didn't want to be seen talking to Savannah.

"Sorry?"

Her voice was deeply Scottish.

"Take the stairs down a level. Follow the corridor, and you'll find the records administrator. He's frosty, but he'll help you."

Savannah didn't speak.

"Got it?"

"I think so."

Following her instructions, Savannah took the emergency exit stairs down one floor. Unlike the lobby, this floor was industrial and functional. Coloured pipes ran across the ceiling snaking off into different directions. White, square floor tiles reflected the faltering light beams hanging from the ceiling. Further ahead a bucket collected droplets of water dripping from leaking pipes above. With nowhere else to go, Savannah walked forward, moving her head from right to left as doors went by on both sides. She assumed that this was the basement of the building. Each and every door was marked with danger signs and stickers warning not to enter. Savannah was approaching the end of the corridor and could not yet see if it continued. With no warning, the lights behind her powered off. She hoped they were motion-activated. Despite the darkness, she felt no fear. Moving forward, Savannah noticed the corridor turn to the left into near darkness. A small square of light seeped through a window and onto the floor, two-thirds of the way down the corridor. As she walked, the lights, detecting her presence, systematically flickered into life. Her footsteps echoed as she walked. Reaching the square light, it was as she had expected. On the door, a small plaque read "Records Administrator"; the light an indication someone was inside. Without hesitating, she knocked on the glass part of the door, rattling the frame. She waited but heard nothing. Again, she knocked. Still nothing. Spurred on by a mix of confidence and anxiety, she turned the knob, opening the door.

"I don't see the point in knocking if you refuse to abide by its practices." Savannah immediately pulled the door shut, muffling the booming, American voice. He spoke again.

"Come in."

Sheepishly, she, again, turned the door knob. As the door opened, Savannah was greeted by the sight of a pudgy, bearded man alone in a small closet-sized office. Piles of paper were scattered around the worktops and stacked high on the floor. Rising from his seat, the man flustered as he cleared a chair of mess before gesturing for Savannah to sit. For a man locked away in a basement office, he looked smart. A red checked shirt that fitted well despite a slight pot belly was tucked and belted into a pair of dark trousers. His beard, tinged with grey, met a long, slicked haircut before his ears. He stuttered before speaking.

"What can I help you with?"

Savannah could tell that he wasn't used to visitors. Nervously, he sipped his steaming coffee.

"I was told to come here…"

He interjected.

"By whom? I'm not known to many of that lot."

"A lady. I think she was Scottish."

He looked puzzled.

"My mum. She used to work here."

Savannah had assumed he would know exactly who she was talking about. He didn't speak up.

"She died quite recently. I just wanted to know some more about her. Hear some stories. Get to know her."

He relaxed instantaneously.

"I'm sorry to hear that sweetie."

"It would help if you could point me in the right direction?"

"I have everything you'd want to know."

After Savannah's rejection upstairs, she was glad to have found someone willing to help her.

"Seriously?"

His teeth, coffee-stained but still all there, formed a smile in between his beard.

"Of course. Now, what was her name? I can check the system."

"Annabel. Annabel Bancroft."

"And your name?"

"Savannah."

"A pretty name for a pretty girl. You can call me Chuckie."

Savannah, upon extending her arm to shake, was met with a clammy palm.

Moving his coffee from under his arm, Chuckie powered on his computer screen and squinted his eyes. Much like Bernadette, he was a one-finger typer. From her seat, Savannah could see the back of the screen, and a puzzled look flash across Chuckie's face. He tried again, confirming the spelling with Savannah as he did so.

"Nope. Still nothing."

Savannah felt stupid.

"Try Staggs. Annabel Staggs. Her marriage name."

"That might work."

He turned back to his computer screen and typed aloud.

"S. T. A. G. S."

"No, double G."

"S. T. A. G. G. S"

"That's right."

"Still nothing."

Savannah didn't understand what was happening. Chuckie looked at Savannah waiting for instruction. She didn't move.

"Let me check the hard copies."

Standing up, Chuckie sipped his coffee, then scanned the room for what he was looking for. It was a mess, yet it seemed an organised one at that. He lifted a large stack of papers and set down them down on his desk. His fat fingers flicked through the pages at some speed. As he did so, he repeated Savannah's mum's name over and over again. Rejecting the pile, he picked another.

"Ahh."

Savannah sat up in his chair. He pulled a slim folder from out of the chaos. He opened the file as he slumped back in his chair. Chuckie's face was expressionless as he read aloud.

"Annabel Bancroft. British. Payroll number BJ250596. Application for payroll submitted, that's when she joined the company, 29th November 1992."

"Yeah, that sounds right. She was working here for nearly 20 years."

Chuckie ignored Savannah and carried on reading from the file.

"Resignation approved, March 3rd, 1993."

"Resignation?"

"When she left."

Chuckie realised that wasn't what she was querying.

"That can't be right."

"Let me check the outgoing log."

Chuckie hurried to a filing cupboard nestled behind the door. He pulled it open and thumb-flicked through the files. Upon finding the outgoing log, he traced his finger down the list.

"Outgoings, 1992."

The list was in alphabetical order meaning it didn't take long for Chuckie to find her name.

"Annabel Bancroft. Finance. March 3rd."

"I don't understand."

Chuckie took a bottle of water from the mini-fridge underneath his desk and passed it to Savannah. He was nearly as confused as his guest.

"Your mother left the company at the start of 1993 meaning she worked here for.."

He did the calculation in his head.

"…just over 2 months. Worked in Finance for that period."

"2 months?"

"The end of November ninety-two until the start of March ninety-three."

"Can you check again?"

Chuckie obliged. His computer produced the same results. He read from the screen.

"No results found."

Savannah refused to believe the computer. She rose from her chair and twisted Chuckie's screen to face her. Snatching the keyboard, she repeatedly searched her mum's name. Only after the fifth attempt did she relinquish control of the computer. Chuckie wasn't sure what to say. He had wished his door had remained locked. Still, he tried to comfort her.

"I'm not sure what this means, but I know—"

Savannah couldn't bite her tongue.

"Well, I'll tell you shall I?"

Chuckie flushed red. Savannah had no problems using him as a verbal punching bag.

"What it means is that my mum has lied to me about where she has been every day for the entirety of my life. For 20 years, she's been pretending to work here. 20 fucking years."

Chuckie wasn't a fan of swearing but in light of his guest's recent revelations, he decided against speaking up.

"So every week, every bloody week when I kissed her goodbye at the airport, and she'd board a flight to Germany, she wasn't coming here. So that begs the question, where on earth was she going?"

"She might have worked elsewhere? Are you sure it was this organisation?"

Chuckie instantly regretted interrupting.

"Are you sure? Yes, I'm fucking sure. I had SchulzVossen notepads, SchulzVossen pens, I even had a SchulzVossen calculator."

As she spoke, Chuckie shuffled his papers across to hide the branded stationery that littered his deck. He wasn't used to diffusing these sort of situations. He lived alone with his wife in an idyllic cottage on the outskirts of town. They had no kids, no drama. As her tirade continued, he did nothing but listen.

"What a mug. I believed it all. I used to sit by the window, my legs squashed on the sill, to keep watch when she'd come home. As soon as I saw her pull up, I'd rush downstairs and see how many pens she had brought me this week. Never once did I think to question it."

"You'd never to have known…"

Savannah contemplated her mum's second life. However she had imagined it previously was wrong. Chuckie's niceties interrupted her thinking.

"Is there anything I could do to help?"

"Well yeah. You could start by searching that magic computer and telling me what the hell she was doing for 20 years. I'd like to know what job was worth missing my childhood for. That's what I want to know."

Savannah's voice was croaking as a result of her shouting. Despite her own inner turmoil, she felt bad for taking it out on Chuckie. He had been nothing but gracious. Taking a minute to calm herself, silence took hold.

"Chuckie. I'm sorry. I shouldn't have been so rude. I just wasn't expecting this."

"Now, now. Don't go apologising. I can't say I relate to what you are going through, but I can understand how hard it must have been, and still is."

Savannah felt no less guilty. Chuckie stood and filled up a kettle with the bottle of water Savannah hadn't yet touched. Chuckie chuckled.

"I'm no Brit, so I don't have any of your Queen's favourite tea but how does a coffee sound?"

Savannah forced a smile.

"I'm not usually allowed coffee."

"I won't tell anyone."

He pushed the plug into the socket allowing the water to bubble away. Chuckie tried to change the subject.

"Are you enjoying the city? It's simply splendid in the winter too."

"I haven't had much of a chance to look around. It was a long journey. I just wanted to get here right away."

"Did you fly?"

"Not quite."

"Drive?"

She shook her head as the Chuckie poured granulated coffee into two stained mugs.

"I'm more of a traveller."

"A traveller tells tales."

Savannah laughed it off. Chuckie attempted an English accent.

"Where does one travel to next?"

Savannah, with a steely grit in her eyes, answered from the heart.

"I've got an idea."

"Is it far?"

"Perhaps too far. But that hasn't stopped me yet."

Chuckie, watching as he poured the hot water, let Savannah continue. "Nothing will."

CHAPTER EIGHTEEN

Chuckie walked Savannah to the door, past the gawping receptionist, and into the hot German afternoon. It was nearing tea time yet the heat showed no signs of relenting. Savannah continued without realising the American had stopped at the door. She turned.

"Thank you for your help Chuckie."

"It's been a pleasure. Something a bit different I suppose."

"And for the swearing?"

"Not the usual office chat, I must admit."

Both Savannah and Chuckie giggled.

"I'm sorry. I have a good excuse."

"You do."

Chuckie took a deep breath before rushing his words.

"You know where you're going right?"

"Straight. One left. Two rights."

He smiled and held his arms open. Savannah had missed hugs. Chuckie squeezed Savannah tight. She now felt warm on the inside, not just the out. Walking away, she waved as Chuckie disappeared into the office building. Her planned journey, formed quickly out of desperation, was not where Savannah saw herself heading. There was only one other place the answers could be found. Latvia. Her mind was clear on the facts. She knew her mum's death place can't have been random. Whatever she was doing while claiming to work in Germany, happened in Latvia. Savannah was sure of it. Her naive mind didn't consider anything else. With an unfounded determination, she set her interior compass for Latvia. Geography wasn't her strongest subject yet even Savannah knew that the Baltic state was thousands of miles away. Her journey would be long and emotionally daunting. As she headed for the bus station, Savannah considered if her journey was worth the potentially, unnecessary danger. Were the answers she needed for her own self-vanity worth risking rape and abuse. Savannah had weighed up her options. It was unlikely that she'd ever get this opportunity again. Once home, her auntie wouldn't let her leave the house. Getting home would be just as hard as carrying on. At least once in Latvia, once with the answers, she could ring home. She could leave satisfied. Her plan had banked on getting to know her mum and prying a return air fare from her friends. She had failed on both accounts. Her head was whirling, but her heart was settled. Savannah with five euros to her name hoped a bus fare would cost no more. She'd rather be penniless at an airport than on the streets of a German city. Ahead, the bus station blocked the road. A convenience store, another McDonald's and a pharmacy occupied units at the base of the depot. The smells of chicken burgers did nothing for her. Articulated buses huffed into the station, rounding the corner by an information booth, into the designated stops. Savannah, not wanting to waste her money on the wrong bus, headed to the booth. It was empty of people but full of leaflets. She searched the desk, finding one marked for the airport. A brightly coloured pamphlet promised 'Quick, reliable and regular' services to the airport leaving from the same station. A picture of the grey bus matched the one pulling into the station as she read from the leaflet. The bus was entirely silver, barring the tinted windows, with large decals of planes and the promised journey time affixed to the outside. As it pulled into the stand, a Chinese couple disembarked, gazing at the cathedral view as they did so. A flashing screen displayed Düsseldorf Airport as the destination. She took the five euro note from her pocket and handed it to the smartly-uniformed driver. He gave her a printed ticket but no change. Sitting down, she mourned the last of her money. The bus was surprisingly full. Nearest the front, a row of elderly ladies, their scarfs and coats defying the weather, nattered quietly. A bunch of school kids, presumably truants, held the back row terrorising the tourists in front. Savannah decided against the back, choosing instead to sit next to a moustached man holding a messenger bag on his lap. Rolling out of the station, the driver ignored waving latecomers, desperately flagging the bus to stop. They hit the road, building speed as they headed out of the city. Soon, the bus turned onto the motorway. The city skyline grew distant on the horizon as they followed the curves and bends of the river down below. A water damaged sign

thanked them for visiting Cologne and wished them a safe journey.

Another welcomed them to Langenfeld. Savannah's mind turned to her

plan once she had arrived at the airport. She had nothing to her name

and no idea of how to get to Latvia. Despite it being a shithole, flights

there would still cost more than they perhaps should. Ideally, she

wanted to avoid begging in such a public place. It would be hard but not

impossible. Slowing, the driver pulled up on the hard shoulder alongside

a heavily graffitied underpass. Savannah cursed her luck. A broken down

bus wasn't the end of the world yet it hampered her progress at a time

she wanted to get going. The driver glanced in his mirror. He shouted.

"Wiir haben angehalten, da das Mädchen den Bus verlassen muss."

Moustache-messenger man shifted forward in his seat. He looked

across at Savannah. She didn't have to speak German to know he was

talking to her. He moved his head in the direction of the door. Savannah

froze. The driver continued.

"Ihr Ticket ist nur für die Stadt Route gültig"

Nobody said anything. Even the youths had been hushed into silence.

"Ist das si schwer zu verstehen?"

With the elderly ladies thriving on the drama, the moustached man

spoke softly, in broken English.

"He says, your ticket."

"Mine?"

"It is only for the city. Not this place."

The driver, wanting to keep to the timetable, raised his voice.

"Bitte erklärt es ihr!"

"You have to leave."

A path was cleared for Savannah to exit the bus. Resigned to defeat, she rose from her seat. Her fear of the driver was far greater than that of embarrassment. She hurried past and stepped down onto the tarmac. As she showed the driver her middle finger, the doors shut and the bus sped off into the distance. She had seen signs for the airport while gazing out of the bus windows. Alone in her company, she spoke aloud. "It can't be far."

Emerging from the underpass, Savannah could feel the heat burning on her neck. The sun was low in the sky yet the heat was almost unbearable. Still, she walked quickly on the side of the road. Cars and bikes whizzing past tooted their horns as they passed the poor, penniless teenager. Cut back trees provided little relief from the sun as she continued on the hard shoulder. Giant, metal signs marked the airport as 6 kilometres away. Savannah felt no encouragement by the sign. She worked in miles. 6 kilometres meant nothing to her. Reaching a junction, Savannah blocked the sun with her hand and waited for a gap in traffic. Cars were hurtling towards the junction at excessive speeds. It wasn't designed for pedestrians. Spotting a gap, she sprinted to safety. Her legs were tiring. Her head was aching. Itching her neck, Savannah could feel the heat radiating from her skin. It was too hot to touch. As the airport signs disappeared, Savannah's focus dwindled. Sweat dripped from her face; her blouse drenched through. She could see an underpass up ahead. Its shadowy coolness would save her from the heat. A respite she craved but would never reach. She could feel it coming before it happened. Darkness enveloped her sight. Savannah's legs gave way, and she fell to the ground. Her head smacked the concrete.

CHAPTER NINETEEN

They were travelling at top speed when they spotted her. She was faced down on a track of gravel that bordered the edge of the Autobahn. Seeing her, both the driver and his passenger decided to stop. Checking his mirrors, he slowed the car down, stopping 50 metres away from her body. As they stepped out of the car, the passenger grabbed a bag from the boot. She swung the bag over his shoulder and caught up with the driver. They both looked at each other as they approached her body. Dropping the bag on the dusty floor, she knelt down and pressed her fingers against the girl's neck. She had a pulse. Zipping open the bag, the much older male watched as his colleague pressed her ear to the girl's chest.

"Sie lebt."

Deducing that the girl had fainted, he took an ice pack from the bag, snapped it into life and held it against her forehead. The afternoon sun was unforgiving. She had found that out the hard way. Once cooled, they agreed to lift her to the car. Putting the ice pack down, he grabbed under her arms and lifted once his colleague had hold of her legs. Together, they shuffled along the hard shoulder before dropping her into the waiting car. As they belted the lifeless body into the passenger seat, the younger lady grabbed the first aid bag then questioned what next.

"das Hospital?"

"Nein. Blick auf ihre Haut." *No. Look at her skin.*

"Ihre Haut?" *Her skin?*

"Keine Tasche. Kein Handy. Am Straßenrand?" *No bag. No phone. On the roadside?*

Catching his drift, the female officer stepped back inside the police car. She didn't like the process but was obliged to abide by it. Her superior officer slammed his door shut and pushed hard on his accelerator. Feigning interest, the two exchanged niceties as they headed for the airport.

***

As she woke, Savannah's heart beat shot up. Her eyes had barely been open a second yet she had already spotted the metal grate in front of her. She was caged. Her breathing turned to panting as she watched the pedestrian-less hard shoulder fly past at extreme speed. She was in a car. A fast car. Past the grate, Savannah could see two people chatting away. One was driving, his eyes firmly on the road, his hands firmly on the wheel. The other, female-voiced, was hidden behind a headrest. Feeling claustrophobic, she instinctively screamed at the top of her lungs. Her deafening scream startled the two police officers.

"It's okay. Please."

Savannah ignored the police officer's attempts to calm her down.

"Police. We are police."

Hearing the p-word alone turned Savannah from extremely scared to uncomfortably anxious. Her overtly paranoid mind went into overdrive. *Police. Fuck. What have I done? Fuck. They are sending me home. How did they find me, I can't go back now. This can't be happening. I'm going home. Home. Fuck.*

Savannah did nothing but shake back and forth as she considered the consequences of going home. Fear engulfed her entire body. As her lungs struggled to breathe, her young heart pounded against her rib cage. She felt for bruises. This time her pockets were empty of a passport. For the first time since leaving home, Savannah had nothing to her name other than the clothes on her back. Paranoia and panic did not mix well. Savannah, not wanting to waste her energy, snuffled her tears almost as soon as they formed. She watched as the police car left the motorway and followed the road through an underground tunnel. Emerging, Savannah relaxed. The road split into two lanes, signposted to the left for departures and to the right for arrivals. Her eyes refused to believe the sight. She read from the sign. *Willkommen im Händel Internationalen Flughafen. Welcome to Handel International Airport.* Set back from the road, a crescent-shaped concrete megastructure dominated her view. Over the years, smaller sections had been bolted on, yet the original structure had stood the test of time. Savannah wasn't sure how the police officers knew that this was where she had wanted to go but thanked God that they did. As the only car on the road, it wasn't long before the police vehicle had navigated the winding roads and reached the door to the departures area. As they stopped, the female officer opened Savannah's door, taking the teen's hand as she helped her from the car. Her paranoia-induced panic attack had subsided but she was grateful for the fresh air. With the afternoon cooling into early evening, there was a notable chill in the air that soothed Savannah's warmed skin. The concrete concourse was long yet Savannah was the only one stood on it.

"Auf Wiedersehen."

The policewoman was stepping back in the car. As far as they were concerned, their job was done. Savannah could only muster a smile. Unnerved by her surroundings, Savannah waited on the pavement to collect her thoughts. Only the sound of the police car struggling through the gears broke the silence. Soon, they were gone from sight. It hadn't been the bus journey she had been expecting yet Savannah had still made it to the airport. On reflection, that was all that mattered to the teen. With this new-found confidence, she took strides towards the automatic doors. Despite being close enough, they didn't open. Undeterred, she walked further down the concourse and tried a different pair. Their refusal to open worried was more irritating than worrying. She tried pushing but to no avail. They wouldn't budge. Only once she had knocked, did she hear movement from within. Hoping they could hear her too, she called out.

"Hello?"

Four individual fingers appeared between the middle of the doors. They disappeared but were soon replaced by a pair of bigger hands attempting to pry the door open. Or at least trying. Savannah hadn't seen this at Heathrow. After a series of attempts, and finger substitutions, the left-sided door was yanked open. The noise it unleashed was deafening. Savannah was greeted by a ghostly pale fair-skinned woman wearing a frayed polo top.

"Hi."

"Hallo."

She was German.

"The police just dropped me here. Is this the airport?"

Ignoring her completely, the German lady grabbed Savannah by the hand and led her into the hall.

"Come, we will find you a bed."

The door opened onto a balcony that spanned the entire perimeter of the hall. Below them, Savannah looked down at thousands of beds, partitioned into homes with temporary walls. Between the walls, fabricated alleyways teemed with children squeaking and squawking in play. Directly beneath them, a queue zigzagged across the gigantic space to a medical tent in the top left corner. Savannah, internally and perhaps facetiously, drew comparisons with a giant sleepover. The room buzzed with activity. Savannah let go of her guide's hand and let it drop by her side.

"This isn't where I wanted to be."

"I understand. But, for now, you must. We will re-house you soon."

"Rehouse?"

Savannah's repetition was ignored. The German lady took Savannah's hand and led her across the balcony to a flight of stairs. At the bottom, another man waited ready.

"This is Franz. He will process you and then show you to your bed. Is that okay?"

Savannah, through both exhaustion and confusion, had no idea what was going on.

"Okay."

Franz pulled out a chair, welcoming Savannah to sit down. His desk was small but practical. His hairline was receding, and the little hair he did have was straying in all directions. Moon-shaped glasses, that covered half of his face, sat nicely on his long, slightly crooked nose. He appeared proficient in using the laptop on his desk judging by his mastery of the two-hand type. Franz looked intelligent.

"Hello. My name is Franz. Do you speak English or do you need Arabic translator?"

Savannah had changed her mind. He repeated himself, slowly.

"A—RA—BIC?"

"No. I speak English."

"Okay. No problem. Are you here alone?"

"Yes. I was brought her by the police. I think it—"

"Don't feel bad. A lot of our friends here come from the police."

"Friends?"

"We are all friends."

Savannah wasn't sure if Franz was lost in translation, dumb, or simply too happy for his own good.

"I must ask some questions now that might be quite upsetting."

Savannah had no emotion left.

"Try me."

"Are you parents back home or—"

"They're both dead."

"Okay, that's no problem."

"Phew."

Savannah's sarcasm wasn't registering behind the glasses.

"Do you have any preference in where you would like to be rehoused?"

"I don't know what rehoused means."

"Where you'll move to. After your stay here."

"Latvia would be nice."

"In Germany only, I'm afraid."

She said nothing.

"No preference. And finally, your age?"

She wasn't sure whether to lie or tell the truth. She wondered which would be more advantageous.

"17."

"Very well."

Savannah's naivety had been diminishing ever since the interview had started. Looking around the room, she noticed that nearly everyone had a similar skin tone. The questions; are you alone, how old are you, who are you with, these were questions for refugees. Savannah had been mistaken for a refugee. Again. Franz stood and pointed his arm towards the first lane of the makeshift housing estate. Standing, she waited for him to lead. As they walked, a group of children, heavily invested in a game of tag, pushed through them.

"Remember, no running kids," shouted Franz in vain. Savannah's new home was found halfway down the aisle nearest to the back wall. Each of the prefabricated dwellings had enough room for families but, travelling alone, Savannah would have to share. Franz stopped just before a black curtain acting as a door.

"The family in here, they have just lost someone. Please be kind."

Savannah could relate. She hoped that common grief would help them bond. Franz knocked his knuckles on the plastic wall.

"Hallo Mrs Chehebar. It's Franz. We have a new friend for you."

A tired, middle aged woman snatched back the curtain. Mrs Chehebar wasn't a typical Syrian. She was strong in views and even stronger in her actions. Her outfit was mismatched and stereotypically Western yet her face, wrinkled towards the edges, showed little signs of caring. Greasy,

184

thin hair came to her bare shoulders, where a lilac pashmina kept her warm. Without saying a word, she visually scanned the girl stood before her. Franz let out a noise of cowardice as he stood near silent on Mrs Chehebar's front porch. She motioned for Savannah to turn, her inspection near finished. Doing so, Savannah heard a small mumble and the apparent invitation into her home. Franz, staying outside, wished her well.

"Okay, thank you Mrs Chehebar. Goodbye."

Savannah attempted to break the ice.

"That man is a fool."

"That man is your elder, and you must respect him, young lady."

Savannah squeezed her lips together, mentally noting to not say anything ever again.

Mrs Chehebar walked Savannah to a well-made bottom-bunk in the corner of the 6-bed makeshift apartment.

"Above you, sleeps my son, Sayid."

Gesturing to the opposite bunk-bed, Mrs Chehebar pointed out where her daughters, Amena and Rasha, slept.

"And the last bed is for myself and my husband, Mr Chehebar."

"3 kids. I bet that's fun."

"I have 4 children, thank you."

"And where do they sleep?"

"Jannah."

Savannah hadn't heard of it but assumed it was somewhere in the Middle East. Despite failing the first time around, she tried once again to be funny.

"Jannah. Sounds like Savannah."

Mrs Chehebar did not look impressed.

"That's my name."

"You must be tired."

Savannah wasn't full of life yet she didn't need to sleep.

"Not re—"

"I'm sure a short nap would help."

Savannah, not wanting to aggravate the situation, ducked into her bed. Surprisingly soft, her bunk was covered with a crisp, clean bed sheet. As she pressed her head against the square pillow, Savannah fell into what would be her first night's sleep of many in the refugee camp.

***

"Amena? Amena....wake up!"

Amena hadn't intended to oversleep yet the loud awakening wasn't pleasant. She would be late, and Savannah wasn't happy.

"Amena! We have to go."

Savannah had woken much earlier. Worried that they would miss their appointment, her sleep had suffered. Amena, rubbing her eyes awake, reluctantly jumped down from her bunk. Rasha, awoken in the commotion, kicked her sister as she stole her clothes.

"Amena, if you are going to steal my clothes, steal them quietly. I need my beauty sleep."

"Yeah, you do."

Rasha's groan was louder than the girl's laughter.

"Are you ready?"

With time a premium, Amena could only manage to step into her converse before Savannah pulled her away. Dr Williams was overworked and undervalued. His cobbled together doctor's surgery was never not busy. With a doctor's certificate required for the rehoming application, the wait for an appointment would often stretch into the weeks. The girls had known to make their appointments at the earliest possible times. If they had left it any later, the queues outside the makeshift medical tent would be hellish. As they arrived, Dr Williams was still setting up. He smiled at the girls, moved behind the curtain and checked his list. Savannah, knowing too well the limits of living in a refugee camp, asked Rasha for a favour.

'Rash, try and steal some paper and a pen for me?"

Before she could nod her response, the Doctor called out.

"Rasha Chehebar please."

Rasha pushed through the curtain and greeted the doctor. Their conversation was, quite rightly, muffled through the layers of fabric. Savannah waited patiently for her turn. Her friend had been with the doctor for little over five minutes by the time she had returned. Rasha clutched a box of medicine alongside an almost, illegible hand-written scribble.

"You're up, Sav."

Dr Williams titled his glasses as Savannah sat herself down on the examination bench. Not until he had finished writing did he acknowledge the teen's presence. His voice was soft yet commanded respect.

"Hello. What is the problem?"

"'I've been having aching pains across my stomach."

"How long for?"

"Since I've been here really."

"And how long has that been?"

"Just over half a year."

"Are you eating well?"

"Not particularly. I can't eat the shit they give us. It's vile."

The doctor leant forward in his chair.

"I understand it's not the nicest, but you must try and eat."

Savannah had heard it all before.

"And are you menstruating?"

"Irregularly and not as much."

"That will be down to the starvation and likely stress."

She nodded.

"Well, my doctor's advice is to rest, eat, and look after yourself. If the pain increases, come back and see me."

It seemed futile, yet Savannah had been worrying about the pain.

"Thanks, Doctor."

She moved to leave before the Doctor spoke up.

"Over half a year? That's a long time here. Have they not tried to rehome you?"

The question prompted a lie.

"I'm not leaving until the Chehebars are found a home. Until then, I'll be here."

"Very well."

As they left the temporary surgery, the girls compared doctor's notes. Rasha, who had just been given antibiotics for an infected spider bite, had pulled through on Savannah's request.

"A pad of paper. And a chewed pen."

"You're the best."

"I know…I know."

Rasha and Savannah were very similar in age if not anything else. Savannah had grown up in a middle-class, semi-detached home in Bath while Rasha had fled a war-torn country where her father was vilified. Yet both girls had arrived at the same place; a disused airport near Düsseldorf, currently used as a refugee camp. Rasha's parents had left their home country hoping for a better future with their children. They knew it wasn't healthy to live a life in fear of persecution. Leaving Syria, their journey was volatile and dangerous from the outset. A voyage across the Mediterranean claimed the life of their youngest daughter. As the battled in vein to resuscitate their pride and joy, the news cameras continued to roll. Their grief was for the world to see. Once they had buried their daughter, their sister in a Northern Greek town, the family resumed their journey for safety. The rest of the family arrived in Germany six weeks after they had left their home in an affluent suburb of Aleppo. With nowhere else to go, the slept on the streets of Berlin for weeks. It was a far cry from their usual surroundings. As the harsh winter approached and the streets became unbearably cold, they were picked up by the authorities and moved across the country to the former airport. Initially, they were told it was a temporary move. Soon, a house would become available, they'd be granted asylum status and the integration process would begin. Two years on, still they cramp into the temporary accommodation they were allocated on arrival. Mrs Chehebar had seen people, friends, come and go yet her family remained. Her stoney-faced exterior, coupled with unprocessed grief, built a notoriety as the feared matriarch of the camp. It was a perception she hated but one she was known by. In her first days in Mrs Chehebar's company, Savannah daren't breathe out of line. Every step she walked was in trepidation. Yet, as the months ticked on, Savannah learnt how wrong were her early assumptions. She was welcomed into the family as if she was one of their own. Often, they'd share stories with such brutal honesty that their tears could be heard five rooms away. Both Savannah and Mrs Chehebar helped each other, filling the voids that death had created. Yet recently, Savannah yearned for home. She'd been away far longer than she prepared herself for. Her homesickness didn't stay secret for long. A conversation with Mrs Chehebar had encouraged Savannah to write a letter. She'd told Savannah, 'to send a letter is a good way to go somewhere without moving anything but your heart.' It was advice, Savannah would savour.

As they arrived back from the doctors, the girls were greeted with an empty home before they both slumped down on their bunk beds. It was a moment of rare quietness in the home. Rasha was rereading the label to her antibiotics. Savannah, staring down at the notepad and pen, was contemplating not bothering at all. Looking across, Rasha studied her friend's emotionless face.

"You should do it, Sav."

Savannah didn't move.

"Even if you don't send it. It will help you."

She knew Rasha was right. Picking up the pen, Savannah searched her mind for the perfect starting sentence.

Auntie Jules,

I don't really know how to start this. You are probably quite shocked to get this from me. I don't know whether you've been looking for me. I'm guessing you have. I left home with honest intentions Jules. I want to know who my mum was. I had my own money, I had a plan. It was the cheapest way to get to Germany. Once I left home, everything went wrong. But I didn't give up. I didn't want to. I made it to Paris and then to Cologne. I saw the building where she worked. I went in, spoke to some people and left empty. She'd worked there for 3 months, twenty years ago. She lied about where she had been for my entire life. What was so secret that she couldn't tell her own daughter? I knew then I'd have to get to Latvia. I spent the last of my money on a ticket for a bus that kicked me off in the middle of nowhere. I walked, fainted and was brought to a disused airport/refugee camp where I write this today. That was 7 months ago. When you get this letter, I'd have left this camp and the people that have looked after me. I've waited patiently for the right time. Refugees dream of the UK. The wait to be rehoused in Germany is endless, they don't want them. As people leave in lorries to get to the UK, the police here turn a blind eye. Not many people want to go where I'm going. I've had to be clever but that meant waiting. Now, I can see the way out and I'm getting closer to the truth. Once I find that? I'll be home. Until then, know I'm safe and well.

All the love in the world,

Sav.

Folding over the paper, Savannah tucked the letter underneath her mattress. Deep down, she knew she'd never send it.

CHAPTER TWENTY

In the seven months that Savannah had lived in the refugee camp, she could name countless people who had disappeared overnight with no trail. Friends she had made, others she'd just seen around, vanished with no warning. It was the unspoken truth. Germany's efforts to rehome the refugees was slow and futile. For those unwilling to explore other means, a prolonged stay in camp was a distinct possibility. Most, however, were impatiently realistic. They knew their only chance of leaving was to engineer it themselves. Like in any group of people, there existed a seedier, well-connected section operating in the peripherals of the camp. Savannah had discovered him by chance. His appearance didn't match his actions. She had queried his job and got little in return. It wasn't until Rasha pointed him out, that she realised who he was. Savannah visited him every week and heard the same answer each time. At times, it seemed impossible. He told her so. One night, he grabbed her arm in the cafeteria.

"Denmark. Take it or leave it?"

Savannah didn't hesitate.

"Take it. When?"

"2 days. Early morning. Be ready."

"I will be."

Her conversation hadn't gone unnoticed. Mrs Chehebar had refused to talk to her in the days that followed the cafeteria meeting. Rasha had also been uncharacteristically quiet. Their family believed in abiding by the rules, following the processes to a tee. Savannah's actions were intolerable. Mrs Chehebar understood why she was doing what she was yet the matriarch was still mindful that their new friend's actions would cause mutiny in her family. Seeing someone so close leave the camp, and before them, would turn the heads of her children. As Savannah prepared herself for leaving, she packed a bag full of clothes she had accumulated during her stay. Thankfully, fashionable clothing wasn't a requirement for the next part of her journey. She had arrived at the camp wearing a blouse and smart trousers. Her money, phone, passport; all gone. Yet while she was departing without the same, she was leaving with friendships that could never be broken. She came splintered, she left whole. As the night darkened, Savannah decided against saying goodbye. Their hostility would only increase, and her heart couldn't take it. Rasha was awake when she left. She wanted to say something, but for once, her head ruled her heart. Waiting alone outside of her home, the man spotted his target even in the darkness.

"Come."

He waved his arms towards her and pointed out to a door nearest him. As she walked towards the silhouette, she looked around at the place she had called home. It hadn't been the greatest period of her life yet Savannah would miss the comfort it brought. Heading outdoors into the bitter night, the well-travelled teen was alone once more. She had never been this side of the camp. What was once a runway expanded in all outward directions. It was a deathly cold February night. Savannah's warmed breath lingered in the air ahead of her. She wasn't alone on the tarmac. Ten or so refugees, huddling like lost penguins, shivered to her right. Soon, he returned with another young family. Savannah looked to be the only solo passenger. She had her reasons for travelling north. She wondered there's. As they waited in the cold, silent air, she scanned the apron for any vehicles. It was empty barring an abandoned plane that stood derelict in the distance. The signs weren't good. She considered the likelihood he was all bravado. This man had promised so much for so little. Just as the panic began to set in, the sound of a roaring engine echoed through the air. A horn, showing no regard for the refugee's still asleep, tooted its arrival. With nothing to light the pitch black night, the vehicle was mysterious until it pulled closer. As it did, Savannah gulped. The vehicle was still unlit yet from the shape, she knew what was approaching. Looking across, Savannah could see worry flashing across the faces of the soon-to-be passengers. Savannah didn't expect luxury but had she have known that this would be their method of transport to Denmark, she would have reconsidered her options. As the vehicle stopped, the driver jumped down from the cab before greeting his apparent friend. They exchanged pleasantries in a foreign language, as the waiting refugees nervously watched on. Still speaking, he pointed at

Savannah. The driver nodded in agreement. Savannah was being summoned over.

"You will go in first. Come."

She followed the driver the length of the oil tanker before stopping at the back. He jumped, grabbed hold of a ladder and pulled it down to ground level.

"Don't worry. It is empty."

"Is it clean?"

"It is empty."

His repetition did little to calm Savannah's nerves. Sliding her bag onto her shoulders, she tightened the straps and grasped the bottom rungs of the ladder. After making easy work of the climb, Savannah struggled to open the hatch.

"Pull harder, girl."

She didn't think she could pull much harder. Not wanting to look feeble, Savannah mustered all of her strength and managed to pry open the hatch after serious effort.

"Good. Push yourself in."

If the night was dark, the inside of the tanker was darker. With families watching on, she wanted to prove her worth. As she jumped, the smell of oil filled her nose. The fall was heavy, yet Savannah was glad to feel the floor dry. As she stood to her feet, the driver called down through the hole.

"You must catch the kids. Be ready."

Savannah helped six children into the tanker. Each was scared of the fall and impending darkness yet the teen had little time to comfort them before another appeared through the hatch. Savannah stood back as the parents joined their children. Too small to catch them, Savannah helped by keeping the kids out of the way. It was clear that the adults spoke no English. Hugging their children, they smiled at Savannah in way of thanks. As the driver slammed shut the hatch, the small shred of light, that had already struggled to be effective, disappeared and the tank was plunged into darkness. Her senses were heightened in the absence of light. The smell of oil had subsided yet it was still hung in the cool air. The other passengers were whispering hurriedly in a language Savannah couldn't place. It was spacious inside yet the fear of darkness kept them all close together. Within minutes, the vehicle started its engine. The sound, deafening inside the tanker, exasperated the young children. Accelerating forward, the lorry exited the airport and joined the motorway. Inside, the ride was smooth. Curved walls allowed Savannah to slump against the sides of the tank. Her eyes were tired, yet the whispering voices irritated her ears. Comfort wasn't optimal yet if she could sleep, the journey would go by much quicker. Using her bag as a pillow, she stretched out into the open space. By now, it was early morning, and she hadn't slept since the previous night. As the conversation next to her softened, Savannah let her eyes close, and her mind wander.

***

Savannah's stomach, screaming out in pain, yanked the teenager from her dream world and back into reality. Her aches had been less frequent since visiting the doctor yet the pain she had just experienced was the worst of its kind. With no warning, her belly spasmed, shooting a sharp pain through her entire body. It was lighter inside the tank now the sun had risen. Morning light seeped through a small gap in the tank's curved wall. Her audible pain was attracting the attention of those lying to her

196

left. As the pain increased, her stomach pushed the feeling upwards. She tried to keep it down, but her mouth wasn't tight enough. Initial vomit trickled through her lips and fell to the flow. The second retch was intensified. Savannah gave up, letting the puke fly from her mouth forming a pool of sick between her legs. Out of the corner of her eye, she could see the other passengers sliding away from the vomit, and its source. She should have been embarrassed yet with the pain so much, Savannah had no energy left to give a shit. Reaching across the gap, the young mother held out a tissue in her hand. Holding the cloth to her mouth, Savannah caught the last droplets of vomit falling from her lips. Her stomach was worrying her. With the smell of vomit now taking over that of oil, Savannah hoped, for vanity's sake, the destination was near. As she attempted to push the pool of sick away with her feet, the young mother rubbed Savannah's shoulder.

"Okay?"

Her accent was strong. Savannah was unsure of it's origin. Regardless, she appreciated the sentiment.

"Yes. My stomach, that's all."

"Denmark?"

Savannah nodded. She wasn't aware if the tanker had multiple destinations.

"We also."

After waking up, cramping up and throwing up, Savannah was in no mood for a conversation, let alone with someone who barely spoke English. She didn't consider the inside of an oil tanker as an appropriate place to break the ice. With the tank rumbling on, wide-awake Savannah had no option but to await their arrival. Catching her focus were the blurred colours, appearing through the gap in the wall almost as quickly as they left. Her pool of vomit on the floor, half-illuminated in the light, rolled towards the back as the lorry accelerated uphill. Beyond the sound of the struggling engine, Savannah could hear the sound of breaking waves. Mindful of the sick, she moved onto her knees and pressed her eye to the gap. It was hard not to blink yet for the brief time her eyes remained open, Savannah could see the coastline. Her view of the ocean, interrupted by sparsely placed trees, extended into the horizon. On the tanker's side, a promenade ran the length of the foreseeable road. As she pulled away from the gap, the families looked to her for information. They looked tired.

"Ocean."

Their faces were still emotionless.

"The sea. Water."

Her words were redundant, and despite her reluctance, she felt obliged to mime her sentences. Mimicking the waves, Savannah weaved her hand through the air then touched her fingers together in the universal sign for okay. One of the men seemed to understand her actions as he translated the information to his family. Savannah, scheming in silence, hoped their time in the tanker was near complete. Her onward journey would be much easier if the tanker arrived near water. Crossing the Baltic Sea out of Denmark would be an ideal way for the now cashless, passport-less teenager to reach Latvia. Every minute spent in the tanker diminished Savannah's chance of being close to water. Now her mime show was over, she resumed her spying role by peering through the gap. To her relief, the water still hugged the side of the road. The tanker soon veered to the left where the sight of the ocean was replaced with that of a city. Slowed by traffic lights, Savannah was treated to a view of the overwhelmingly brown streets. As they passed through a ringing railroad crossing, the buildings became industrial in nature. Random concrete plots laid empty between corrugated iron barns fenced in. Moving further down the road, graffitied shipping containers replaced the buildings, allowing a view of the ocean in behind. At speed, the tanker swung out, pulling on the tarmac nearest an industrial unit. Hearing the beeping, Savannah braced herself for the tanker's reversing. As they inched backwards, the gap returned to darkness and the tank followed suit. It was all quiet as the vehicle slowed to a stop. Within minutes, the hatch had been cranked open, and the driver popped his head into the tank-cum-cabin. It was too dark to see his face yet Savannah could sense the grimace from his voice.

"What is that smell?"

Not wanting to stay behind and clean, Savannah blamed those unable to speak.

"One of the kids was feeling unwell."

"Fucking kids."

He extended his arm down from the hatch and called out for Savannah to grab hold. Dodging her sick, Savannah reached his arm and gripped tightly as he pulled her out of the tank. Savouring the fresh air, she stood atop the tanker, looking around at the empty hanger. Not wanting to halt progress, she slid down the ladder onto the stained floor. Stretching her legs, Savannah lapped the tanker breathing deeply as she reached the edge of the space. Turning, she shouted to the top.

"Thanks."

The driver, raising his head out of the hatch, turned and waved his hand nonchalantly. Through the gap in the hangar doors, Savannah exited the building into the crisp morning. Nerves had crept into the space the stomach pains had left behind. It had been seven months since Savannah was alone in a city. The feeling was familiar. With purpose in her stride, she roamed the dockside in search of anything to give her hope.

CHAPTER TWENTY-ONE

Outside of the hangar, the path followed the water's edge. Gentle waves sloshed over jagged rocks lining the sea wall below Savannah. In the distance, temporary cranes, not in operation, loomed large. Piles of aggregate, similar in height to the permanent dockside machinery, dotted the industrious surroundings. To each side of the pathway, shipping containers, mostly derelict, were seemingly randomly placed. It was nearing the hottest part of the day yet the air was still fresh. A zephyr breeze swept in from the sea bringing a salty, chilling air. Decaying cars, now too worthless to consider selling, were strewed about the seafront. The area was vast yet undeveloped. Savannah followed the unnecessarily wide roads that avoided the ocean's natural curve. As she rounded the corner, rows of lorries stood parked in a fenced area away from the road.

Smaller, functional cars parked in front of them, nearest a ridged, grey building lit from within. Mysteriously tall concrete blocks rose from the ground with no clear usage. Still, the road continued on, straightening out as the ocean did. Past the building, a bent sign curled into the shadows. Its paintwork was chipped yet Savannah could see make out the writing. *Velkommen til Aarhus havn.*

There was no English translation yet the boat logo was universal. Aarhus port stretched across multiple acres of concreted land. At the far end of the harbour, modestly sized ferries operated passengers services to Scandinavia. On the opposite side, much smaller fishing boats emptied their morning catches into boxes. Her success would be far greater on a bigger boat yet Savannah was in no mood to risk smuggling herself onboard. She had tried it once before and despite making it across, she had been broken in the process. Eyeing the bobbing trawler boats returning to dock, Savannah headed that way. For a major port, the lack of activity was surprising. She was able to cross roads without glancing to see if it was safe. High fences caging restricted areas along the waterside stopped her route becoming the most direct. Despite seeing the boat docking straight ahead, her path twisted between buildings and through car parks. Two men, stacked top heavy, sat on a sodden bench attempting to ignite a cigarette. Spotting the bench, Savannah sat, reached into her bag and pulled out a jumper. Her t-shirt was too thin for the coastal coldness. Ignoring the men's efforts for a conversation, Savannah carried on towards the dock. Eight boats of varying size floated in the harbour. A group of buildings stood close to the dockside, dwarfed in size by construction of a tower behind them. Approaching the dock, the boats rocked back and forth in the gentle wind. They were empty but for the squealing seagulls resting atop. For the most part, the boats were well-kept yet the furthest from the dock called out for loving. Peeling paint adorned the sides while the mast, holding a ripped sail leant over to one side. Savannah wondered if it had travelled much further than the port. As she pondered her next move, a fat man wearing ripped, dirty overalls climbed out of the ripped, dirty boat and stepped onto the wooden walkway. He limped as his heavy feet trounced towards Savannah. Getting closer, she could hear huffing with each steep. As he walked past, the smells of alcohol and body odour followed him. Despite walking close by, he didn't look at Savannah before he pushed open the door to a predominately wooden building. In doing so, the raucous noise of a tavern spilt out onto dockside. She was afforded a slight glimpse at the pub as the door swung back and forth. The afternoon was only just beginning yet the tavern was full of similarly-dressed men. Savannah was realistic about her chances. Desperately wanting to cross the Baltic sea, it became clear that her best chance would be in one of the boats bobbing in front of her. With no passport control or strict security, blagging her way onto a small boat would set her on the path to Latvia. As she mulled over the plan in her head, a slightly larger cargo boat appeared on the horizon. Unlike the sailboats parked in the dock, the advancing ship was a motorboat. An orange hull glided through the water leaving a turbulent wake in its path. While no expert on ships, Savannah could see that the incoming boat, complete with onboard cranes and navigation systems, was no match for the smaller boats in the same harbour. Cutting off the engine, the boat spun itself neatly into the moorings with ease. From out of the cabin came a crew of seamen who leaped down from the deck onto the gangway. In unison, they tied a series of ropes to the deck securing the boat in the wind. With the boat now stable, the gang of sailors, led by their much taller captain, strolled onto the pavement. As they passed Savannah, their conversation quietened. Again, jolly drinking sounds spilled out onto the street as the crew headed into the popular tavern. Seeing two separate boat-owners head into the same establishment was enough for Savannah to deduce that the pub was a popular drinking spot for sailors. She needed a ride and the teeming tavern was the perfect place to find one. Languishing between a corrugated steel warehouse and the SOC boat repair workshop, the Vandkanten tavern looked far from welcoming. Strips of cheap wood, painted haphazardly in a smokey shade of grey, stacked on top of each other forming a rustic frontage. Faux windows, painted with pictures of welcoming interiors, were stuck into the front wall above a saloon-style door in need of oiling. Three barrels, formerly home to gallons of beers, were left outside the door for collection. As she walked closer, Savannah could hear booming voices engaged in frivolous conversation inside. She felt uneasy around male company yet her options were limited. Pushing open the door, Savannah held her breath and entered the tavern. A smokey haze, both in smell and sight, was evident as she left the sea air behind. The tavern was mostly dark, lit only by four lamp bulbs hanging spaced across the length of the room. To her immediate left, a busy bar cramped itself into the corner. A solitary draught beer pump was in constant use as thirsty sailors competed with each other as to who would have their muggy glasses refilled first. From the bar, the tavern continued for some distance. With tables on either side, the tavern's slender walkways forded the fatter sailors to congregate together nearest the entrance. Most of the beer-drinkers were too preoccupied with their slightly warm pints to notice a mixed-race teenager girl enter the pub. However, those that did had put down their drinks and stopped their conversations to stare open-mouthed at

Savannah. Soon, the entire tavern, hushed to near silence, looked on in unison at their new visitor. A television, screwed to the wall in the corner, the only source of noise. It played the news channel yet little of the tavern's customers showed much interest. Instead, they gawped at Savannah, who now regretted even coming in. Despite the silence continuing for what felt like an eternity, the pub soon resumed to full noise and the conversations were continued. With no money to her name, Savannah ignored the bar completely, instead walking the length of the room into the darkest doldrums of the tavern. Reaching the end, a long bench welcomed the bums of the sailors, Savannah had seen disembark from the orange cargo boat. After time spent at sea, the crew welcomed not just the beer but the arriving hot food brought from the kitchen by a tired-looking waitress. As she dropped the plates of steaming fish stew on the table, she looked at Savannah as if the teenager was on fire. It was clear that the waitress did not often see other females at her workplace.As she searched for somewhere to sit, Savannah noticed the paint-peeling boat owner engaging in a arm-wrestle on a nearby table. Despite starting strongly, he succumbed to his opponent's strength and was forced to drop a krone into his cup. Leaving the table, the baying crowd cheered for the victor. Spotting a vacant table, Savannah sat and rested her legs awhile. To her relief, the tavern looked to be full of sailors meaning Savannah wasn't short of potential rides. Encouraged by her discovery, Savannah shifted her focus to the new challenge, interrupting their drunken conversations before talking herself onto a boat. She knew it would be harder than it seemed. To grow her lagging confidence, she scanned the room for friendlier faces to start her hunt. Crowding around a small table, a group of slimmer men sat in silence as their friend made a phone call. They were much younger than any of the other drinkers in the tavern, and for Savannah, that made them much more approachable. Once she had twisted past chairs and between tables, she confidently taped one of the young men on their shoulder. He turned quicker than she had anticipated. His wart-covered face was scrunched tightly into an expression, that had she have seen before, would have warned her away. His eyes tightened as he waited for her to speak. She wasn't entirely sure what to say.

"Do you have a boat?"

"Yes.

He spoke with a strong, hardened Eastern Europe accent.

"I'm looking to get to Latv—"

"But not for you."

He turned back around and faced his silent friends. Savannah was disappointed but not despondent. Knowing he was just one of many sailors in the pub meant his rejection wasn't hard-hitting. Immediately to their right, an older man, balding between his ears, sat alone looking into his pint. He hadn't moved in the time that Savannah had been looking at him. He seemed desperate for conversation. She approached him differently than she had with his neighbours.

"I'm looking to get to Latvia."

His accent was instantly recognisable.

"Latvia?"

"That's the one."

"That's some way from here little one."

Savannah hadn't always liked the Scottish accent yet miles away from home, the almost poetic sounds were comforting to hear.

"Not too far. A boat would get me there."

"But from here? No chance."

"Are you Scottish?"

"No. Jamaican."

His Caribbean accent was rubbish. Savannah laughed out of politeness.

"I know what you're thinking, what's a Scottish man, pasty as fuck, doing out here in Denmark?"

Savannah hadn't thought that. He didn't wait for a response.

"I came out here on a cargo boat. Stopped off here before heading home."

'Home?"

"Aye. Back to God's own country."

"Not Latvia then."

"No lass, I'm sorry."

"Safe trip."

"You too."

With another denial under her belt, Savannah wondered if she was ever going to find someone willing to ship her across the Baltic Sea. As she moved her way around the room, her message spread quicker than she could. Reaching the other side of the tavern, sailors were answering before Savannah had a chance to speak. She grew frustrated with the sailors as they made their decisions before listening to her story. Savannah was running out of options. Away from the noise and past a dart-less dart board, a small but tall table cornered into the walls. An older man, his hair ruffled untidily, sat at the table on a wobbling barstool. He kept a distance from the rest of the tavern's punters. They knew something Savannah didn't. In peace, he sat reading a folded newspaper while he cut, chewed and swallowed a tough, overcooked slab of steak. If her options were plentiful, then Savannah wouldn't have dared to interrupt him. Yet, with the confidence of somebody in a far greater position than she was, she tapped his shoulder. Neither, the man or Savannah moved at first. She tried again. He dropped his fork onto his plate. If people hadn't noticed Savannah before, they had now. Still, he refused to turn around. She tried verbally.

"Excuse me?"

Clasping his beefy hands together on the table, he pushed back on his chair and stood to his feet. His head moved quicker than the rest of his body. Somehow, his muscular frame was obscured when sat. Once stood, he towered over the teenager. Even if he agreed to her request, Savannah would fear for her safety. His chest exhaled smoky breaths as his teeth repeatedly bit down on his lips. With Savannah too scared to speak, he coughed up a sentence.

"What do you want?"

"I'm trying to get to Latvia and I—."

Moving his broad index finger across Savannah's lips, he shushed her in to silence.

"No."

His refusal didn't register with the teenager.

"I've come a long way to get here. I'm getting close. Just help me."

He had turned back to face his steak, newspaper combo leaving Savannah talking to his back.

"All I need is a seat on any boat. Anywhere. Just not here."

Still he ignored her.

"Not even a seat. I can fit into a box. Anything."

He rolled his shoulders to his neck and back down. She could hear the bone click.

"Please."

"I will not help you. Now I wish to enjoy my food in peace."

Savannah stared back at the on-lookers. She remained polite in defeat.

"Thank you for your time."

"Safe trip, Savannah."

The little focus she had held was smashed to pieces. *Safe trip, Savannah.* She was tired but sure of what she heard. *Savannah.* Turning back to face him, her brain worked double time.

"What did you say?"

Savannah's question was answered only by an overly audible chew of his meat. As he swallowed, he flicked the page in his newspaper. She went again.

"Answer me."

Without moving, he spoke to the wall.

"What are you asking me?"

Savannah felt no fear. She was angry.

"How do you know my name?"

He raised his arm and circled it in the direction of the watching tavern.

"We all know your name."

"You don't."

"Savannah Bancroft. England's missing orphan."

Savannah felt the colour drain from her face. Lying had become second nature.

"That's not me."

"You think some cheap clothes and a fat stomach will fool me?"

Spitting out her breath, Savannah felt aggrieved. She couldn't dispute that the clothes were cheap, but she certainly hadn't gained any weight. Without saying anything, he slid the newspaper along the table for Savannah to read. It was open on the sports page and while she liked swimming, Savannah didn't currently have an interest in the World Championships.

"Page 7."

Her fingers, greasy from touching the tavern's tables, flicked to the double page spread. Hurriedly, her dubious eyes scanned the blocks of black ink. Savannah followed his finger as he pointed to a column of text below a grayscale, dated picture of her school prom. The entire newspaper was written in Danish. Some words, her name, her aunt's, stood out of the article yet the rest was incomprehensible. Pushing the newspaper back across the table, Savannah gritted her teeth.

"Read it."

The man scrunched the newspaper in his hands as he pulled it closer. He continued chewing as he translated the text aloud.

"Possible sighting for England's missing orphan. Police in Austria say they are investigating possible sightings of missing teenager Savannah Bancroft who disappeared from Dover Port, England in August of last year. Investigators in England are offering a £250,000 (*2,000,000kr*) reward for information. After disappearing from England, possible sightings in Paris, Madrid and Zagreb have been followed up. Savannah's maternal aunt, Jackie Bancroft is still considered the prime suspect due to her suspicious behaviour and serious financial motive. While she now believes Savannah has been kidnapped, her coy-ness when cooperating with the investigation led officers to arouse suspicions. The investigation is ongoing. Please call +10121995 with any information."

Savannah didn't want to believe what she was hearing. There was far too much for her to process. Her aunt. The reward. Austria. With a look of pure glee on his face, the chewing man turned back to face Savannah. He reached into his pocket and pulled out a small flip phone. Opening the phone, he typed in the number from the newspaper and held the phone to his ear. Savannah grabbed his arm and pulled the phone away from his ear. She was riled.

"What the fuck are you doing?"

His licked lips opened to show a jagged, toothy smile.

"2 million kroner for some dirty bitch? Happily."

"You dare."

His laughter at Savannah's empty threat turned to coughing.

"Or what?"

Since the newspaper's harsh revelations, she hadn't been thinking clearly. As she reached for the knife, regret set in. It was too late to stop. Her dainty hands wrapped around the wooden handle below the blade. He flinched as she moved the knife from the table to below his neck. Her hands were shaking as she pressed the blade to his oily skin.

"You press call, and this knife is going through your airway, and you'll be hooked to a machine for the rest of your life."

He didn't react.

"Or you can put the phone down and walk out of here, a healthy, albeit fat, man. It's your choice."

A crowd had gathered around the altercation. Any chance of slipping out unrecognised had been dashed. She waited for him to move. Savannah pressed harder. Droplets of blood squeezed out of a tiny cut she had made. Her days were surely numbered. An aproned man pushed his way through the watching crowd.

"If you even whisper my name to anybody, I will find you and finish what I started."

He roared with sarcastic laughter as Savannah pulled the knife away from his bleeding neck.

"Right, you. Out!"

With the landlord's hand on her shoulders, Savannah dropped the knife onto the plate and eyeballed the fat man. As she was pulled through the crowd to the door, her eyes remained locked on her previous target. Standing at the door, the landlord spat words towards Savannah.

"You come back here again, the police will be called."

Despondent, and now increasingly paranoid, Savannah sat down on the rock wall along the dockside. If her penniless journey wasn't hard enough, she would now have to contend with a £250,000 ransom on her head. Wherever she went, her face would be known. The sooner she got to Latvia, the better.

"That was some fight."

Savannah, hearing the voice, turned to face its source. He looked shorter now not surrounded by his crew. She pointed to his orange hulled boat.

"That was some parking."

He suppressed his slight laughter.

"Cargo boats aren't easy to move."

"Cargo?"

"Nothing but."

Savannah sensed an opportunity. He was there for that reason.

"Room for a special package?"

"A dangerous package, you mean."

Savannah could sense a rejection coming. She remained silent.

"Why should I take Europe's most wanted girl on my boat?"

The question was rhetorical. He walked towards Savannah as he continued speaking.

"I shouldn't…"

Her manners forced a smile.

"..but if I don't, your story is lost forever."

Savannah's ears pricked up.

"Tomorrow morning. 4am. We leave to Poland. If you can stay in the shadows long enough, there is a seat for you. Don't be late."

CHAPTER TWENTY-TWO

The refuse bag that she had used as a pillow had split under the weight of
her sleeping head. Rotting food swimming in a yellow liquefied stench
seeped out through a tear in the plastic. Decaying meat was easy enough
to flick off, yet the pool of unidentifiable grease stained Savannah's
slightly smelly top. Knowing it was time for a change, she reached into
her drawstring bag and pulled out a blue fleece. Her underwear hadn't
been changed for days yet Savannah resisted to urge to dirty another pair.
In a state of darting paranoia, Savannah slept only in ten-minute shifts.
She had made camp in an enclosed cul-de-sac, a short walk from her
Danish departure point. From her vantage point, Savannah could watch
not just the entire road for unwelcome visitors, but also a weather
information board flashing the wind speed, temperature and crucially, the

time. Savannah's journey would soon continue on a boat, leaving in just under an hour. Her sleep had suffered for the lack of an alarm clock. With a bag full of other clothes, Savannah chucked the stained top into the torn bin bag. Leaping to her feet, she began the journey to the dock. Overhead, the moon and a plethora of stars kissed light into the dark night's sky. The walk, this morning, was easy. Last night however, with the new knowledge of her wanted status, Savannah's path was frenzied. She rushed between factories and docks, desperate to find somewhere obscure enough to rest her head without being spotted. Savannah longed for anonymity. Until yesterday, she was a nobody. Today, she was an expensive somebody. In the earliest hours of the morning, the port was surprisingly busy. Cargo cranes lifted shipping containers from storage across into waiting, impatient boats. Under the darkness, Savannah's identity was safe. Golf carts, ferrying people to and from the gigantic ships, whizzed past those walking. Consisting of concreted roads and tarmac through-ways, the port was a confusing place, not least in the darkness. As she passed a particular hanger for the second time, Savannah stopped to focus her thoughts. Usually outstanding, her memory had become distorted by her tiredness. Most of the possible routes were restricted meaning Savannah only had a few paths to choose from. Following the water's edge and past the car park, the area felt familiar again. Soon enough, the blip was forgotten, and the boat came into the distance. It was winter in Denmark, and despite the sun not due to be rising for a few more hours, Savannah felt visible as she passed the tavern. In front, the dockside was empty. She hoped she was early rather than late. Sitting on the same rock wall as she had done so yesterday, Savannah pulled the fleece's hoody over her head. Nearer the water, the morning breeze was much colder. With her hearing muffled by the fabric, she didn't hear the advancing footsteps.

"You are early."

It didn't take much to startle the already on-edge Savannah. The captain, followed by his crew, paced onto the walkway.

"I didn't want to miss it."

"Come. We have work to do."

As she headed down the ramp and onto the wooden walkway, Savannah couldn't help but feel relieved. Boarding a boat with a crew of five, strong men was enough to calm her palpable nerves. Arriving at the gangway, she waited for the order aboard. Dominating the much smaller boats in the harbour, the orange-hulled beast swayed in the wind. Recently painted lettering named the boat *Izabela*, a friendly name for a boat so big. Climbing aboard, a crew member grabbed a rope ladder, chucked it over the side and moved to let the rest of his comrades on board. With one hand holding the ladder, the Captain encouraged Savannah to pull herself up on to the ship. As her strength wavered, one of the crew members grabbed the teenager below the waist and plonked her onto the ship's deck. With the ground beneath her now swaying in the wind, Savannah clutched the side railing as the crew went about their business. The Captain stayed and extended his arm.

"I'm the Captain here but please, call me Piotr."

"Savannah."

There was no need for Savannah to introduce herself. Piotr and his crew knew who she was.

"Come and sit inside."

Savannah followed the Captain across the ship's slippery deck to a thick, bolted door cut into the steelwork. Twisting the door handle, Piotr unlatched the door and pushed it open revealing the cold interior. From the compact kitchenette across to the short bunk beds, the entirety of the cabin was panelled with varnished wood. It was cheap-looking but seemed practical. Piotr invited Savannah to sit on the foldable sofa that squeezed between a wall and the plywood table. He took a rusty, metal kettle from a cupboard underneath the plastic sink and filled it from the spluttering tap. The cabin was not much warmer than the deck outside.

"Including me, we have 6 crew."

Savannah wasn't sure of his point.

He tapped the wood twice, on two separate cupboards.

"Tea..Mugs."

With nothing more said, Piotr, left the cabin and let the door slam shut behind him. Savannah was left alone in the room with a boiling kettle and tea order to fulfil. As it whistled, the kettle clouded the room in wispy steam. Moving to the kitchen, the heat was welcoming. Her chilled breath cut through the warming air. With shaking hands, she reached underneath the sink, pulling out enough tin mugs for the crew. After grabbing the tea from behind a stack of playing cards, Savannah cupped the boiled kettle to warm her hands. As she poured the tea, a crackling radio buzzed from near the table. Speaking in what she assumed was Polish, the voice spoke at speed, in a way that was surely incomprehensible to native speakers. Savannah, unable to carry all of the drinks took only the captain's as she unscrewed the door. Emerging onto the deck, she was encouraged by their progress. Either side of the boat, the vast ocean rolled out for as far as her tired eyes could see. Seeing Savannah leave the cabin, Piotr jumped down from a crane to divert her path.

"Give this to the crew. I will come inside for mine."

Savannah collected the rest of the teas and climbed the stairs to the upper deck where the crew were working. Her arrival hadn't stopped the conversation. With no place to leave their drinks, Savannah knocked on the side of an empty cargo container as if on a doorstep. Hearing her beat, the crew, in near unison, grabbed the teas from Savannah's weakening hands without so much of a glance. She wasn't made to feel welcome. Savannah wondered if she wasn't. Heading back inside, Piotr had taken a seat at the sofa and was just finishing his tea.

"You don't like tea?"

Savannah craved a hot drink yet wasn't she wasn't sure if the Captain would allow her one.

"I'm British."

Piotr laughed as he rose to re-fill the kettle. He faced the sink as he spoke.

"You are British, but your skin? It's darker."

"My Dad was born in Zimbabwe."

Piotr was confused.

"And he came to Britain?"

"As a child. Went to school, got a job, met my mum and then voila, I came along."

He poured her tea as she spoke.

"That radio went off earlier."

"Good, it's working. What did it say?" quipped Piotr.

Savannah bit back.

"I don't speak Polish."

Piotr remembered who he was talking to. He passed Savannah a tea before sliding into the sofa next to her. As she sipped, Piotr took a piece of paper out from his pocket. Once unfolded, the annotated map covered the whole width of the table. Unlike most maps she had seen, Piotr's was centred on the Baltic Sea. Using, what seemed a complex series of drawn lines and measured angles, he had plotted their journey out of Denmark and into Poland.

"You see, here."

Savannah listened as he traced his finger across the highlighted route.

"We leave Aarhus. We will sail past Copenhagen, under the bridge. Then, we are out in the Baltic Sea. Overnight, we travel along the Polish coast into Gdansk. Then we come back."

Both Piotr's map and route cut off at the Polish eastern border.

Savannah's knowledge of Latvia was limited.

"So I can get off at Gadanse?"

"Gdansk."

"Gdansk."

"Yes. From there, you will have just Lithuania in your way."

"Is Latvia close?"

"Very."

Savannah scanned the map to feign interest while Piotr gained the confidence he needed to question his guest. He pulled his hands away and took Savannah's hand in his.

"Tell me. What does Latvia want from you?"

Despite being slightly scared of the contact, Savannah knew he was a man to please.

"It is more a case of what Latvia can do for me."

Savannah liked the sound of her own sentence. With her face recognised across Europe, she wondered how much of her story was known. The press had a tendency to spin the news to whichever angle they liked. It was unlikely she was considered heroic or noble in her quest for truth.

Instead, Savannah considered her likely media persona. A runaway girl, stricken with grief, locked away under the care of a tortuous Auntie. Even Savannah could admit it sounded better. She'd been asked her story many times over the course of her journey. In the camp, her history became well-known even if her face didn't. It was a tale that captivated the coldest of hearts. Sitting next to her was another inquisitive mind. Yet Savannah was tired, not just physically, but of telling her story. For once, she wanted to listen.

"A Captain aboard a ship must have some interesting stories. Indulge me."

Piotr was slightly taken aback by the request. Polish people, sailors especially, were hardened souls. Not often before had he been asked to tell his own story. His life experience was one that had shocked those whose ears had heard it. He was grateful that somebody was willing to listen. He jumped to his feet.

"Wait."

Piotr left the cabin and sprinted across the deck. Up a small flight of stairs onto a much smaller upper deck, he found the ships' bridge, a room crammed with the controls that led through to his Captain's office. While in no rush, the urge to tell his story quickened his hands as he searched through the desk draw in search of the photograph. Finding it, he paced back to the cabin where his visitor waited. Savannah, seeing the speed at which he left the room, had wondered if there was something wrong with the ship. Considering her luck, it wouldn't have surprised her. It wasn't until he returned with the photograph that her worry subsided. Once again, Piotr squeezed onto the sofa. He placed the photograph down onto the table, inviting Savannah to look. Torn at the edges with blobs of water-damage, the Captain's photograph captured the subjects in laughter.

"Who are these people?" Savannah asked.

"My family."

As he spoke candidly, he pointed to each of their smiling faces.

"This is my beautiful wife, Natalia. We have one daughter. Her name is Aleksandra."

"And they don't mind you spending your life at sea?"

"It is because of them, I am here."

While confused as to what he exactly meant, Savannah, sensing an incoming explanation, stayed silent. Focusing his eyes on the photograph now in his hands, he spoke softly.

"We emigrated to Moscow. I worked in investment banking as an analyst. For my job, it was the perfect place to be. We enjoyed living there. Moscow is a very beautiful, friendly city."

He spoke with fancy and quaintness that hinted at a loss.

"My daughter, she was similar to your age.."

Savannah noted the was.

"..and on her way home from school. We lived in a lovely area of Moscow. It wasn't a gated compound, but it was nice. We thought it was safe. Aleksandra came home as we, our home, were being burgled. She called out for her mother. She was dead. They had shot her hours before."

Savannah could see his eyes cloud over with tears. She rubbed his shoulder, attempting to comfort him. His story had little order.

"I'm so sorry, Piotr."

"Aleksandra. She had seen too much."

"What do you—"

"They took her, left a note telling me. They demand money that I didn't have. My clients, yes. But me? No."

"What did you do?"

"What I could only do. Nothing. I waited for the police, but they knew nothing. Police on this side of Europe don't work for the people. One day, nearly two months later, she comes to me."

Savannah let out a gasp of pure happiness. She felt her story align with his. Piotr's voice was firm.

"No. She came to me not whole but piece by piece."

Her mind painted a picture that she hoped was untrue.

"Piece by piece?"

"First, her hand. Then, the other. I still had hope. But then the rest."

Savannah tried to be compassionate, but her outburst at the attackers sounded like a response to his story.

"That's disgusting. Utterly vile. Why did they do it?"

"It is the Mafia. They want me dead."

"Mafia?"

He nodded.

"So now I live in Russia with people who want me dead and a family that are dead. I need to think. No better place to think than the ocean."

His previously clean-cut face looked aged by the telling of his story.

"How long have you been here?"

"That was six years ago."

"And you are still thinking?"

"I think now that I am too scared to go back. The world is full of dangers. It is hard to trust anybody."

Savannah knew his sentiments all too well.

"Tell me about it."

CHAPTER TWENTY-THREE

As the night grew more, so did Savannah's boredom. Despite powering through the ocean, the view was monotonously similar. Standing on the edge of the deck, the sea's chilled wind swept her backwards. Gripping to the railing, her shivering body begged for the inside yet the splatters of salty water rising up from the sea sobered the teenager into a state of absent mindedness. With nothing to focus on, her mind felt empty. She knew it wasn't. Still, she cast doubt over the rest of her journey. It was only a matter of time before she was recognised and taken home to face her fate. After coming so far, she was hoping not to fall at one of the final hurdles. Savannah had quietly struggled with aspects of her ever-changing personality as she travelled across Europe. Like any teenager, there were facets of her identity she hated. Most were new. Forced upon.

For a young woman, Savannah's trust in strangers was dangerous. Each time that she was compelled to lean on a stranger for support, she felt uneasy. With each day that passed, Savannah had become more and more naive in her interactions, especially with men. Since being raped, Savannah had entered into every conversation with less confidence than before. She now viewed every man differently however friendly they seemed. At first, she believed it hadn't affected her. While the violent, physical abuse was scarring, she considered herself lucky to still be able to function. Yet, deep down, she had changed. Mentally, she was weaker. Her confidence was fake. Every ounce of bravado was unnatural and false. Gazing out at sea, Savannah questioned herself. As the boat crashed through waves, her fragile emotions conflicted with her seemingly unstoppable body. Inside, she was broken. Part of her, the much cleverer side, wanted to be caught. She wanted to go home and forget that any of this had happened. Her gutsy, perhaps stupid, side, wanted to carry on. Her inner torment was in danger of causing problems. For now, Savannah was stupid. Soon enough, and once she was comfortable with herself, she would be forced into confronting her feelings. But for now, surrounded by a crew of unfamiliar men, she couldn't rest. A vicious splash from the ocean slapped the teenager out of her thoughts. Above her head, the cloud's stretched out into the horizon. As they grew distant, the pale, wispy floaters darkened into heavy, grey gloom. Behind her, the conversations heightened into shouting, their Polish voices carrying a degree of alarm. Savannah wasn't a meteorologist, but even she could sense a storm incoming. Soon enough, the last dregs of daytime slipped from the night's grasp. As they did, a bold floodlight boomed down from the upper deck. It pointed both forward and backwards, lighting not just the route but the deck behind.

Savannah could feel the gentle heat of concentrated light on the side of her left arm. Unable to ignore the intensifying shouting behind her, she turned to confront it. Piotr cut a lonely figure as he reasoned with his crew. All bar one of the ship's workforce were demanding answers. Savannah wasn't comfortable interjecting. Instead, she answered her body's calls for heat and headed inside to the relative warmth of the cabin. Judging by the licked-clean plates still on the table, Savannah's pasta dinner she had cooked earlier had been well-received. Promising to herself to wash the plates in the morning, she stacked them by the sink before slouching on the sofa. With boredom and tiredness setting in, Savannah wanted to sleep. Not only would she feel refreshed after resting but the morning sunrise would indicate that the boat was nearing its destination if Captain Piotr's estimates were to be believed. She could feel her eyes wanting to shut but the noise outside stopped them from closing. As she widely yawned, the radio in the corner crackled into life. Again, it spoke only in Polish, yet Savannah knew this time to alert the captain. Pushing open the cabin door, she couldn't see Piotr. His crew stood watching the advancing rain clouds. Savannah shouted over their innocuous conversations.

"The radio is going again."

A few of the men turned to face the teenager. She repeated herself only this time louder.

"The radio. Someone is speaking."

With a look of worry, followed by hurried steps, the entirety of the crew pushed past Savannah into the cabin. Not wanting to catch a chill, she squeezed back inside and sat down on the sofa. Piotr's crew gathered around the radio waiting for it to speak once more. As it did, the crew listened intently. Any murmurs were shushed down straight away. Once the message had finished, the group turned and consulted each other. They spoke quickly stopping only to laugh and slap each other on the back as encouragement. Upon seeing Savannah, the conversation ended.

"Out. Out."

The skinniest sailor was tasked with kicking Savannah out of the cabin. Their expressions told her that this was a conversation she wouldn't be allowed to hear. She wondered if they realised she didn't speak their native language. Outside, Savannah could see Piotr gazing through a pair of binoculars from his vantage point on the upper deck. His focus was locked on the now advancing rain clouds. Dropping the binoculars, he spotted Savannah shivering by the door. He talked as he tiptoed down the steps.

"There is a storm coming. Go into the warmth."

"Your crew just kicked me out of there."

His expression read confused even from a distance.

"Kicked you out? Nonsense."

Savannah wanted to hint at their shiftiness.

"They are talking on the radio. Not something for my ears apparently."

Hearing the revelations, Piotr walked past Savannah and into the cabin. Although Savannah could listen to the conversation through the door, they spoke solely in a language she didn't understand. After a few minutes of muffled speech, Piotr emerged with several of the crew members. As his sailors walked past, the Captain stopped and spoke to Savannah.

"You were right. Another ship is warning us about the weather. It sounds like a strong one."

"Can't we go around?"

"Not one this size. It will only be a short distance of turbulent waters. We have good sailors."

Savannah wasn't sure she believed him.

"Stay in the cabin. Jedrek will keep you company."

Savannah stepped back inside to be greeted by Jedrek crouched in the corner. His hair was much patchier than his colleagues while his arms were much smaller. He looked young, but his face was aged with experience. Unless Savannah was painfully unaware of facial hair fashion, he was in need of a shave. Savannah, now knowing his name, broke the silence.

"Hi, Jedrek."

As he darted his eyes across to the teenager, Savannah could tell he wasn't expecting conversation. He grinned his jagged teeth before speaking.

"Hi, girl."

She was unsure whether his greeting was rude through a lack of English or chivalry. It seemed that his job, manning the radio, was one of the easier onboard tasks. Savannah wondered if that was a blessing or a curse.

"You've got the easy job then?"

"It isn't easy."

His English seemed fine, she thought.

"Listening to a radio message?"

His silence conceded defeat. Savannah provoked more conversation.

"Do you speak English?"

He retorted quickly.

"Do you speak Polish?"

She answered resolutely.

"No."

"Well, it is good then I speak both."

"Quite."

As he went to speak, the radio crackled softly. He twisted a dial and tuned his ear. Leaning into the machine, he listened intently. Hearing the message now finished, he lifted the microphone and spoke softly. His tone was much different to his with Savannah. Her boredom provoked inquisition.

"What are you saying?"

"None of your business."

"Thanks."

"You should concentrate on yourself."

Savannah's thoughts mirrored her words.

"What do you mean by that?"

His response, coupled with his strong accent, sounded threatening.

"You know."

She didn't like his menace.

"No, I actually don't."

"If I told you then you perhaps wouldn't sleep tonight."

Savannah liked the sound of the challenge.

"Try me."

"I don't know many girls who get on a boat alone with this many men."

She had heard it all before, and while it confirmed her trust issues, Savannah wasn't in the mood to hear it.

"You don't know many girls like me then."

"In my country, in other countries nearby, we have serious problems with girls."

"Girls? What about them?"

He turned to face Savannah as he spoke with a vapid expression.

"They are taken. By men."

"Taken where?"

"For sex. These girls are kidnapped and then sold around Europe for the highest price. They become prostitutes. Never again do they see their mothers."

"Why are you telling me this?"

"Why? Because you are at risk. A pretty girl will go for big money."

Savannah regretted starting the conversation. Once she arrived in Poland, she was alone again. With a bounty on her head, and now the possibility of a kidnapping, her journey to Latvia would be riddled with nerves. He looked glad to have told Savannah his information. Jedrek thought his story would have acted as a warning. Perversely, he was looking out for the teenager. Yet, Savannah could see only scare-mongering. While the threat was genuine, her plan couldn't change. Moreover, she took comfort in the realisation that her mother had been in Eastern Europe and evidently never been kidnapped. Her need for conversation had been relinquished as more messages hissed through the radio. Even though she was silent, Jedrek hushed Savannah as the voice spoke. Until now, the journey across the ocean out of Denmark had been smooth. With little advance notice, the seas intensified. From the rear of the boat, Savannah could hear the waves crashing into the ship's hull. Thunderous rain pattered against the tin roof of the cabin creating a noise that silenced that of the radio. Whistling wind spun past the door outside leaving an eery feel in its path. For a boat of its size, the ship's shake came as some surprise to Savannah as she gripped the table tightly. Jedrek, crouching on the floor with his ear pressed against the speaker of the radio, shouted into the handset. His face told Savannah this was far from usual. As the boat ploughed through the waves, the thumping rain amplified. At home, Savannah found the sound of rain against the windows comforting. There was no greater feeling than that of snuggling into a duvet as the skies opened above her house. However, on a boat struggling through the Baltic Sea, the sound was far more ominous. In times of similar danger, Savannah had closed her eyes to sleep, yet even a heavy sleeper like she was, would struggle to doze off in this storm. With the door shut to the deck, the length of the storm was a mystery to the pair inside. Even Jedrek with his radio wasn't sure how much longer the shakes would continue. Suddenly the dirty plates beside the sink were shaken onto the floor, smashing into dozens of sharp pieces. Jedrek clung to the side panelling, his fingers wrapped around the handset. The radio still buzzed with messages yet with the rain hammering down on the roof, it spoke too quietly to make any sense. While it felt like an eternity, just minutes had passed before the rain had softened to a slight shower. Jedrek, now able to stand, attended to his radio. The boat's shaking mellowed to a more familiar rocking. Savannah hoped the storm was over. Not ten minutes had passed before a drenched Piotr swung open the door and greeted the pair.

"That was a big one, eh?"

Savannah nodded as Jedrek spoke in Polish. Piotr interrupted his subordinate.

"In English, for our guest, Jedrek."

He repeated himself.

"Sir. Is the ship okay?"

"The ship is fine. Jedrek, go help secure the load."

"Yes, sir."

With his reply, Jedrek left the cabin alone to just the Captain and his guest.

"Are you okay? We don't often get weather like that," asked Piotr.

"Fine. Just tired."

He sat down on the sofa next to Savannah.

"We will arrive into Gdansk in the morning. Hopefully, the storm won't delay us."

"Yeah, I remember."

"My friend, Wojciech will meet us at the dock. He will take us to our hometown of Elbag."

"Us?"

"I go too. I need to return home. But whether you come with us, that is your option."

"Elbag. Is that closer to Latvia?"

"Closer than Gdansk. From there, you go through Lithuania into Latvia."

Savannah, thinking his plan was too good to be true, voiced her concerns.

"Where's the catch?"

"This isn't a fishing boat."

With that, he pulled the door open and straddled the doorway. He had work to do.

"Get some rest. When you wake, we will be close to land."

Piotr turned off the room's only light as he shut the cabin door behind him. Savannah wasn't sure what to think. While the plan seemed sound, Piotr was unnecessarily hospitable. She hoped his kindness was driven by grief and not by cupidity. For now, her only option was to sleep. With the boat now in calmer waters, her sofa-cum-bed was comfortable enough to rest her head. Once horizontal, she stretched her legs, closed her eyes and hoped for the best.

CHAPTER TWENTY-FOUR

Judging by his route calculation, Piotr expected the port of Gdansk to appear on the horizon imminently. Since the storm midway through their journey, the sailing into Poland had been much calmer if not lonely. He had allowed his crew a break once the chances of stormy conditions had been nullified. With the boat nearing its destination, Piotr needed his crew awake and ready to prepare for a docking. With his left hand still on the controls, he reached for a stringed whistle hanging from the ceiling. Pulling the string, the tooting noise woke the crew from their slumber but not the guest in the back cabin. Seeing his men emerge from below deck, Piotr slung open the door and shouted down to prepare the ship. A series of disgruntled groans told the Captain his crew had heard his command. Turning back to face the open ocean, the promised dock began to reveal itself in the distance. Ahead, with the morning sun just high enough, the ocean glistened ever so slightly. Approaching the harbour-side, the captain slowed his boat to meet the signposted speed limits. His crew had readied themselves on the edges of the cargo deck. Piotr had thought of waking Savannah yet with the destination nearing, he trusted only himself on the controls. As they rounded the curve into the dock, Piotr's heart sank. Along the entire width of the sea wall, a convoy of flashing blue vehicles serenaded their arrival with sirens. Towards the middle of the wall of police, a larger vehicle, complete with speaker system on top, shouted orders towards the boat. Piotr, too far away to hear, continued into the dock. He looked down towards his crew. They had spotted the commotion, but their faces showed no signs of alarm. Piotr pushed down the side window and shouted in their direction. "Wake the girl. Wake her."

Jedrek went to move but was immediately hoisted back by the crew. They stood still. Piotr repeated himself before realising his orders were being ignored.

"What have you done?"

In that split second, the realisation he had feared set in. It was clear that his crew, the men he had trusted for so long, had radioed the police. Each knew the bounty placed on Savannah's head, and together they had betrayed their superior officer. If not for the adrenaline, Piotr would have frozen in shock. Once more he pulled down on the whistle in an attempt to wake his guest. He hoped she was awake. To be sure, he tooted the whistle again but this time much longer than before. Little did he know that inside of the cabin, Savannah was awake and focused. Her sleep has been interrupted by the shouting from outside. In her stirring state, her awakening mind whizzed with ideas. While she had no clue as to what was happening, she knew that something was up. Jumping to her feet, she listened with her ear against the door. It was muffled, yet she could hear Piotr calling her name. Without thinking, she pulled open the door getting a slap in the face from the crisp, morning breeze. Her eyes, blurred from her fast awakening, made out the figures of the crew lining the side of the boat. Piotr was on the upper deck and hadn't noticed Savannah emerge from the cabin. As she moved forward into the middle of the deck, she saw the reason for panic. Less than a hundred metres away, a seemly impenetrable barricade of police cars stood between Savannah and the red transit van that presumably carried Piotr's friend. Not one of the crew had afforded Savannah a smile as they sailed through the seas yet now their faces were flooded with pure happiness. She knew what they had done. For now, the path was clear to the upper deck. With her eyes firmly locked on Piotr, she darted past the traitorous sailors. Reaching the bridge was a temporary relief yet still the police posed a sizeable threat. Seeing Savannah, Piotr turned and apologised profusely in panic.

"I'm sorry. My crew, they want your head."

Savannah didn't care for apologies. She needed a way out.

"Listen to me. How I can get past?"

"The dock, it curves around."

"What are you saying?"

He glanced down at the ocean in front of them and mimicked breast stroke. Savannah wasn't the most proficient of swimmers, but her life and subsequent quest for truth depended on it. Nearing the water's edge, the police orders were much clearer.

"Surrender yourself. This is an order from the police."

Savannah was in no mood to surrender herself. She hadn't done anything wrong yet at that moment, she felt worse than a murderer. Eight silver and blue Policja cars, each with two accompanying officers, stood waiting for the catch of the day. Lurking behind, the red transit van had moved back out of sight. From their upper deck vantage point, Savannah could see that all of the officers were heavily armed. Piotr accelerated the boat past docked ships and smaller sailboats. He lacked a clear plan but knew that he wasn't going to stop. With his eyes fixed ahead, he shouted at Savannah in the glass reflection.

"Go! What are you waiting for?"

"They'll see me. I can't go now."

"I'll distract them. Jump on my call."

Piotr shut off the engine and let the boat glide for the final few metres of its journey. Leaving his office, he stood on the corner railings, waving his arms at the police below. As he did so, the armed police took aim. Savannah squeezed through the bridge and out onto the deck's highest point. Standing atop a box of cargo, she gasped at the size of the fall. It was no time to be a wimp, but still, her breathing quickened. Above the sounds of sirens, she heard Piotr's command.

"Jump, Savannah."

Savannah's trembling legs ignored their own advice and leapt from the ship. Her fall felt endless until the water engulfed her flailing body. Immense coldness washed over her entirety. Weighted by her clothes, now soaked through with dock water, Savannah battled to stay afloat. Her mouth filled with water as she gasped for air. Kicking her feet, her body refused to float to the surface. Her eyes, stinging with salt, struggled to make sense of the surroundings. Bringing her arms together, she pushed away the water and broke through the surface. Savannah spat out the water before enjoying the ocean-less mouthfuls of air. Now stable, she looked around for help. She had floated further from the boat than her jump had suggested. From her bobbing point, Savannah could see the orange-hulled ship nearing the sea wall. With her energy restored, the teen started swimming away from the drama. Her ears, filled with water, muffled the shouts and screams. As she neared the dock, Savannah spotted a ladder extending into the ocean. It clung to the sea wall a safe distance from the shouting Police. Savannah, feeling the effects of the spontaneous swimming, stopped her stroke and let the gentle tide push her towards the ladder. Reaching the first rung, Savannah stepped up and pulled herself out of the chilly water. Once atop, she was privy to the action unfolding several hundred metres away. Piotr was standing tall beside the upper deck's perimeter fencing. Below, his crew huddled together in a sign of apparent surrender. Still, the Police shouted at Piotr to shut off the boat. He didn't listen. Even from a distance, Savannah could hear the whimper. It had happened with no prior warning. He fell to his knees, blood seeping through his uniform. Another shot pinged off the side of the boat. Another hit him once more. He cried out in considerable pain. On land, the police continued shouting, but to no avail as their commands were drowned out by the noise of a revving engine. Savannah flashed her eyes across to the police barricade. They had dropped their guns in favour of binoculars. She had been spotted. He called at her from the safety of his dulled red, transit van.

"Come on! Get in."

As the police moved towards their vehicles, Savannah jumped into hers. He floored the accelerator even before the door had slammed shut. Unable to buckle her seatbelt before speeding off, Savannah grabbed hold of the door handle to steady herself. She glanced in the winged mirror on her side of the van.

"Wait, we have to get Piotr."

He didn't listen to her. She raised her voice.

"What about Piotr?"

Again, as his ears refused to listen, she shouted louder.

"What are you doing? He's supposed to be your friend?"

With the road straightening ahead, the driver looked deep into Savannah's eyes.

"He's dead."

Savannah, switching her gaze back to the mirror, watched as the boat faded into the distance. Ringing wet, cold and numb, she felt like shit.

CHAPTER TWENTY-FIVE

Wojciech kept his gaze on the road and not on the convoy of flashing police cars accelerating behind them. His furrowed brow caught the cold sweat that trickled down his stressed forehead. Ahead, the road to Elblag was congested.

"Psiakrew."

He corrected himself almost instantaneously.

"Sorry. I shouldn't swear with children here."

Savannah was too preoccupied with the chasing police cars to snap back. With her clothes soaked through, the teenager stuck to the chair as the van accelerated through gaps between slower traffic. With only Wojciech knowing the route, Savannah's eyes scanned for the first sign of refuge from the chase. Wojciech's clammy palms slipped on the wheel as he cursed for the other cars to move out of the way. He had driven from the port to his hometown more times than he could remember however this journey would force the van and its inhabitants onto unfamiliar roads. Savannah was jolted across her seat as the van swerved down a narrow lane spurting off from the main road. Laden with stones and smaller rocks, the dirt track offered little comfort to the passengers bolting down it. Wojciech had forced the police cars to follow in single file as they flew after the van. On the bumpy terrain, the distance between the chasers and the chased grew. Savannah had stopped checking the mirror. Her focus honed in on the road ahead. Taking the uneven track had appeared the best option yet with the road seemingly endless and straight, there was no place to lose the coppers.Sparse hedges, under tall oak trees, lined the side of the track with their branches swinging down into the road. As they sped past, the branches slapped the side of the van littering tiny pieces of bark over the windscreen. In her mirror, Savannah watched as the furthest police car back dropped off from the chase and turned around. His intentions were clear.

"He's going to block us off, we need to find a way out."

Savannah's worried voice croaked under pressure. Wojciech nodded, taking on board the teenager's remark. As they continued on, the police showed no signs of relinquishing their grip. Wojciech was hesitant to carry on for much further. They had been driving for near ten minutes on the same stretch of road, and he didn't want to stray too far from his mental map. Past a derelict piece of farmyard machinery, the road curved out of sight. Refusing to slow down, Wojciech held his breath as the van, not made for speeds this fast, rounded the corner. To his relief, the road straightened out once more as it approached a series of barns. With the distance even bigger, Wojciech slammed on the brakes and spun the van across the grass verge and behind a considerably large barn. Only through Wojciech's mirror could they see the three police cars approaching. With the road ahead straight, and now sign of their targets, the front police car slowed considerably. Inside, the officer crawled the car while scanning her eyes across the farmland. As Savannah went to speak, Wojciech shushed her back into silence. He whispered without moving his focus.

"Keep still. We won't move from here."

Wojciech's heart was beating faster than the teenage girl's. From his position, he watched as the leading police officer grabbed her radio and started to speak. As she did, her eyes darted across the landscape. Within seconds, the exhaust blasted a plum of smoke, and the police car had accelerated forward. One car remained behind as the two leading vehicles disappeared into the distance.

"What do we do?"

"Wait."

Savannah didn't trust Wojciech as much as the recently-deceased Captain. His oily forehead was covered in acne while his teeth were a bright shade of yellow. A patchy moustache added to the little hair he owned. Nothing about Wojciech exuded confidence. As they waited, both driver and passenger locked their eyes on the last police car. After a few minutes of ogling, the flashing car followed his colleague and sped off down the lane. Savannah felt her relief was premature.

"Are we safe?"

"Not yet. They could come back."

"So we'll wait?"

Wojciech looked across at Savannah and smiled at his passenger for the first time. With the hurried departure, there was no time for proper introductions.

"Wojciech."

He held his arm out for Savannah to shake.

"Savannah."

Noticing her soaked clothing and lack of luggage, Wojciech broke the ice.

"You are the first girl I have met who doesn't have a handbag."

Since jumping into the dock, pulling herself out and embarking on a high-speed car chase, Savannah hadn't realised that she was once again bagless. With her clothes hesitant to dry in the cold winter air, she resigned herself to death by pneumonia. Savannah thought of her bag that she had left in the cabin where she slept. It was most likely still there. As was his body. In Savannah's name, someone had lost their life. A body, a person's memories and experiences had been destroyed. She thought of his friends, what was left of his family. Remembering her own grief compounded her guilt. Savannah's self-obsessed hunt for normality had killed somebody. As the bullet pierced Piotr's skin, every last piece of resolve Savannah had cherished for so long, dissipated. Yet, even after death, Savannah excused her own actions. If she stopped now, Piotr's death would be in vain. A man of morals, as he was, would surely rather die for the truth than for nothing. Savannah wasn't reasoning with herself, but with opinions of people she would never meet. Soon, it would be on the news, and England's missing orphan would be a murderer. Savannah's ruthlessness would soon be her downfall. Before this trip had started, Savannah had thought of herself as a sensible and nice person. Now, despite an admiration for all she had achieved, she hated herself. For now, her concentration was vital. Wojciech was waiting for a reply.

"It's on the boat. Along with a crew of bastards and a dead man." Wojciech made a noise that politely conveyed his understanding. He crept open the door and jumped out of the van without saying a word. Savannah waited in silence assuming he had forgotten they were wanted by the police. She heard the van door open at the rear followed by echoing footsteps behind the interior partition. Within a minute or so, Wojciech got back in the van holding an extremely large t shirt.

"This will be okay until my home."

He passed the t-shirt to his passenger before turning and facing away. On his cue, Savannah slipped out of her squelching, now smelly, clothes and pulled the shirt over her head. While Savannah had never heard of the Krakow Half Marathon, she was very grateful to the organisers for the t-shirt. Down to her knees, the t-shirt eschewed her modesty effectively given the lack of options. As she reached for her seat belt, her stomach reminded her that life wasn't content. Again, it cramped into life. She scrunched her eyes tight as the pain kicked in. Buckling over, she reached for her stomach as if to squeeze away the torment. Rumbling uncontrollably, Savannah hunched motionless in a bid to conserve her energy. Gulping her breaths, she sampled the familiar taste of sick. Reaching for the door handle, she swallowed the first upheaval of vomit. With the door now open, she leant out of the van and allowed gravity to suck the sick from her. It felt relentless, but as she spat the last drops from her mouth, the pain subsided. Wiping her face, she turned back to Wojciech and slammed the door on her vomit. Judging by his smile, he found the experience a lot funnier than she did.

"Travel sickness but not moving or sea sickness but on land?"

Savannah wished she knew. Without consulting his passenger, Wojciech stuck the van into gear and moved off from behind the barn. After moving slowly onto the road, he accelerated away from the farmlands back towards the main road. If the police were to follow, they find themselves behind the van once more. Wojciech felt confident in his chances. He followed the lane in its entirety until arriving at the junction with the main road. There, they found the traffic much calmer than before. Pulling out, he swerved onto the right side of the road and accelerated to near top speed. Despite no longer having police on his tail, Wojciech was aware that a red transit van would be easy to spot amongst much smaller, sparser cars. Indecisive by nature, he struggled to decide between the slow, lesser roads or the fast route via the main but watched roads. Feeling gutsy, he followed the signs directly towards Elblag. It was a journey that would normally take an hour of Wojciech's day however with the barnyard pit stop and chasing, it was nearing two hours since the boat faded from view. Savannah gazed out of the window at meadows stretching out of sight. Despite not planning to visit Poland, the beauty of its countryside was becoming a highlight of her journey. While pretending to be care-free, Savannah admired the modest river that followed the road. Crossing over the water, she was greeted with the hallmarks of western civilisation. A McDonalds jolted to the side of the road in front of a cold, dreary block of flats. Soon they left the urbanisation behind and continued through smaller villages and towns with trees that refused to lose leaves despite Winter. Further ahead, the previously lost river appeared much wider and grander beneath a well-fenced bridge. Flowing at a much faster velocity, the river pulled branches and logs downstream. Savannah preferred the much smaller, calmer incarnation.

Grass verges filled the space that narrowing roads had left behind as they approached the outer suburbs of Elblag. Wojciech eased the speed as the traffic became tighter. Looking across at his passenger, he spoke quietly. "We are close. We will cut through the city, and my home is not far." Either side of the road, quant cottages reminded Savannah of home. Of all the places she had travelled, it was unexpected that Poland would be the place to provoke the symptoms of homesickness. With winter nearing its end, planted flowers showed early signs of new life as they sprouted from the ground. Past the pretty houses, the standard of architecture dropped. Driving through, what she assumed was the ghetto of Elblag, Savannah held her breath that the van wouldn't slow to stop. Dilapidated homes, abused by years of disregard and ruin, yearned for better days. Local youths, riding their bicycles in wide circles overlapping the road, ignored the horns and shouts from frustrated car drivers. To her relief, Wojciech kept his foot on the gas, crossing a bridge over the river. In the city, the buildings were consistently coloured. White blocks, broken up by identical, black windows, were roofed with an orangery red tile. A bell tower, the only signs of height in the modestly-sized city, chimed as they entered the urbanised streets. Hindered by red light after red light, the van made slow progress through the city. Soon enough, Wojciech indicated to the left, and they slowed awaiting a gap in traffic. As they turned into the side street, Savannah watched as a smile washed over the driver's face.

"Just up here."

With his hands clasped on the wheel, he pointed his finger toward a square, red house that cornered the street and smaller alleyway. Pulling up, Wojciech switched off the engine, jumped out of the van and opened the gate onto his front garden. Savannah followed sheepishly. Standing on the doorstep, Wojciech rattled his knuckle against the wooden door. From inside of the house, both Wojciech and his guest could hear footsteps coming closer. Wojciech grinned as the door swung open.

"Papa!"

CHAPTER TWENTY-SIX

Klaudia kept herself busy as her child slept. In a rare moment of quiet, alone time, she gathered together the ingredients onto the worktop. Taking a large bowl from out of a cupboard, Klaudia washed her hands before reaching for the smallest knife from the block. Ripping open the packet, she sorted the dirty potatoes into size order then swept them all into the bowl. Her hands were muddied as she cleaned away their imperfections. Taking her knife, Klaudia peeled the skins then tossed the cut potatoes back into the bowl. Her husband should have been home by now. Ignoring the worry, she prepared the cabbage in much the same way. Having guests was a rarity in her household, especially for lunch. Despite having made golabki more times than she could remember, Klaudia felt an immense pressure to deliver. Her dainty hands were shaking as she filled a pan with cold water. As a housewife, her stress was another man's relaxation. Since the birth of their child three years previous, she held a secret resentment towards her husband. He was able to leave the house, leave the monotony of domestic life and experience a normal working day. For Klaudia, her day was almost identical to the previous. Today, however, it was different. Late, last night her husband received a call from one of his closest, longest friends. After he had moved away, their friendship deteriorated yet tragedy brought them closer. He knew her husband worked in port couriering. He knew their house had room for one more. What he asked for wasn't unreasonable. It was whom it involved that caused friction. Klaudia wasn't interested. Her refusal, on the grounds of legality, was well-merited. Yet, her husband made the decision, and his word was final. Klaudia was fully aware of her own selfishness yet with a family to feed, she didn't want her husband endangered. As the clock ticked on, she started believing her own worst nightmares. With the pan near boil, Klaudia dropped the cabbage and potatoes in and moved onto the next step. Before she had a chance to chop the top from the first carrot, her quiet time was disrupted. Her son had awoken from his nap and was demanding some food. Klaudia wanted to install chivalry and gentlemanly respect into her child yet it was clear he was taking after his dad. Banging his hands on the table, the child hurried Klaudia along. Her stress levels had risen. Stood at the sink, her view outside onto the street was perfect. It was from here that near an hour later that she watched her husband pull in. Parking the van on the side of the street, he jumped from the driver's cab and welcomed his guest through the gate. He knocked loudly igniting their son's excitement. Composing herself, Klaudia straightened her apron and paced to the front door. Behind the wooden frame, she practised her smile. With her lips in position, she pulled down on the handle. As the door opened, their son rushed through her legs and into the improvised arms of his dad.

"Papa!"

"Mój piękny syn" *"My beautiful son"*

She stood on the door step without saying a word. Klaudia took the initiative.

"Please. It is warm inside."

As the girl stepped inside their home, she grinned at Klaudia through her teeth. It wasn't the housewife's ideal situation yet she was determined to still be hospitable and courteous to her guest.

"And your name?"

The girl looked at Klaudia as if she was stark naked.

"Savannah."

Klaudia, much like everyone, knew her name beforehand. Noticing her outfit, or lack of, Klaudia rushed to the cupboard under the stairs. Sifting through the pile of clothes, she found a pair of leggings that would most likely never be worn again.

"Here."

Wojciech, speaking in Polish, explained to his wife how she had fallen into the water. He omitted the death from his version of the told story. As Klaudia went to speak, her husband interrupted her with a line of hypocrisy.

"In English. It is rude otherwise."

Klaudia didn't appreciate being undermined in front of their guest. It was rude, and her tone told him so.

"Fine. Lunch will be ready shortly. Little girl, shall we sit?"

Before she opened her mouth, Savannah remembered she was a guest in their home.

"Sure."

As she sat on the blanket-covered sofa, Savannah watched as the married couple moved their conversation into the kitchen and out of ear shot. A little boy, not much older than three, pulled himself onto the settee and jumped into Savannah's lap. She had grown up without brothers and sisters so the presence of a toddler startled her. He wasn't shy, babbling at Savannah in his native tongue. With no Polish phrases to hand, she smiled, tickling his tiny stomach. Savannah needed the infectious, innocent laughter more than she would care to admit. Hearing the roars of laughter coming from the living room, Klaudia poked her head around the door frame. Seeing her son smile was her life's own elixir. Now her son was occupied, Klaudia was free to finish the cooking. Her husband, who had nipped upstairs to change, thought it best to feed Savannah with Polish cuisine. Klaudia agreed to that at least. Her meal was healthy, hearty and wholesome. It was certain to please. Now properly dressed, Wojciech, seeing his wife plating the food, grabbed cutlery from the draw and started laying the dining table in the adjacent room. Once done, he walked to the sofa and grabbed his son from Savannah's lap.

"Lunch is ready. It smells good."

Savannah internally disputed that claim. She followed Wojciech and his son through to the dining table where his wife was serving the food. Her hands were full with ceramic bowls brimming with steaming food of different types. Klaudia couldn't hide her pleasure as she stood looking at the table full of food. Wojciech kissed his wife on the cheek as Savannah and their son took their seats.

"Wow, my darling. It looks brilliant."

She smiled as silence took hold. Savannah assumed the pause was a polite place to speak up.

"Thank you, it looks delightful."

Savannah was lying through her teeth. Scanning across the metal table, she could see nothing but bowls of beige food sloshed in sauce. Somehow, the cook had managed to turn red cabbage, grey and the cauliflower, green. If Savannah had learnt anything on her trip, it would be to not judge a book by its cover. It was a cliche in every sense yet one that was important to remember at this moment. Taking her fork, Savannah shunted the relatively safe-looking potatoes onto her plate while mentally assessing the other options. Reaching across the table, she picked up a bowl of cabbage and piled it on top of the potatoes.

"You must try this. Classic Polish dish."

Wojciech passed Savannah a silver plate, wide enough to hold six rolls of stodge. Savannah's expression gave away more than she hoped. Klaudia defended her honour.

"It's called golabki. I wrap cabbage leaves around pork."

The description was far more appetising than the aesthetic. Again, she tried to sell it to the teenager.

"With the sauce, it is best."

Without agreeing to try it, Wojciech pushed one of the rolls onto her plate before dousing it in the creamy, tomato sauce. They watched as she picked up her cutlery and sliced off a mouthful. It tasted marginally better than it looked yet Savannah still struggled to swallow it down. They looked to her for approval.

"Really nice."

Klaudia didn't decipher her lie. She grinned from ear to ear.

"Please, have more. You must be hungry."

As she spoke, Klaudia picked up the plate and slid another roll onto the teen's growing portion. Looking down at her food, Savannah regretted lying. Klaudia hadn't finished.

"You look well? Big. Have you been eating a lot?"

While grateful for their kindness, Savannah wasn't entirely convinced their hospitality merited being called fat. She laughed it off.

"I eat when I can."

"Yes. Very good."

Klaudia's comment coupled with the mountain of carbohydrates in front of her caused Savannah's appetite to disappear. Noticing his guest's indifference towards the food, Wojciech changed the conversation.

"Now, you must tell us. Where are you off to next?"

"Latvia, hopefully. If I find out where it is."

Wojciech excused himself from the table before returning moments later with a furled map of Europe. He made space at the end of the table then unrolled the paper map securing its corners with empty bowls. He circled the eastern border of Poland.

"We are here. Elblag…"

Savannah traced an imaginary route to Latvia. To her surprise, the route was much shorter than she had expected. Just Lithuania stood in the way.

"…and this is Latvia. The capital is Riga. Just here."

He pointed out the starred capital city. It was on the coast on a near, 45-degree straight line from their current point. Passport-less, the borders scared her.

"I don't have my passport. How can I get into Lithuania?"

He looked to his wife and confirmed something in Polish. She nodded but said no more.

"You do not need."

"My passport?"

"Yes."

"From Elblag, there is a bus. It can take you to Kaunas."

He circled the city in Lithuania with his finger before continuing.

"The journey is long, maybe nine or ten hours but it will get you into Lithuania."

Savannah looked at the distance between Kaunas and Riga. It was still a considerable length.

"And from there?"

"From there, I do not know. I cannot help you other than tell you that it is a popular route for freight trains."

Savannah could sense his point. Despite scanning the map for alternatives, Wojciech's proposed route seemed most reasonable. Other than the food still on her plate, her biggest worry was now how'd she get on the bus to Lithuania.

"Do I need a ticket for the bus? To Lithuania?"

Both Wojciech and his wife laughed aloud.

"Of course."

"How much?"

"Let me check."

Once more, he rose from the dining table. Klaudia's darted eyes followed him as he grabbed his laptop from the coffee table in the living room. Returning, he sat and flipped open the screen.

"Let's look."

He searched the internet for the PolskiBus website. Over his shoulder, Savannah watched as the site loaded pictures of happy couples and families ready to board the bright red buses. He searched for the next available bus. His connection was much slower than Savannah was used to.

"Ninety-three złoty."

Savannah was still none the wiser.

"How much is that in pounds?"

After searching for a currency converter, he calculated the price in sterling.

"Twenty pounds."

Savannah stayed calm, but as always, she was realistic. Klaudia, as she started clearing the plates, cut in.

"How much you have?"

"I'm ninety-three złoty short."

Klaudia stopped what she was doing.

"You have nothing?"

Wojciech pushed back his chair and rolled up the map. He looked at Savannah with sympathetic eyes.

"Please help my wife clean."

Klaudia motioned for the largest plates to be taken first. Rising to her feet, she followed the orders and carried the stacked crockery to the kitchen sink. As Klaudia emptied the food into smaller containers, Savannah started washing the plates. Soon enough, the last of the plates were clean and tidied away. It had taken shy of ten minutes yet Savannah was exhausted. Drying her hands on an ageing tea towel, Klaudia admired the clean kitchen.

"Good job."

"Thanks for the food. It was very kind."

Klaudia could only nod as she swapped places with her husband. Wojciech was tall enough that he was required to duck as he entered the kitchen. It was an old house and as such all of the door frames were built for much smaller people. He too, like his wife, admired the cleanliness.

"You did a good job."

He handed Savannah a folded piece of paper. It wasn't until she had unfolded the note that she realised that it was a twenty złoty bank note.

"If you keep the house clean and look after our son then soon ninety-three złoty will be yours."

For her ten minutes of cleaning, Savannah didn't deserve the equivalent of just under five pounds, but she was more than happy to receive it.

"I have booked you the bus out of town on Tuesday night."

Five days away.

"If you work well, I will let you go."

With her heart a flutter, she wrapped her arms around Wojciech and hugged him tightly. Klaudia appeared from behind of the doorway.

"If you are to stay here for five days, you must pretend to like our food much better. It can't be that bad."

Savannah laughed until she cried. The end was near.

* * *

Pulling the handles of her plastic shopping bag together, Savannah swung her legs out of the car. As she shut the door behind her, she caught his glance across the body of the car. Wojciech felt a tinge of sadness as he pointed out the best route to the bus station.

"You know, I'll miss having you around."

Savannah was immensely grateful but to say she would miss the domestic work would be a lie.

"I can't thank you enough."

"No need. You worked hard for it. Klaudia has enjoyed the time off," he joked.

After a slow journey to the station, she was conscious of the time.

"Down here and to the left?"

"That's it. Do you want me to walk you?"

"No. I should be fine."

He looked coy as he shuffled on his feet.

"Well, I guess this is goodbye."

"I guess."

She walked around to Wojciech's side of the car and into his open arms. While unlikely, Savannah hoped to see the family again.

"I'm sure I will meet you again one day, Wojciech."

"I think we will."

He hugged Savannah tight before releasing her into the world. As she walked away, he shouted the directions louder than need be. Clutching her new bag of spare clothes, Savannah grabbed the ticket from her pocket as she turned left into the coach station. At the gate, a guard checked her ticket and welcomed her aboard. With a press of a button, the gate opened, allowing Savannah to board the double decker, red PolskiBus. On the bottom deck, each of the window seats were taken forcing Savannah upstairs. It was much quieter on the upper level with a large section of empty seats nearest the back. Dropping her bag on the aisle seat, she slumped down beside the window. From her seat, she watched as a similarly aged teenage boy climbed the stairs and trounced down the aisle. He eyed Savannah before squeezing himself and his brimming backpack into the pair of seats adjacent to hers. Sliding the bag from his shoulders, he slipped his mobile phone out of his pocket. Holding it to his ear, he began to speak with a heavy Essex accent.

"Hello…police, please. I'd like to report a crime. There's this girl on my bus."

His eyes narrowed on Savannah.

CHAPTER TWENTY-SEVEN

"There's this girl on my bus…"

He waited and said nothing. Savannah kept her eyes to the floor. She cursed her luck.

"yeah, that's right. She's just stolen my heart."

She scoffed aloud almost as soon as he had delivered his line. Her pretend arrogance masked the softening nerves.

"Do you talk to all of the girls like that?"

Savannah wasn't impressed with his chat but couldn't deny that he was very good looking. A creased t-shirt struggled to contain his muscular torso that framed his slightly small pointed face. He smirked holding his lips tight together.

"Just the pretty ones."

Savannah, her teenagers year stunted with grief, had little chance to become fluent in men. Not many of her friends had boyfriends, so her inexperience was hardly uncommon. For all of the boy's attractiveness, Savannah knew that now, wasn't the time nor place to discover boys. She was on a mission. But still, the conversation with another English teen was rare and welcoming. Savannah's silence prompted him to start speaking once more.

"I'm Dave. David. My mates call me Chappy."

His accent and name weren't straying from the preconceived stereotype.

"Chappy."

"Yeah. And your name?"

Despite being known across Europe, Savannah felt he was slightly too close to home for the truth.

"Katie."

"Nice to meet you, Katie."

She nodded back.

"So what you doing out here then Kate?"

It wasn't even her real name yet Savannah already resented him for calling her, Kate. She thought of a lie quickly.

"Just doing some travelling. Gap year."

He imitated her voice and mocked in the usual way.

"Ahhh gap yah."

Savannah had seen the Youtube video and couldn't stop herself from laughing. It felt good. She asked him the same question.

"More of the same really, Kate. Just on the search for cheap beer."

"And how's that going?"

"It's sick. Literally. I found a place this afternoon with 50p beers. Next level."

Savannah was slightly impressed.

"Hungover then I'm guessing?"

"Just a bit. Once this fucker starts driving, I'm off for the count."

And very soon after, he did. The last of the waiting passengers clambered on board, the doors shut and the bus pulled out of the station onto the open road. Once out of the city, the road widened onto motorway allowing the bus to accelerate to a surprisingly quick speed. On the tannoy, the driver spoke both in Polish and English explaining the trip they'd be taking. With stops at most major cities on route, the journey would take nine hours and forty-five minutes, a length that worked perfectly for Savannah. If she slept now, the teen would wake in a new country at the crack of dawn feeling refreshed and energised. For once, the world was working with her. With the windows offering little in the way of view, Savannah looked across to her fellow Brit only to see him slumped across his backpack. Judging by the nasal snoring, he kept true to his word. With the day consisting solely of waiting around for the overnight bus, Savannah didn't feel tired or in need of sleep. Upstairs, the majority of the seats were empty. It had darkened quickly, and now with just the above seat lighting providing relief from the darkness, the bus felt cosy. Taking a jumper from her plastic carrier bag, Savannah rolled a makeshift pillow and pushed it against the window. With her head softened by the fabric, she curled into a foetal sleeping position and knowing a big day was ahead, she shut her eyes and willed for her body to fall asleep.

* * *

Dave had been watching her sleep since his head banged on the window as the bus took a tight turn. He had understood why she called herself Katie but not why she hadn't disguised herself. What's in a name. Since leaving the UK a few weeks ago, Dave had seen pictures of Savannah in almost every city. When she went missing, nobody believed she was alive. Even when she had allegedly been spotted, nobody believed it was her. Dave had to believe it now. He had no choice. If the thought of the reward money in his bank account didn't attract Dave, then he'd be lying. As he looked at her sleeping, it was all he could think about. Yet, he knew the story and wasn't sure what to make of the runaway. Everyone did. Dad died of cancer, Mum died abroad. Nobody knew where. He wondered if it was Lithuania. What other reason would she have for travelling from Poland to Kaunus. Another announcement sounded out as the bus arrived at the penultimate stop. Dave spoke aloud. "Another shithole."

His words were accurate. This town, much like the previous, was identically grey. It was a long way from Dagenham. Pulling out of the stop, the town dropped away to reveal the rising sun over a field of dead crops. In the amber light, even death looked pretty. He caught the reflection of Savannah in the window. She looked nice enough but with the plastic bag of old clothes, she stood out from the other passengers. He watched as she suddenly lurched forward in her seat. Her body moved before her eyes had opened. Dave didn't believe in ghosts, but right now he did. Savannah looked possessed. Now awake, she screamed out in pain. Her hands reached around her stomach. After so much ache, she was well rehearsed in her actions. Still in a semi-sleep state, she feared a sudden expulsion of sick. There was nowhere to run, no bucket to catch it. Savannah could see Dave staring at her as she wrestled with the pain. His lingering stare didn't help proceedings. Squeezing her belly tight, the pain subsided. She took a deep breath of warm, regurgitated air. Dave looked on in disbelief.

"Are you alright Kate love?"

He had remembered to use the correct name. Savannah knew she wasn't. Her belly bulged with what felt like wind. It spun around, pushing pain upwards. She self-consciously yelped. Now mellowing, she turned to Dave and apologised.

"Nah, don't apologise love. You look white as a sheet."

"I think it's appendicitis. I've had it for weeks."

His voice deepened in seriousness.

"You should go to a hospital. That ain't normal."

"I will if I get a chance."

"Have you got insurance?"

Dave's question was a loaded one. Savannah lied once more.

"Yeah."

"See, I don't think you have."

Savannah spun her legs out of the window seat and spread across the pair. Her voice was sharp.

"What?"

"If I were going to run away from home, I don't think I'd get insurance."

Savannah had been rumbled. As she decided whether to continue the lie or admit all, Dave jumped in.

"Because that's what you've done isn't it Savannah. Run away from home. I know who you are, everyone does."

She said nothing. He carried on.

"I thought you were dead. Most people still do. What are you doing?"

It was a simple question and one that Savannah had contemplated many times over the months. Still, she remained silent.

"Just by wearing a hoody and getting on the bus in the middle of the night isn't going to fool me. I could dob you in, get some handsome dosh and I wouldn't have to worry about the shitty fifty pence beers."

She tested his resolve.

"Do it then."

"Alright."

He reached for his flip phone and held it to his ear.

"Police, please. I've got a stupid girl here who think's everything is dandy."

Dave chucked the phone onto the seat. After calling his bluff, Savannah held all of the cards.

"You've already done that joke. It wasn't all that funny the first time around."

"Next time it won't be a joke."

Savannah laughed in his face.

"I'm serious. I've seen your Auntie on the telly. Crying her eyes out, begging for you to come home. Begging for you to be alive. I don't think any of this is to be laughed at."

Savannah scoffed at the suggestion.

"They're crocodile tears. She was one of the reasons I ran away in the first place."

"Not her, your other Aunt. I can't remember her na—"

"Jules?"

"Yeah, Julia."

"She was crying?"

'On Crimewatch, yeah."

Savannah didn't like the thought. She had never wanted to hurt her Auntie. Her eyes felt heavy under the weight of emotion.

"I thought she understood."

"They want you home."

The conversation had faltered by the time they had arrived into Kaunas. Savannah was left to reflect whereas Dave regretted going in hard. Both gazed out of the window as the countryside developed into city streets. Her silence said more than any words could. As the coach slowed into the stop, the doors opened and the few remaining passengers took to the cobbled streets. Dave went first down the steps and out of the bus before waiting on the pavement for Savannah to disembark.

"Where are you off to next?"

"Why do you care?"

"I want to help you. You are clearly on a mission."

Savannah couldn't help but be charmed by Dave's familiar voice and good looks.

"The station. I need to get a train."

"I'll walk with you."

As they walked, the pair resumed their conversation but with a subject matter far less contentious than before. Stopping at a street map, the duo admired the tree-lined avenues kissed with light by the morning sun. It was still early, and as such, most of the cafes and bars that made up the street were still opening up. Following the signposts, Dave and Savannah rounded the corner onto a much smaller street. In the middle of the walkway, three telephone boxes stood unused. They were red, much like the ones back home, only these were capped with what looked to be concrete bowler hats. Savannah was attracted to their quirkiness. Feeling in her pocket for the converted money Wojciech had given her in exchange for cleaning the house, Savannah ran towards the box.

"Two minutes."

He knew what she was doing before Savannah had a chance to pull close the door. He grabbed her wrist and yanked her out of the telephone box. "No. They'll track you."

Flushing red, she realised the errors of her ways. Dave let his bag fall from his shoulders then leant it against the wall. He pulled out his phone from the top pocket.

"Use this."

"I can't. It'll cost you a fortune."

Dave was willing to take the cost. Savannah still objected.

"They'll be able to track you though?"

"We aren't going the same way. They can track me all they want."

Reluctantly, Savannah took the phone and began typing in the number engrained in her mind. Dave could tell Savannah wasn't well travelled.

"You need the country code. It's plus four, four instead of the zero."

After retyping, Savannah pressed the green call button. She heard the dial tone ringing as it attempted to connect cross-country. Soon, it was ringing. Savannah listened as the person on the other end of the line picked up. She sounded tired.

"Hello?"

"Jules, it's me. I've got to be quick."

"Sav?"

"Yeah, Jules, it's Sav.

"Oh my goodness, Sav. Are you okay?"

"Yeah, I'm fine. I'll be home soon I promise. I didn't ever think it would take me this long. I'm so sorry."

Jules' voice was rushed.

"Sav, where are you?"

"It doesn't matter just know that I'm safe. Nobody needs to look for me or try and find me, I'll be home as soon as I can."

She didn't believe Savannah at all.

"Are they making you say this? Who are you with?"

"No, Jules. I'm fine. Honestly. Just know that I'll be home soon, and I miss you."

"Sav, come home now. Please."

Savannah was resolute. She could feel the tears beginning to form.

"I can't. There is something I need to do. Look, I've got to go. I love you."

Savannah slammed the flip phone shut and forced it back into Dave's hand. Unable to contain her emotions, she let the tears flood from her eyes as she slid down the wall next to Dave's bag. If the streets were busy, it would have been some scene. Yet, with just the pair of Brits present, Dave felt helpless. He waited for Savannah to compose herself. Thankfully, he was in no rush.

CHAPTER TWENTY-EIGHT

Kneeling on the floor, Dave patted Savannah's shoulder as she snuffled the tears back up her nose. He swept the hair from her face and tilted her chin towards his face. He waited until she could fully open her eyes.

"Let's go. At least cry on a bloody train."

She didn't take her eyes off of his. Realising what he said was true, she wiped her eyes with the palm of each hand and stood up from the floor. As she did, Dave heaved his backpack onto his defined shoulders. Without waiting for Dave, Savannah picked up her bag and walked ahead. It wasn't the appropriate time to be emotional. Savannah had to man up and plough on. Catching up with her, Dave grinned as he spoke.

"So you're good now?"

"Yeah I feel much better," she lied. "Thanks for letting me use your phone. I appreciate it."

"Hey, no worries, you were quick." he chuckled to himself.

"Hopefully it won't cost you the earth."

"If it does, the first beer is on you."

"What's to say they'll be a first beer?"

The final signpost put on them on course with the station.

"I'm heading home soon and hopefully so are you."

"Am I?"

Her sarcasm didn't break through. Approaching the station, the pair stopped before the main door.

"Yes, and once you do, I'm going to come find you."

"And how are you going to know when I'm home?"

"I'm sure we'll hear about it."

With that, he spun away from Savannah and walked off. Turning, he walked backwards before shouting.

"Top story, England's missing Orphan is found….,"

He made the dun, dun, dun sounds himself.

"…ALIVE!"

If the concourse were busy, Savannah wouldn't have been laughing nearly as much as she was now. As he turned the corner back the way they came, he shouted down the road.

"See you Sav."

Less than twelve hours after she had met Dave, he had gone. It was a fleeting meet but once she was grateful for. Now alone, she turned and faced the steps leading to the three wooden doors. Near the roof of the building, giant letters spelt out *Geležinkelio stotis* which Savannah hoped was native for train station. Pushing open the door, the station was much quieter than she had anticipated. An ornate grandfather clock stood tall in the middle of the modestly-sized concourses ticking with every second. As she moved closer, Savannah read the time to be just after eight in the morning. In the small plaza, the floor was tiled with marbled slabs. Faux columns formed a spaced perimeter around the room leaving gaps for the ticket office opposite the door. It drew serious differences between itself and the other stations that Savannah had visited or travelled through. A departure board, large enough to display just three lines of information, was affixed to the wall above the glass ticket booth. If the information was to be believed, then no trains were currently scheduled to depart. Savannah hoped it was broken. Unlike in Paris, there were no ticket barriers or gates onto the platforms. Instead, another wooden door, marked to the trains, was propped open by the base of a signpost. It seemed too easy. Savannah, checking for any watching staff, scanned the room. It was empty if not for a couple of seemingly lost travellers consulting a map at the furthest end from the teen. Squeezing between the door, she followed the hallway to another ajar door which opened out onto a platform. Moving through the space, Savannah looked across the empty tracks to a train a few platforms away. As she emerged, a family of three younger girls and their mother gawped at Savannah. Disliking their stare, Savannah quickened her pace as she walked down the length of the platform to a set of stairs that crossed over to where the only train waited. Walking over the tracks, Savannah could smell nothing but the pungent fumes of diesel lingering in the morning air. It was a smell that Savannah had once liked yet now the slightest irritant in her noise caused significant discomfort. Descending the second set of stairs, Savannah arrived on the platform. If not for the train, the entire length was empty. Walking forward, she peered into the carriages and wondered if this was the train Wojciech had spoke about. Nearest the stairs, it looked normal. Eight passenger carriages connected together, pulled by an engine at the front. After the eighth carriage, the train looked less welcoming to customers. Cargo carriages, each open and containing a plethora of boxes, latched themselves onto the passenger trains. Savannah was confused by its destination. Nearing the end of the track, she stepped into one of the trains and instantly regretted it. Not before her foot had touched the deck, a booming voice shouted at her from behind. He was speaking in a language Savannah assumed was Lithuania but its origin was unclear. She sprinted from the carriage, bolting down the length of the platform. As she reached the stairs, she held the rail and leaped over a number of steps at a time. Only when she reached the first platform did she stop running. Savannah's panting and struggle to catch her breath gave more reason for the family to stare. With her options limited, Savannah resigned to momentary defeat by slumping onto the long wooden bench. From there, she watched as the mother to the young girls crept to the edge of the platform. She leant her body with the curve of the track and kept still. Her ears warned her eyes. Seeing what she had wanted to, the mother hurried her children from their seats and held them tight on the platform edge. Savannah could hear what they were waiting for. She moved from the bench to garner a better vantage point. In the near distance, a slow moving cargo train crawled along the tracks. Inside, Savannah saw only cargo stacked high on top of each other. It didn't look fit for human travel. Disappointed, she returned to the bench to rest her legs. As the train crawled past, the mother of the girls flickered on the spot. She was kissing her children on the head while playing with their ponytails. Since entering the train station, Savannah felt nothing but confusion. Just as the last cargo carriages rolled past, the mother and her children began to run in the direction of the train. Slightly faster than the train, the oldest daughter held on to the side of the wagon before jumping into the carriage. Scooping her youngest child into the arms, the mother encouraged the middle daughter to do the same. As she did, the woman leapt with her child into the carriage. Savannah, seeing the last of the train's carriage disappear down the platform, was dumbfounded. If she had known the unusual boarding procedure, Savannah would have been on a train out of Lithuania. She hoped for another chance. With the bench her only company, Savannah extended her legs and waited. There was no clock on the platform yet she wasn't waiting for long. After numerous false calls, Savannah rose from the bench on the sound of an engine and peered down the platform. Only then did the trepidation set in. Holding out her hand, she waited for the right carriage to roll into grasping distance. Rejecting the first few carriages out of fear, Savannah waited until one took her fancy. Midway through, a set of wagons each with wide openings as doors, trundled past her. As they did, she began to run. Reaching the carriage, she grabbed her hand onto the handle and held tight. Her feet moved quicker than she had thought possible. With the end of the platform approaching, it was now or never. Letting go of the handle, Savannah leapt into the carriage, crashing onto the floor. Bringing her head from the floor, she looked into the carriage. Stacks of cargo were spaced out leaving plenty of room for Savannah to inhabit. Once stood, the picture changed completely. From behind a large tower of boxes came a young girl and her much older mother. They looked to be of European descent but the mother had much darker skin than her daughter. Each smiled at Savannah as she stared at their faces. She asked for information.

"Is this to Riga?"

"Riga. Yes."

As they nodded, Savannah could tell they spoke little to no English. The lack of potential conversation didn't worry the teenager in the slightest. She was on route to Riga and nothing could stop her.

CHAPTER TWENTY-NINE

Savannah tore a chunk of bread from the loaf that had been offered around the carriage. A family; a mother, father and teenage daughter, had come well prepared for the journey. In their bags, each had enough food to last for a journey around the world let alone across the Lithuanian border. They had watched Savannah jump onto the carriage and seeing her alone, they moved out from behind of the boxes in the far corner. Along with the other young girl and her mother, the carriage homed six passengers as it rattled down the tracks. Unfortunately for their boredom, it seemed none of the groups spoke in the same tongue. They attempted to converse in English but with only one native speaker, the trying was tough. Savannah was grateful for the food, and truthfully the silence. She hadn't eaten since the evening of the day previous and her hunger had recently become increasingly unsatisfiable. With the train still rolling through the urban areas surrounding the city where Savannah had boarded the train, it was wise for the group to cower in the corner of the carriages. From behind a box, the view outside was obstructed but crucially it was impossible to be seen by onlookers. It wasn't until near thirty minutes of train riding that the exterior scenery transitioned into greenery. Savannah took the first steps towards the wide opening in the side of the carriage. She could see nothing but coniferous trees and pylons whizz past the now, much faster train. The morning was a foggy one. Whispers of lingering grey hung in the air limiting their view to the tree line. In mid-February, the temperature inside of the train was cold. Nearest the door, it was infinitely colder. Savannah noted to wait for the sun to burn away the fog and heat the day before she stood admiring the view again. With no conductor, information screen or onboard announcements, the length of the journey was a mystery to the teen. She knew not if the train would be home for an hour or a day. Whether they had meant to or not, both groups of people had carved out their own space, their own territory, on board. At the far end, the family of three spread themselves across the long boxes that were pushed against the wall. Opposite, the young girl rested her head in her mother's lap as they laid together on the floor. Any sound outside rushed the groups further into the corner. Savannah had seemingly been allocated the middle ground. Atop an empty oil drum, she sat dangling her legs and waited. As she rested, her mind wandered to Latvia. Since leaving the SchulzVossen building in Germany, the country had been her ultimate goal. Everything she had done, every person she had met, every country travelled through had been building to Latvia. And now she was close. She felt it. If the other passengers were right, this train would take her right to the capital, Riga. Right where she needed to be. Casting her mind back to her meeting with PC Nichols, She had never forgotten the details of her mother's death. The cause of death, suicide, was, to Savannah at least, contentious. It was an act of cowardice she knew her mother wasn't capable of. Yet still, Savannah wanted to see where she hung from, where she orphaned her only daughter. From Riga, she would go there first. The name was clear; AgriLab, the route from Riga not so. If she was made to walk, she knew that the journey, however long, would be bearable. It would put the teen in touching distance of the truth she so craved. Savannah felt giddy, filled an odd mix of emotions. At one end, her journey was nearing the conclusion and for that the excitement was evident yet the goal she had been working towards was the place her mother had died. Whatever the truth, Savannah was fearful of bringing month-old emotions back to the forefront. For now, she daren't worry herself into a frenzy. Every so often, the train would rumble through urban areas. As the train approached a station, it slowed to a crawl as it did in Kaunas. Past the town of Siauliai, the train stopped only at the platform of Joniskis. Peering out through the opening, Savannah, noting a similar style of sign to the previous train stations, assumed they were still in Lithuania. Progress was slower than she had hoped. With the platform empty, Savannah took the opportunity to stretch her legs. She managed just one loop of the space before the train started moving again and Savannah had to jump on back. The others looked at her as if she was crazy. Climbing back onto the barrel, the boredom set in. With little to do other than think, Savannah tapped her fingers against the echoey oil can. She created a beat that at first, played well with the sound of the train against the tracks but soon became an irritant to those with her. Both the mother and daughter sat up from their slump to stare Savannah into silence. She was irritating herself as well as the others. Dropping onto the floor, she stood by the opening and let the wind rush over her body. Leaving behind the towns and cities, the train roared through the countryside at an impressive speed. Her view was that of flat, arable land. Too cold to grow crops, the fields laid bare, awaiting their use. From the height of the tracks, Savannah could see for miles. It was a view that only amplified how far she had travelled. After a period of nothingness, the train snaked through a small settlement on the edge of the woods. Soon, the flat, barren land become a busy, luscious forest. Tall, wise trees stood littered through the forest in a planted pattern. Their style and deep velvet colour reminded Savannah of Christmas time. Her dad would take Savannah to a local farm to pick out the tree that would take centre stage in their living room. These trees were identical in style just much taller than they had ever picked. With a dusting of snow on the forest floor, the view was plainly magical. However, the beauty of the view didn't stop Savannah from shivering as the sun was obscured behind the pines. If her bag wasn't more than an arm's length away, she would have reached for her hoody to keep herself warm. The young girl had joined Savannah in admiring the view. Her mother was sleeping and much like Savannah faced boredom. As she stood at the opening, Savannah watched her face light up. Her mouth was open in pure joy, her eyes brimming with happiness. She went to speak. "Snow. My first."

Her accent was heavy and her English barely recognisable, but Savannah could still understand her point. Seeing the young girl's face light up at the sight of snow reminded Savannah how the little things in life could provide so much happiness. Much like the young girl, Savannah couldn't take her eyes from the scenery. Everything seemed well. An hour had passed since the train last slowed through a station. Approaching the next, Savannah hid behind her drum and focused her eyes on the platform. Missing the first, she concentrated hard on the second sign. It was shaped and coloured differently to the Lithuanian style. White text printed on circular red background read as Jelgava. She was in Latvia. It was an assumption, but a merited one. Soon after leaving the city, the forest resumed. In this area, however, the snow that had created such a pretty scene miles back, was nowhere to be found. Another set of tracks had appeared to the left of the train as the forest path widened between the trees. Above, hanging wires resumed their flow from pylon to pylon between the tracks. Overgrown grass rose up through stones lying next to the sleeper boards. Unlike the beauty of the forest's natural symmetry, the train's path was messy, manmade decay. It continued on in uniformity for miles, keeping regular distance with the forest to either side. Past the densest part of the forest, the train's brakes screeched in an attempt to stop the hurtling train. Ignoring the howls of the underbelly, the train carried on forward. Relenting to the squeals, the train heaved to a stop pushing Savannah back into the carriage. The family looked to Savannah as if she was omniscient. She knew that the nature of the stop, unexpected and quick, wasn't a good sign but, there, in the moment, Savannah refused to acknowledge the fact. Despite the forest being clear of onlookers, she decided against peering out of the window. The silence was unnerving. Her heart rate started to quicken. As they waited motionlessly, Savannah reassured herself in an attempt to calm down. It wasn't working. Abruptly, the birds cackling in the trees took flight and flew away from the area. They had heard something the carriage hadn't. Moments later, their ears made no mistake as the sound echoed down the track. Again, they heard the same although now, the sound of reflecting metal followed soon after. Somebody had a gun, and they were firing it. Stood nearest the door, Savannah leant her head back onto the metal with her ear in the open air. Closing her eyes, she listened to the shouting voices. They were yelling in English. It wasn't their native language yet they spoke it well. She could hear a voice ordering people out of the train and instructing others which cargo to take it. He seemed in control. A few minutes since the train had stopped, the voices became much clearer. They were coming closer to Savannah's carriage. She had moved to the corner where the families had come together. Despite not being the eldest there, she took it upon herself to comfort the children. As they cried, she curled their hair around her finger, wiping away the tears.

"Don't worry. It is only a robbery. They will get the cargo they want and leave us."

Savannah, addressing those who didn't understand English, spoke more to comfort herself than her neighbours. With the engine switched off and silenced, the group could hear movement in the carriage next to theirs. The robbers were close. Soon enough, a gun-wielding thug appeared at track level. He pointed the gun into the carriage and shouted his orders.

"If you move, you die."

You didn't have to be a proficient English speaker to understand what he was asking of the carriage's inhabitants. As he pulled himself into the carriage, another armed man followed him. Savannah hoped the parents didn't pull any brave moves. However poetic it may be, she didn't want to die in the same country as her mother. Ignoring the cargo, the two men advanced towards the corner where the group had huddled. Both men were dressed solely in black from the heavy, steel-capped boats to the balaclava over their heads. Speaking in a foreign language, the first, bigger man laughed to himself. He lowered himself to their level.

278

Casting his eye over the group, the man's actions were unclear. Pointing the gun towards them, he turned back to his colleague.

"Two pretty ones."

Savannah couldn't decipher his accent. She didn't want to. Within a second, he grabbed the hand of the youngest girl and pulled her across the room to the doorway. Scooping her into his arms, he chucked the girl into the waiting hands of another thug loitering on the edge of the tracks. Leaping to his feet, the father screamed out for his daughter. He wasn't about to let his daughter be kidnapped. As he shouted, the gunman turned and pushed the father back. He repeated his sentiments.

"You move, you die."

Still, the father attempted to rescue his daughter. Angered by his attempts, the gunman turned to the side and fired a bullet into the metalwork of the carriage. It pierced a hole all the way through. Undeterred by the warning, the father pushed his way past in search of his daughter. As he went to jump down onto the tracks, the gunman nearest the door knocked him out cold with a punch that wouldn't look out of place in a heavyweight boxing match. His wife screamed for justice. They weren't done. Kicking his unconscious body to the side, the bigger man steamed towards the other girl. Her mother had known it was coming, and having seen the much stronger man succumb to a punch, turned away from the action. Her eyes flooded with tears as her daughter was marched out of the carriage and chucked to the ground. The first gunman looked around the carriage before calling his colleague closer. He pointed towards Savannah.

"Is chocolate too old?"

She could see him licking his lips underneath the balaclava. He walked towards Savannah, crouched to her height and breathed in her face as he spoke.

"A sweet piece of chocolate. All for me."

He grabbed Savannah's wrist and yanked her closer to him.

"You're coming with me, sweetie."

Savannah's resistance was weak. She put up no fight. As he marched her to the doorway, the gunman pushed her onto the tracks. It was some height and the fall not just cut her knees but sprained her ankle also. Forced up, her hands were tied with a piece of muslin while her mouth was gagged with a cut sock. Breathing through her nose was taking its toll on her lungs. From behind, she was kicked forward and guided towards an opening in the forest tree-line. On her sprained ankle, the walk, just a few steps from the train, was agonising. Moving further from the train, the screams of broken hearted mothers gradually softened. No-one was crying for Savannah. Gunshots continued to sound behind her as she struggled into a clearing between the trees. Counting quickly, Savannah realised that six other girls had been tied and gagged in the same way as she had. She could see the girls from her carriage stood together, tears streaming from their puffy, red eyes. Savannah, realising she was the oldest of the group, held back the emotions and tried to portray an image of strength. Internally, she was scared, gutted and broken. Savannah blamed herself. She should have known that her journey into Latvia wouldn't be as easy. Joining the group of girls, her future looked bleak. If death wasn't near, a life of misery surely awaited. In the present day, she stood tall amongst the crying girls as they waited for the last of the captives to walk down the path. The crew of four disguised men formed a human cage around the girls as they led them down the narrow track. Not one of the girls dared to stray from the pack. With the forest all around them, safety seemed a long way away. Ahead, the dirt path snaked beyond the crest of a small hill and out of sight. Their destination was unclear. Near the back, the pace was slower than the captors liked.

"Walk faster you bitch." shouted the tail of the group.

With his command came even more tears. Savannah struggled to stay calm. Her white trainers had become dirtied as the group kicked up dust walking in unison. Once over the hill, the apparent end was in sight. At the end of the dirt path, the forest dropped away and revealed two black vans parked rear-facing. Wherever they were going wasn't near. Getting closer, the lead gunman split the girls into two groups. He dragged Savannah's tied hands over to the van. Yanking open the door, the gunman pushed Savannah into the back of the vehicle. She had been in a similar space before. After three other girls had joined her in the van, the lead gunman reached into his pocket, pulling out four pieces of black fabric. Taking each girl by the hand, he jerked them closer and slid the loose fabric over their heads before tying it at the back. With the hood now obscuring her face, Savannah let the tears flow. Gagged, tied and blinded, the outcome didn't look good. Her heart ached. Slamming shut the door, the engine kicked in, and the van accelerated down the bumpy, rocky road. Unable to move, and now in complete darkness, all the girls could do was scream. They screamed for salvation, for help, for anything other than this. Helpless to the situation, Savannah joined them. Her heart hoped someone would be able to hear their screams and send help. Her head knew they'd never be found. Soon, the other girls realised this brutal truth. There was nothing they could do. From there on in, the van rumbled in on complete and utter silence.

CHAPTER THIRTY

With her ankle throbbing in pain, the journey had been particularly unpleasant for Savannah. Tied behind her back, her hands started to cramp under the tight ligature of the fabric. Savannah sat contemplating how she ended up gagged in the back of a van on the way to her early grave. Ignoring the masses of variables that sent her here, Savannah focused only on the first train at Kaunas station. If she ran, instead of watching the other family leap, she'd most likely be in Riga heading to the factory. Her indecisiveness bugged her at the greatest of times and not least, now she had been kidnapped. Aside from the groan or sniffle every few minutes, the girls sat in silence. It was for that reason that Savannah's scream were all the more audible. Her stomach cried out once more, only this time the pain was exponentially greater than she had ever experienced before. With her hands tied, the pain couldn't be soothed and squeezed as she had grown used to. Her torment was clear to the others even in the pitch black. As the bumpy road flattened out, the van slowed, and her pain eased. Savannah hoped for light but feared the worst. Quickly after, the van yanked to a stop. Within seconds, the doors had been opened, and the girls were yanked from the car. A voice ordered them to stay where they were. In the distance, the sound of a struggling engine could be heard. Once it had stopped, the same procedure followed. The other girls weren't as quiet. As soon as the door had opened, Savannah could hear their screams as they walked closer. Taking their hoods off, the girls were free to look around. Her eyes, now exposed to the sunlight, burned with the brightness of the day. She squinted at her surroundings, her stomach still aching from the outburst of pain in the van. They had arrived at a derelict factory that looked to have been devoid of operation for many years previous. It consisted of three sections. Nearest the group, a 2 story bolt on building, made entirely of chipped red bricks, housed a large door and smashed in windows. Splinters of glass clung resolutely to the frame. A paved patio stepped down onto a dusty forecourt which wrapped around the whole of the complex. Adjoined to the brown building, a wider three-story square stood windowless and graffitied. Remnants of the glass windows, now shattered and crushed, joined the weeds along the base of the wall. Tag signs and cartoon-style artwork adorned the sand-coloured brick walls that formed the factory. A third building, two stories taller than the previous, towered over the rest of the complex. Although made of similar material to that of the first, the building looked much newer with each of its many windows still in place. Graffiti had been washed from the side of the building leaving the faintest of outlines on the hardened brick work. Across the top of the building, an adventurous artist had graffitied over the painted name of the previous occupants. In front of the group, a barbed, electrified wire fence was being opened, leading them through to the furthest building. Shunted forward, Savannah followed a man through the fence and past the middle building. With her ankle hurting move when stood still than walking, she took the time to weave between the pieces of glass and smashed bricks as she led the way. Approaching the building, the man again walked ahead to open a steel door on the reverse side of the building. Once he had it unlocked, he called for Savannah to follow him. Inside, the air was damp and smelly. The door opened into a smaller cupboard-sized room which led into the long factory floor. Half of the room was lit while the other side remained in darkness. On the left side, the broken windows welcomed light into the room. The glow stretched to the centre where steel columns held up the roof. Around the bases of the columns, the concrete had chipped away revealing the foundations below. Torn strays of red tape were tied around the columns warning of danger. To Savannah, this entire place was dangerous. Walking the length of the room, the girls arrived at another unmarked door. He struggled to unlock the door before giving in and asking for help from his easily-frustrated partner. Once open, the girls followed their captors into a much smaller room. In the centre, a hook on a pulley hung from the ceiling above the sandy, dirty floor. Along the left-hand wall, torn boxes and empty oil cans dotted themselves haphazardly. The room was double height with spaces, that were once home to windows, carved into upper walls. It was light and airy but cold and creepy. On the right, a series of three doors, marked with Latvian words, looked locked. Columns, concrete unlike the previous room, protruded from each of the four corners of the room. Now seated along the wall, the girls awaited their instruction as Savannah's stomach, bulged in pain as it faced increased pressure. She looked down the line. In the light, she could see their faces more clearly. With red, puffy eyes, the girls looked much younger than Savannah hoped them to be. Her fellow passengers from the carriage looked at her for guidance. She didn't know what to do. There was no way out. One by one, their mouth gags were ripped from their mouths. Last in the line, Savannah craved a deep breath of air. Untying the fabric from Savannah's mouth, the man spoke to all of the girls.

"If you talk or scream. I will make sure you never speak again. No excuse."

He didn't seem entirely convinced by his own words. While Savannah didn't believe him, the whimpering girls further down the line most definitely did. Saying nothing, he stood motionless, keeping his eyes on the girls in front of him. His focus was so that as a fellow thug whispered into his ear, he flinched. Regaining composure, he listened to the message. He nodded approval as the message deliverer walked backwards and kicked open the third door on the right.

"You little bitches will come here when I say."

He surveyed the line of mostly-crying girls then pointed at a slight girl with short, brown hair furthest away from Savannah.

"You."

Taking her eyes from the floor, she dared to look him in the eye.

"Come here."

As she struggled to her feet, her hands wiped away tears. Her steps were slow and measured. Unsatisfied with her progress, he rushed forward and yanked her through the doorway. It slammed behind her. For now, they were alone in the room. Nobody dared to speak. Savannah scanned the space for a way out. For once, she wanted to be caught by the police. It seemed impossible. If she stood to look for a way out, she'd be spotted by the thugs and most likely punished. If she stayed seated, she would never find a way out. Her bundles of confidence had gone missing. She whispered to the girl sat next to her.

"What shall I do?"

The girl looked at Savannah and said nothing. She was afraid and quite rightly so. A few minutes later, the man returned alone. He called on the next girl to join him. Mindful of punishment, she walked much quicker than the previous. At this rate, Sav would be last through the door. Without knowing what stood behind the door, she wasn't sure if that was a blessing or a curse. Over the next ten minutes, more girls had left than remained. Just Savannah and two other girls awaited the mystery behind the door. Next up was the youngest girl from her carriage. When called, she burst into tears. Her hands trembled as she stood to her feet. Looking at Savannah for help, the girl quivered on the spot. Savannah's encouragement in the form of a smile wasn't working. Across her journey, she had relied on the kindness and goodness of others. When she fell, someone was always there to pick her up. In this factory, amongst these girls, Savannah was the leaning post. She didn't like that the roles had reversed. Fed up of her hesitation, the man grabbed the girl and marched her through the doorway. Just two girls were left. If Savannah were about to be killed, and she considered that to be a strong possibility, these were her last minutes on earth. It wasn't how she had envisaged dying. She was sure her dad felt the same way. As she contemplated the afterlife, he came for Savannah's sniffling neighbour. Truthfully, Savannah was grateful for the peace. Her alone time only lasted for a few minutes before the door swung open and he stepped out of the room. She waited for him to look her in the eyes before she stood to her feet. Taking a deep breath, Savannah felt her heart beat rapidly increase. Feeling the nerves in every step, and the pain in her ankle, she headed straight for the doorway. His balaclava stretched as he smiled. Once the door had shut, the lights flickered on. She followed him down the corridor where another door, cut into the wall on the left, opened into a shower room. Around the square room, shower heads hung from the wall above metal taps covered in limescale.

"Strip."

She waited for him to turn but it seemed her modesty would not be accounted for. He repeated himself but with more force.

"Strip."

He gathered the clothes from the floor once she had stepped out of her leggings before slapping her bum as she moved into the room. The tiled floor, slanted towards the centre drain, was even colder on her feet where the water had run. With ten or so to chose from, Savannah first stood under the corner shower. In the Latvian winter, she hoped for hot water. Turning the tap to its furthest point, she stood aside and waited for the hot water to kick in. Holding her hand under the trickling stream, she realised it wasn't heating. Trying another, the same problem persisted. She could hear his laughs from behind. Knowing it would give him too much pleasure, she didn't turn. Savannah twisted the handle to the coldest point and braved the chill. Her legs were cut and bruised. She was fatter than she liked to be. Her hair was greasy and matted. She was a version of herself unrecognisable from the Savannah of old. Keeping her eyes forward, she resisted the urge to look at herself. It was too much. Frozen to the spot, she let the water trickle over her head and run down her torso. The cold satisfied not a bone in her body but her ankle which welcomed the numbing water. Until the water had shut off, Savannah had forgotten about the pain. Turning, she covered herself to face the perving man leant against the wooden door frame clutching a towel. As she moved forward to grab it, he chucked the towel high above her head. His trick may have worked for the younger girls, but Savannah wasn't that naive. With her hands protecting her modesty, she walked back before kneeling to the towel. His prying eyes couldn't hide his disappointment. Drying herself, she wrapped the towel around her body and followed after the man who had disappeared out of sight. At the end of the corridor, he stood dangling a piece of fabric.

"Wear this."

Chucking the fabric towards Savannah, he held his breath. As she caught it, her towel dropped to the floor. She unravelled the fabric and slipped what appeared to be a nightie over her head before he had chance to get an erection. Most definitely handmade, the dress was cropped just above the knee while the flimsy fabric offered little in modesty. Savannah wasn't stupid, she knew it was designed that way. Now dressed, the perv opened the door to a familiar room. Savannah recognised the chipped concrete and steel columns almost instantaneously. As the door shut behind them, Savannah looked across to see the rest of the girls lined up against the wall. They were all dressed in the same piece of fabric. Most were still crying, the cold water doing little for their puffy eyes. Savannah wondered if they'd all been subjected to the same treatment as she had. She hoped not but feared it true. Pushing her forward, the man barked at Savannah.

"Sit down, choco bitch."

Racial slurs were nothing new. Savannah squeezed herself between two of the bigger girls in a selfish bid for warmth. It seemed that the man who had showered the girls was nearing the end of his shift. He waited until another balaclava-wearing thug entered the room before spinning out of the door. Savannah was happy enough to see him go but was clever enough to know that all of the patrolling twats would be of similar mould. He started afoot.

"You will speak if spoken to."

His voice was firm and sounded much less European than his counterparts.

"You will address me as Igor and nothing less."

Savannah doubted Igor was his real name, but she was in no position to criticise.

"You will be safe here. If you try to escape, you will be punished."

His rules were met with an anxious silence.

"Do I make myself clear?"

After so long in silence, speaking didn't come easily for the captive girls. Igor repeated himself.

"I said, do I make myself clear?"

While some mumbled acceptance, most stayed quiet. He wasn't satisfied.

"Yes, what?"

Savannah, realising nobody else would, went for it.

"Yes, Igor."

Igor smiled as Savannah spoke. His eyes followed the voice.

"Good girl."

Savannah wasn't sure whether to thank her captor. She decided against it.

"Being a good girl here brings reward. Little bitch, you can come first."

He held out his hand as he walked towards the teen. Inside, she was trembling like a leaf in a storm but staying strong for the other girls meant she stood upright and followed Igor confidently. He walked Savannah out of the room and through a different corridor. At the end of the narrow walkway, a door had been left ajar. As they walked, Igor turned to his hostage.

"Be kind to this man. If you act smart, he will hurt you."

Savannah appreciated the warning-cum-threat even though she hadn't planned on pulling any fast moves. Igor had stopped in his tracks five metres from the door. Following his lead, she also froze.

"No. Go on."

It felt as if even the thugs were afraid of this man. Presenting an unfounded confidence, she quickened her pace to the door. Her anticipation was far greater than her fear. Pushing through the door, the hinge creaked as she stepped through the gap. Just a desk separated Savannah from the man gazing out of one of the few functioning windows. Her footsteps echoed on the hard, concrete floor. She waited for him to turn. His attempts at intimidation were working. As the seconds passed, her nerves became palpable. He spoke to the wall.

"My pretty girl. It's nice to meet you."

Turning to face Savannah, he double-blinked. She spoke before he had the chance.

"I believe we've already met."

CHAPTER THIRTY-ONE

It took him a few moments to register what she was saying. He didn't
believe who was stood in front of him. Now her confidence had faltered,
Savannah refused to acknowledge the truth. It couldn't be. It felt
impossible to her. His powerful front had taken a hit. As their meeting
became personal, his ruthlessness became redundant. She knew this too.
Her rigid back relaxed beneath the fabric night dress. She walked
forward and sat at the desk. He followed suit. She waited for him to
speak, to explain himself. He had no words. Not once had he felt this
powerless. He hated it. Savannah, no longer the hostage, took the
initiative.

"I gather you remember me."

He looked at her with a contempt that was pathetically fake.

"I do."

Savannah revelled in her new found position of power.

"Forgive me, your name escapes me."

"Daniel."

"Daniel. That's it. How could I forget that beautiful stew?"

"You liked it?"

"It tasted like dog shit."

Daniel laughed aloud at the thought. He needed to quickly regain control of the situation.

"For that, I can only apologise."

His desk was bare if not for a pen and a pad of paper. Staring at the ground, he flicked the pen between his long fingers. Savannah could tell he was loitering. She let him linger. As the silence drew longer, he lifted his eyes to meet Savannah.

"How are you here?"

"I was kidnapped. I thought you'd have known that."

He didn't enjoy Savannah's sarcasm.

"That I had gathered."

Her confidence was building despite the fact she was mind-numbingly confused.

"Ask a better question then."

"You are in Latvia. How?"

"Do you want to know the short version or the full story?"

"We have time."

Grinning like a schoolboy, Daniel dropped the pen and leant forward into his leather chair clicking his fingers in the process. He listened as Savannah spoke.

"My dad died of cancer. It was fucking tough. He was my everything, the world."

Daniel nodded his head in sympathy.

"Then my mum goes missing, and she ends up dead too."

He remained still in the squeaking chair.

"The police told me suicide. I didn't believe it. Not in a million years. Why on earth would my mum kill herself and orphan her only daughter? It didn't make sense. It wasn't who I thought she was. But I didn't know her. Not well enough."

Daniel coughed.

"I wanted to know who she was. I wanted to know who she was friends with. I wanted to know about my mum."

Savannah was on a roll, and there was no stopping her. He was more than happy to listen. Emotionally, she was running on empty. She had told her story so often, it had become almost second nature.

"I was being forced to move in with my mum's sister. She was a cow. To say I hated living there would be the understatement of the century. So there's that. I couldn't move on with my own life without knowing what had happened. It would have been easy to pretend I believed the official line but I didn't. I never did. The police wouldn't investigate it further, so I took it into my own hands."

"You came here?"

"I thought you wanted the long story?"

He shut up.

"I ran from home. I had planned this whole trip to the bank where she worked in Germany. It was the cheapest way, and it meant that I could see parts of Europe I'd never seen. Only I got to Dover, and I couldn't buy a ticket. They had sold out. It was the last one of the night, and if I didn't leave then, I'd be caught and made to come home. It was my only chance."

Daniel hadn't expected this from the girl sat on the other side of his desk.

"I got into a van and managed to make it on board."

"Into?"

"In the back. I thought nobody had seen me."

"And did they?"

"Just one person. The driver."

Daniel roared with unnecessary laughter.

"I can't imagine he was too ha—"

She interrupted his stupidity.

"I was raped."

Once more, he was silenced.

"He stole everything I had and dumped me on the side of a road in Calais. I walked for miles to find help. Nobody wanted to help a girl they thought was a migrant. That was until I met a migrant. They showed me more kindness than I could ever have wished for. They clothed me and sent me on my way."

"These are not the migrants I have experienced."

"Have you met them all?"

He wasn't learning. Savannah was on a mission.

"I didn't think so. I got to Paris and needed money for a train ticket to Germany. Do you know who gave me enough money?"

"A migrant."

"No, a prostitute. A black, educated hooker. She taught me more about life than I could ever have learnt at school."

"So you got to Germany? How was that for you?"

"It wasn't what I was hoping it to be."

"In what way?"

"I think you know."

Daniel swung his feet onto his desk and leant back further in his squeaking chair. He let Savannah continue.

"A few hours after I arrived in the city, I had left again on a bus. I realised I needed to be in Latvia. My mother's body was found near the capital, in a factory. That was all I had to go on."

Savannah hadn't made the connection though that didn't stop Daniel making the assumption she had. She continued, rarely pausing for breath.

"I got sidetracked. I ended up in a camp for refugees. I've found that my skin makes a lot of people jump to conclusions. Especially when I have no clothes, money or passport. I made it to Denmark a few months later. From there, I got a boat to Poland and there a bus into Lithuania. I knew I was getting close. It was getting easier. Perhaps, too easy."

He scoffed at her self-depreciation.

"I heard you could get into Latvia via a cargo train. I got to the station and watched as a young family did the same. It seemed too simple."

He interrupted her nostalgia abruptly.

"And now you know it was. Only the stupid, desperate people jump onto moving trains."

She looked him dead in the eye.

"I'm not stupid."

"No, you are not stupid. You are desperate."

He waited needlessly before continuing.

"Desperate for the truth."

"You could say that."

"I will give it to you."

She moved forward in her seat.

"I will tell you everything you want to know."

Savannah didn't say a word.

"What would you like to know first?"

Her mind was racing with ideas. She wanted to know everything.

"How you know my mum."

"We worked together for a long time."

Savannah crossed her arms and relaxed her legs.

"I met your mother on a flight. We were seated together, we talked for the entire flight. There was a connection. As we landed, we decided to meet for a drink. I liked her, but I knew our relationship would never work."

"Relationship?"

"I work and live here. She, at the time, worked in Germany and lived with you."

"I wasn't born th—"

"She lived in the UK. With your Dad."

"Happily, married."

"Not so."

"So, wait, you and my mum had an affair?"

"Of sorts, yes. She came and visited me in Latvia many times. Over the years, we grew together."

Savannah didn't like what she was hearing.

"We trusted each other."

"She trusted my Dad."

Daniel sighed in his chair. He wasn't enjoying this nearly as much as he expected to.

"I must warn you, the truth is not always pleasant to hear."

"So what's the point?"

"Because it is the truth. This is what you came here for."

Despite Savannah understanding his point, hearing the truth did not become any easier. She encouraged him forward.

"Then what?"

"I trust her more and more till one day, I show her my work."

He waved his arms around, signalling the factory.

"And what is it exactly you do here? Rape kids?"

"Not quite."

He stood from his seat and wandered over to the window before addressing the wall.

"We regrettably source friends for our clients across Europe."

Savannah couldn't believe her ears.

"Friends? Is that what you call them?"

"They are friends and nothing more. Once they are sold, they are used at our client's discretion."

His sentence contained a multitude of words that Savannah felt disgusted by. However, she was stunned into silence.

"We offer a high-quality service and a much better life for our girls. It is a shame it happens in the way that it does."

"You don't have to do this? It's inhumane. You're a monster."

"A very rich monster at that."

"Is that all you care about?"

"Me? No. I care about the girls. Deeply."

She could sense no joviality in his voice. He was deadly serious.

Savannah had completed the story ahead of time.

"I get it. You showed my mum all of this. Seeing these young girls living in squalor made her feel helpless. She couldn't save them so faced with nothing else, she killed herself."

It made perfect, wicked sense. He turned before speaking sharply.

"No."

Savannah waited for something more.

"No. Quite the contrary. Your mother helped recruit some of our best-selling girls. She travelled through each and every country looking for the best. Most parents were willing to let their children go for a few thousand euro. It ran like clockwork."

"But the train? This whole kidnapping—"

"Only since your mother has died. We are low on stock…"

His disregard for mankind was shocking.

"She was our number one asset."

"I don't believe you."

"You don't have to…"

He walked to the other side of the desk and perched on the wooden top. The power was his, and he was loving it.

"…but there is only one truth. And that is it."

"My mum wouldn't do that. That wasn't who she was."

"Morals don't pay the bills."

"Money isn't everything."

He laughed at the thought.

"For your mum, it most definitely was."

Savannah hated this version of the truth yet still craved for more.

"That doesn't explain how she died."

"I'm afraid it does."

Once more, she waited for Daniel to elaborate.

"She became like you. Nice. She grew closer to the girls that we wanted to sell. As you grew older, she became more sympathetic. Maybe your mother saw you in them. She threatened to shut down the operation, get the police involved."

Savannah knew where this was going. She could feel herself flushing red in rage.

"I couldn't have that. Be rid of this money maker? No chance. So I did as I knew best. I knocked her out cold, tied a rope around a neck and dropped her from the ceiling."

He mimicked a throat slice with his fingers.

"Dead. Nice and quick, no pain, please don't be sad for her. She didn't suffer."

As Savannah's rage forced her to her feet, Daniel ducked out of the way. With unfounded strength, she flipped the table letting the desk draws crash onto the floor. Amongst the failing papers, Savannah noticed the weapon affixed to the underside of the desk. Now exposed, she grabbed the gun and pointed it at Daniel. Darting to the door, Savannah expected the coward to flee, but instead, he slammed the door, bolting it shut. He turned to face the gun.

"Just you and me, little girl."

She had never held a gun before and knew not how to fire one, yet still, adrenaline-induced conviction ran through her veins.

"Come and closer and your brains will decorate the wall."

"Shoot me. Take revenge for your mother's death. It is what she would have wanted, her little girl locked up in jail for the rest of her days."

"You think the police will side with you?"

"The police work for me. Everyone in this town knows me, knows what I'm capable of."

Savannah's hands trembled under the weight of the gun. She wasn't a natural. Despite a gun pointed to his head, Daniel showed no signs of fear. He had her cornered.

"If you think that means I won't shoot you, you're wrong."

"Go for it. What are you waiting for?"

Savannah wanted to do it. Knowing she had killed her mum's murderer would sweeten any potential day in jail. Holding the gun tight, her finger moved above the trigger. Steadying her hands, Savannah swallowed her breath, closed her eyes and pushed on the trigger. His cackle was a sign that it hadn't worked. He could barely finish his sentence over the rapturous laughter.

"You might want to take the safety off before—"

Savannah interrupted his sentence, not with a bullet but screams of her own. She dropped the gun to the floor and grabbed her stomach. It was a pain like none other. Daniel stood motionless, staring solely at her anguish. Savannah's torment was so much, she wondered if she had broken every bone in her body. Her breathing struggled to keep up with her increasing heart rate. Gripping tight of the chair, Savannah waited for the pain to relent. If this was death, Savannah could understand why it was so feared. Daniel watched as Savannah's entire life changed before his eyes. Her feet were drenched. Confused, she reached down and felt for the source. Only then did she realise what was happening. She screamed at the top of her voice.

"How?"

Daniel wasn't sure what to do. Savannah was stuck on auto-pilot.

"How?"

Her screams could be surely heard for miles. Daniel rounded Savannah as he lifted the desk from the floor. Once upright, Savannah felt the murderer pull her body onto the flat surface. Her breathing had become panting. Her hands scratched at the sides of the desk. Her body was too weak to deal with this, her mind too feeble to answer the hoards of questions whizzing around her brain. Savannah's cramps reached new levels of pain. In those intense moments, everything became clear. The sickness, the stomach pains, the bloating. Savannah lamented her stupidity. Now, it seemed so obvious. Nothing could stop what was happening. She let nature take its course. Sweat poured from her forehead, dripped down her face and onto the rolled up nightie. Daniel stood behind offering nothing in the way of support. If Savannah were to do this, she'd be doing it alone. Her pains would come in irregular waves. As they subsided, the teen enjoyed the respite. It was welcoming but short-lived. With every cramp, the pressure increased. Time ticked on quickly and with the hours, the waves of pain intensified. Savannah searched for relief. Knowing to push, largely out of intuition, she did so. Just for a moment, and only with each heave, the pain eased. Wanting to be free from her torment, Savannah listened to her body's calls and pushed. With each squeeze, the pain lessened. It was working. Leaning forward, Savannah tried to see her child. It's head, surprisingly hairy, had appeared out of her vagina. It was a sight she had never expected to see so soon. Daniel, sensing the end was near, walked to her side and cheered her on. Dropping her hands to her waist, Savannah pushed hard for the final time, releasing the baby into her waiting arms. Tears, falling from her eyes, mixed with sweat on her greasy face. Hearing her child's first cry, Savannah rested the baby on the floor and looked up at Daniel's grinning face.

"It looks like Mummy has a new grandson."

With just one hand free, Savannah flicked the safety, took aim and fired a bullet between his beady eyes. Daniel's dangly body collapsed to the floor as drops of blood dripped from the wound. His death was quick. She regretted not making him suffer. Dropping the gun, Savannah took hold of her baby and wrapped him into her nightdress. As her ears filled with the sounds of shouting and hurried footsteps, Savannah did nothing other than stare into the eyes of her rapist's child.

ACKNOWLEDGEMENTS

I'd like to take this opportunity to thank the people closest to me for supporting this story and showing me unconditional love and support throughout this process.

To my parents, thank you for giving me every opportunity in life; for helping me with almost everything I do and allowing me to follow my dreams however stupid and silly they may seem.

To my friends, thank you for inspiring me to better and challenge myself. I'm very fortunate to be surrounded by clever, funny and kind people and I love nothing more than spending time with you. Throughout this book, I've hidden references to you - birthdays, initials, cafes etc - this is a true test of whether you've actually read your free copy!

And to my dogs, Lulu and Tilly, for the cuddles and unwavering excitement. You'll never read this book but I know you'd love it.

ABOUT THE AUTHOR

Callum Noad is an young author who has recently graduated with a degree in Business Management from Cardiff University. He is a keen football fan and has been a season ticket holder at Cardiff City FC for over a decade. When not watching the mighty Bluebirds, Callum enjoys playing the sport for a local 11-a-side team or laughing with his friends at cosy, country pubs.

Familiar Strangers is his first novel.

wildfires

When the body of a young footballer reported missing 24 years ago is found in the concrete foundations of a garage, DCI Fran Hansen is tasked with bringing the killer to justice. As she reopens the case, Hansen starts to dig up the truth - the truth that some would rather be left untouched.

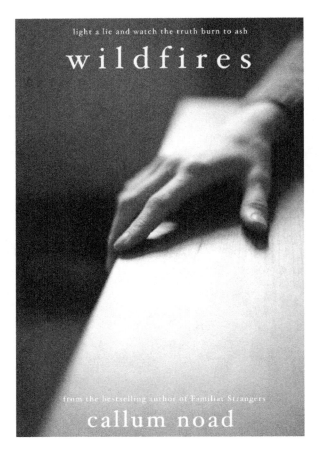

2018

Printed in Great Britain
by Amazon

84575969R00181